EVERY
SINGLE
BROKEN
PIECE

OTHER TITLES BY MICHELLE HEARD

In Reading Order:

MONTLAKE

Things That Break Us

Every Single Broken Piece

MAFIA ROMANCE

Mafia / Organized Crime / Suspense Romance
All books can be read in this order or as a stand-alone.

The Kings of Mafia Series
This series is not connected to any other series I've written, and there will be no spin-offs.

Tempted By The Devil

Craving Danger

Hunted By A Shadow

Drawn To Darkness

God Of Vengeance

Craving Revenge

Forceful God

Possessive Enemy

Vicious Devil

Saved By A God

Mafia Empire

The Hermit

The High Priestess

Death

The Empress

The Devil

ST. MONARCH'S WORLD

The Saints Series

Merciless Saints

Cruel Saints

Ruthless Saints

Tears Of Betrayal

Tears Of Salvation

The Sinners Series

Taken By A Sinner

Owned By A Sinner

Stolen By A Sinner

Chosen By A Sinner

Captured By A Sinner

Corrupted Royals

Destroy Me

Control Me

Brutalize Me

Restrain Me

Possess Me

CONTEMPORARY ROMANCE

Beautifully Broken Series

Beautifully Broken

Beautifully Hurt

Beautifully Destroyed

Enemies to Lovers

Heartless

Reckless

Careless

Ruthless

Shameless

Trinity Academy

Falcon

Mason

Lake

Julian

The Epilogue

The Heirs

Coldhearted Heir

Arrogant Heir

Defiant Heir

Loyal Heir

Callous Heir

Sinful Heir

Tempted Heir

Forbidden Heir

Stand-Alone Spin-Off

Not My Hero (young adult / high school romance)

The Southern Heroes Series

The Ocean Between Us

The Girl In The Closet

The Lies We Tell Ourselves

All The Wasted Time

We Were Lost

STAND-ALONE

Lifeline (FBI suspense romance)

EVERY SINGLE BROKEN PIECE

MICHELLE HEARD

Text copyright © 2026 by Michelle Heard
All rights reserved.

Published by Montlake, Seattle

www.apub.com

Amazon, the Amazon logo, and Montlake are trademarks of Amazon.com, Inc., or its affiliates.

EU product safety contact:
Amazon Media EU S. à r.l.
38, avenue John F. Kennedy, L-1855 Luxembourg
amazonpublishing-gpsr@amazon.com

ISBN-13: 9781662536823 (paperback)
ISBN-13: 9781662536830 (digital)

Cover design by Caroline Johnson
Cover image: © Wander Aguiar Photography; © Pongstorn Pixs / Shutterstock

Printed in the United States of America

For Mom

SONG LIST

Real World—Ryan Star

Bad Thoughts—Rachel Platten

Beauty in the Hurting—Jared Benjamin

Hold Me Steady—Valerie Broussard and Ronen

Safe with Me—Ike Dweck

Fix What You Didn't Break—Nate Smith

Love Me Back—Max McNown

Someone to You—Matt Hansen

Life or Death—Declan J Donovan

Fall into Me—Forest Blakk

Loved Me Back to Life—Céline Dion

AUTHOR'S NOTE

This book contains subject matter that may be sensitive for some readers.

Home invasion and descriptive murder of family (on page)
Grief
Physical and mental abuse
PTSD
Physical assault

There is triggering content between these pages.
Please read responsibly.

Chapter 1

Kelcie

Levi Graye, 32. Kelcie Woodruff, 24.

Taking a sip of my vanilla iced latte, I savor the delicious taste.

"Mmm . . . I could drink it every day and never grow tired of it."

This heaven-in-a-cup sensation became my latest addiction at the beginning of the summer, and every afternoon, I take a walk to Dixie's Coffee.

Mrs. Dixon, the store owner, chuckles as she shakes her head. "I've noticed, but you won't hear me complaining."

She's so used to seeing my face, she now has my drink ready the moment I walk into her quaint little coffee shop. I love the green and lilac décor and always feel at peace when I'm here.

Maybe it's just Mrs. Dixon's calm demeanor that rubs off on me. She might be in her sixties, but she doesn't look it. Her red hair always hangs in perfect curls around her shoulders, and her pale blue eyes remind me of a clear sky on a warm summer's day.

Honestly, she's one of our town's greatest treasures.

I give her a wave as I head toward the door. "Enjoy the rest of your day."

"Tell your mom I'll be at tomorrow's embroidery class," she calls after me while wiping down the counter.

"I will," I reply cheerfully before I step out onto the sidewalk.

While enjoying my latte, I smile at all the familiar faces as I pass them on Main Street. Nearing Mom's store, I glance through the window, and not seeing any customers, I quickly slip inside. When the bell above the door jingles, Mom looks up from the romance novel she's busy reading.

A warm smile spreads over her face. "Hi, buttercup."

I lean against the counter and rest my elbows on the worn wood. "I'm on my way home." I nod at my beverage. "Just got my daily dose of goodness."

Mom takes the cup from me and helps herself to a sip before scrunching her face. "Wow, that's sweet."

Chuckling, I shake my head. "You say that every time." I glance around at all the shelves stacked full of everything a person could ever need for embroidery and other arts and crafts. "How's business?"

Mom reaches over the counter and tucks a few stray strands of hair behind my ear. "It's a bit slow today."

"Mrs. Dixon says she's coming to the embroidery lesson tomorrow. Save her a seat."

Mom's smile widens while she shuts the book she's reading. She's one heck of a bookworm. For as long as I can remember, there hasn't been a day when I haven't seen her engrossed in a novel. I don't share her love for books, unlike Sage and Jordan, my older siblings. Instead, I take after Dad and love whittling wood.

Three years ago, the folks in town found out about my little hobby when Mom asked me to make her bunnies and eggs so she could decorate her store for Easter. Since then, I've been getting orders from our neighbors. I also created an online store, and it's become so successful that I'm able to make a decent living. Even though I can afford a place of my own, I still live with my parents, and I'm in no hurry to move out.

Looks-wise, I'm the spitting image of Mom with my light brown hair and brown eyes, whereas Sage and Jordan got their blond hair and green eyes from Dad. I'm also a head shorter than my siblings, which has contributed to them being overprotective of me.

I tap a finger on the cover of the book. "Are you enjoying it?"

"Oh yes." Mom's eyes light up. She loves talking about books. "This one has a lot of angst. The hero is so swoonworthy."

A chuckle escapes me before I take a sip of my drink.

Laughter sounds up from out on the sidewalk, and I watch as three teen girls walk past the store. They look carefree and happy, and it has my smile growing. They wave at us before they continue down the street.

All in all, Verona is a happy little town with an everyone-is-your-neighbor feel. Sage and Jordan couldn't leave quickly enough, but to me, it will always be home.

Dad was sworn in as mayor last year, and that elevated us to royalty status around here. It took months for me to get used to all the attention, but thankfully, it finally died down, and things are back to normal.

"Did you get that big order out in time?" Mom asks.

I had to whittle and paint one hundred Christmas balls for a store in Virginia. With the festive season a few months away, things are going to be super busy for a while.

"Yes. I plan to sleep for most of the weekend before I get started on the next order."

"I'm happy to hear that. You haven't taken a break in a while." Her eyes drift over my face, then she asks, "What should we have for dinner?"

I think for a moment, mentally going through the short list of dishes I can prepare without poisoning my family. "I can make spaghetti and meatballs?"

"With it being Labor Day on Monday, Sage is coming home for the long weekend."

My eyebrows lift with surprise. "Really? She's actually taking time off work?"

"Thankfully, yes." Mom sighs with relief. "It will be so nice to have her home."

With Sage not liking meatballs, I decide to try my luck and mention, "She loves pizza. I can stop at the diner and get two or three."

Mom grins at me. "It is Friday, after all, and we have plenty to celebrate. Sage is coming to visit, and you've completed your order."

"Definitely." I lean closer with a wide smile. "Think of all that greasy cheese. Yum."

Mom nods excitedly. "That's it. Get us three pizzas." She pulls cash out of the register. "Order a pepperoni for your dad and have them add chilies."

"I'll get Hawaiian for Sage."

Mom nods, holding the dollar bills out to me. "As long as the third one has a lot of cheese, I'm good."

Not taking the cash from Mom, I say, "Pizza is on me."

"Aww, thanks, buttercup."

I finish the last of my latte before moving around the counter to drop the empty cup in the trash can. "I'll see you at home."

"Okay. If there aren't any customers in the next thirty minutes, I'll lock up."

Walking to the door, I blow Mom a kiss before I leave the store and head in the direction of the diner.

Since Dad became the mayor, businesses have been booming in Verona. Even though there's a new restaurant, I still prefer getting all our takeout from Reggie's Diner.

I glance up and down the street before crossing to where the diner is situated on the corner, its red leather seats visible through the windows.

When I step inside the air-conditioned building, the familiarity of a close-knit community wraps around me. I sit down on one of the stools by the main counter and grin at Waverly. Her mother, Jesse-Lee, has owned the diner since before I was born.

Waverly places the glass cover over the last two slices of apple pie, then comes toward me. "It's been a while, Kelcie. How have you been?"

"Same old. I was busy with work." I shrug, then ask, "How are you and Lucas? And your mom?"

"We're good. Mom's visiting my aunt in Florida, and Lucas is going through a stage where he has boundless energy. He doesn't sit still for a minute."

Lucas is the cutest five-year-old I've ever laid eyes on.

"Just let me know if you need a night to yourself and I'll babysit," I offer.

"You sure?" she asks, tired lines pulling at the corners of her eyes and mouth. "I would just love to soak in the tub for hours."

"How about Tuesday night? You can bring Lucas over after your shift, and he can even spend the night so you can get some rest."

Waverly grabs hold of my forearm and gives me a squeeze. "God, Kelcie, that would be amazing. Are you sure your parents won't mind?"

I shake my head. "Not at all. They'll probably end up spoiling him rotten."

She gives me a trembling smile as emotion washes over her pretty features. "I'd appreciate it. How much do you charge?"

I shake my head again. "Nothing."

Her eyes widen slightly. "You can't look after Lucas for an entire night and not charge anything."

I think for a moment, then grin. "You can put extra cheese on my pizza order."

"That's a deal." Digging a notepad and pen from her apron pocket, she asks, "Which pizzas do you want?"

"One pepperoni, one Hawaiian, aaand . . ." I reach for a menu and pull it closer to look over the selection the diner offers. "Make the third one with as many layers of cheese as you can pile on."

"Coming right up." She turns away from me to give the order to Rodney, the cook. Glancing over her shoulder, she asks, "Would you like a soda while you wait?"

I shake my head. "I just had something to drink."

I glance at the other customers in the diner, which is not too busy before the evening rush.

When Waverly brings me the bill, I quickly pay. While I wait for my order, I watch a bit of the football rerun on the TV that's mounted next to the chalkboard menu that shows the specials for the week.

A hand settles on my shoulder, and my head snaps to the side. Seeing Colby Adams, who graduated the same year as me, I smile.

He was the most popular boy in school due to him being the quarterback. After we graduated, he became a reporter for the Sugar River Valley area. I was actually surprised. I always thought he'd move to the city.

"Hey," he says as he takes a seat beside me. "How's the prettiest girl in Verona doing?"

"I don't know," I chuckle. "You should ask her."

The corner of his mouth lifts. "How are you?"

I let out a burst of laughter at his harmless flirting.

"I'm good. I haven't seen you around much."

"I was covering a story for the historical society in Mount Horeb." He reaches for my hair, which is caught in a low-hanging ponytail, and tugs a few strands. "But now that I have some time, I was hoping you'd reconsider and go out to dinner with me."

Colby's been trying for five years to get me to go out with him, and even though he is attractive and a good man, I just don't feel a spark between us.

"You need to stop asking. My answer isn't going to change." I give him a smile to ease the blow of rejection. "I'm way too busy with work, and dating is the last thing I'm interested in."

I even made Jordan go with me to my prom so I didn't have to accept any of the invites I received. I'm one of those people who are perfectly content with not being in a romantic relationship. My life is full and happy, and it doesn't feel like it's missing anything.

Not accepting my rejection, Colby smirks and leans forward. Sounding too sure of himself, he says, "I'll get you to change your mind at some point."

Waverly sets the three large pizza boxes down in front of me, and it prompts Colby to ask, "Can I give you a ride home?"

"Nope, but thanks for the offer." I lift the boxes and turn my attention to Waverly. "See you on Tuesday."

"I'll drop Lucas off at six p.m."

"That works for me."

I can feel Colby's eyes resting on me as I walk out of the diner and let out a sigh. Hopefully, he'll stop asking me on dates.

I cut through the town square, admiring the baskets of colorful flowers hanging from antique lampposts. As I head down my street, the three boxes grow heavier, and by the time I reach the cul-de-sac where my family home is, I let out a breath of relief.

I take the steps up to the porch, which is decorated with a hanging chair and potted flowers. It's my parents' favorite spot to sip on a glass of wine while they watch the sun set.

The front door opens, and Mom grins at me. "Let me take those."

When she rids me of the boxes, I shake out my arms and rub over the red marks left on my skin.

"Sage called to let me know she was able to get away from the office earlier than expected. She'll be here any minute," Mom informs me as we head into the house.

"That's good news." I blow a loose strand of my hair out of my face while following Mom to the kitchen. "I offered to babysit Lucas, Waverly's boy, on Tuesday night."

"That's so nice of you."

After the walk home, I make a beeline for the fridge and grab a bottle of water. After quenching my thirst, I ask, "When did you last hear from Jordan?"

Mom thinks for a moment before replying, "He called on Monday. His construction business is keeping him busy, and Natalie and Brady are doing well. He said they'll come through for Thanksgiving."

Jordan met Natalie a month after he moved to Naperville, and they've been happily married for five years. We took a trip to visit them when Brady was born, but that was two years ago.

"Boo . . ." I scrunch my nose while putting the bottle down on the counter. "That's still two months away."

"Right?" Mom lets out a huff. "I'm just happy that we'll get to see them this year."

Moving closer to Mom, I place my arm around her shoulders and press a kiss to her cheek. "Hey, at least you're stuck with me."

A smile widens over her face. "The house would be empty without you, buttercup." Her expression grows serious. "But I don't want you to feel like you're stuck here."

"I don't feel that way at all. I love living with you and Dad."

Mom pats my cheek. "One day you'll meet someone who'll make you feel differently."

I shake my head. "Nope. I have zero desire to date."

"You might change your mind a few years from now."

I peek into the pizza boxes until I find the Hawaiian and quickly steal a piece of pineapple. When I pop it into my mouth, I say, "Don't tell Sage."

It's always been our thing where I'll pick off the pineapple from my pizza to give to Sage because she loves it so much. It's something special between us.

Mom walks to the stove and begins to prepare a pot of chamomile tea.

The front door opens, and a second later we hear Sage calling out, "I'm home."

Shrieking happily, Mom barrels out of the kitchen. I follow after her and grin when I see Mom hugging the life out of Sage.

"I missed you so much! It's been too long since we last saw you," Mom says.

Sage basks in the attention Mom's giving her, and only when they pull apart do I step forward to give my sister a tight hug.

"Missed you," I whisper.

Sage rubs her hand up and down my back before pulling away. "I've missed you too. I'll definitely try to come home more now that the case has been settled."

Just then, the front door opens again, and Dad steps into the foyer.

"Sage!" He rushes forward and engulfs her in a bear hug. "Dang, sweetheart. It's so good to see you again." He pushes her backward, his eyes sweeping over her before he asks, "How's work? Your mom told me you won the case."

"It was a difficult one, but we got a billion-dollar settlement," Sage replies.

Dad's chest puffs out, and he gives Sage a look filled with pride and love. "That's such great news. I knew you could do it."

While Dad presses a kiss to Mom's lips, I say, "We got pizza. Are we eating in the kitchen or the living room?"

"Kitchen," Mom replies.

Dad wraps his arm around Sage's shoulders and walks with her. As they take a seat at the breakfast nook, decorated with the matching blue and white throw pillows and tablecloth Mom just finished making, I grab glasses from the cupboards and fill them with water and ice.

Once everyone has something to drink, I take my seat beside Mom and grab a slice of Hawaiian pizza. When I pick off the pineapples and place them on Sage's plate, she gives me a loving smile.

"Mom said you had a huge order," Sage mentions before laying into the food on her plate.

"I had to make a hundred Christmas tree decorations for a mom-and-pop store in Virginia."

She reaches for my right hand and checks my fingers. "Did you use the gloves I got you for your birthday?"

Nodding, I reply, "That's why my hands aren't covered in blisters. They're a godsend."

The conversation turns back to Sage's life in Madison, and while I stuff my face with pizza, my heart is filled with happiness and a sense of peace.

Chapter 2

KELCIE

Sitting at my dressing table, I squeeze all the excess water out of my freshly washed hair before dropping the damp towel on the floor beside me. I'll throw it in the laundry basket once I'm done blow-drying my hair.

Just as I reach for my brush, there's a knock at my bedroom door, and Sage peeks in. "Are you almost done? I spotted chocolate cake in the fridge. Wanna share a slice?"

"My hair can wait," I say while quickly getting up from the stool. "Chocolate cake always comes first."

Laughter bubbles from her, and when we head downstairs, she asks, "So, besides work, how's everything?"

Entering the kitchen, Sage prepares two cups of tea while I grab the cake from the fridge.

"You know me. Nothing changes much." I cut a thick slice and plate it before adding two forks, then shoot my sister a grin. "Which is exactly the way I like it."

I take a seat on the bench while Sage sits down on one of the chairs across from me, and I break a piece of cake off before popping it into my mouth. A crumb falls on the tablecloth, and picking it up, I drop it on the side of the plate.

"Are you really happy living here with Mom and Dad? You can always move in with me."

I shake my head. "Unlike you and Jordan, I love living here. I'll never be happy in the city, and I have my workshop set up exactly how I like it."

She lets out a huff, her fork pausing right by her mouth. "It was worth a try. I've been thinking about getting a roommate and hoped it would be you."

"Sorry." I take in Sage's beautiful face, then ask, "Why don't you move in with Derek?"

She starts shaking her head before I'm even done asking the question. "No. We've only been dating two years."

"That's a long time." I give my two cents.

Sage's eyes lock with mine, and I can see she's unsure about something.

Leaning forward, she drops her voice to a whisper. "Don't tell Mom and Dad, but I broke up with Derek last Saturday. He started getting too controlling for my liking."

"Dang, Sage!" My eyes widen at the unexpected news, and I reach across the table to give her forearm a squeeze. I look for any signs that she's heartbroken but don't see any. "How are you holding up?"

She spears another piece of cake. "I'm doing okay. I'm just struggling with the loneliness."

"Last I heard, Marla was thinking about moving to the city. I can ask her if she still wants to go and would be interested in sharing a place with you."

Marla was my best friend in high school, but when she left to attend college, life pulled us in different directions. Even though we're not as close as we used to be, we still keep in touch.

"That would be great!" Sage exclaims.

"Hmm . . ." Dad playfully grumbles as he walks into the kitchen. "I hope you left some cake for me."

Grinning, I reply. "Of course. We wouldn't dare eat it all."

Dad pulls the container from the fridge and gets a fork from the drawer before he leans back against the counter and starts eating.

"No, Harry!" Mom snaps. She makes a beeline for him and grabs the container from his hands. "Cut yourself a slice instead of eating like a barbarian."

Dad steals another bite, and when she tries to slap his shoulder, he darts out of her reach.

With a playful scowl, Mom cuts two slices and places them on plates.

When they join us at the table, she asks, "What are you talking about?"

Sage gives me a panicked look, which has me answering, "I told Sage about my workshop. I want to get another table and more shelves."

"I'll have some time next month, then I can help you build the shelves," Dad offers.

I nudge my shoulder against his. "That would be great. Thanks, Dad."

"Do you still have enough space for all the shipping materials?" Mom asks.

"For now. But at some point, I might have to build onto the workshop."

"How about we add a second floor because I'm not giving up more of my garden?" Mom replies.

"Oooh . . ." I smile happily. "I love that idea."

Sage glances at Dad and changes the subject by saying, "I read in the newspaper that you're clamping down on drugs and crime. How's that going?"

Dad lets out a huff, a frustrated expression passing over his face. "You know how it is. You cut off one head of the snake, and two grow back. It feels like a never-ending battle."

"You're making a difference," Mom says, her voice filled with pride.

Dad smiles at her before turning his attention back to the last piece of his cake. "I know. I just wish things would move faster and not at a snail's pace."

"You're doing things for this town no one else has ever done," Sage says. "And people are noticing."

"Thanks, sweetheart."

I lift my hand and rub Dad's shoulder before gathering the empty plates. While I load them into the dishwasher, Mom says, "I'm calling it a night. I want to read a little before bed." She presses a kiss to the top of Sage's head, then comes to do the same to me. "Night, girls."

"Night, Mom," Sage and I reply.

My sister looks at me. "Do you want to watch a movie?"

"Sure. Just give me a few minutes to dry my hair."

"Great!" She darts to her feet and heads for the pantry. "I'll make popcorn."

"You two enjoy the movie." Dad gets up from the chair. "I'm going to lock up, then I'm turning in as well."

"Night, Dad," I say as I leave the kitchen.

"Night, buttercup."

When I reach my bedroom, I shut the door so the noise of my hair dryer won't bother my parents. I take a seat at my dressing table and pull the brush through my hair to get rid of the knots before I begin to dry the strands.

I have thick hair like Dad, and if I leave it to air-dry, I'll end up looking like Hagrid from *Harry Potter*.

Halfway through the tiring process, I hear a sharp sound, and switching off the hair dryer, I frown as I listen more carefully.

"Noooo!"

Mom's scream makes shock shudder through me. Dropping the hair dryer, I jump up and run out of my bedroom.

As I burst into the landing between the three bedrooms, where Mom's bookshelves decorate the walls, I see a man with a ski mask grabbing hold of Mom's hair and dragging her out of the main bedroom.

Paralyzing shock hits me so hard that the air leaves my lungs in a whoosh, and intense fear pours through me.

Mom's face is bleeding, and she looks completely dazed as she tries to claw at the floor and walls to keep the man from dragging her with him.

Not thinking at all, I charge the man while a horrible-sounding cry tears loose from me. Icy pins and needles erupt over my skin, and as adrenaline fills my veins, it feels like I'm running down a long tunnel.

I lose all sense of time. Colors dim, and I swear my hearing sharpens until I'm able to hear every single sound in the house.

Dad's grunts from downstairs.

Sage's sobbing.

Mom's wheezing.

My breaths saw over my lips, and as I jump onto the man, hooking one of my arms around his neck, another wave of shock saturates every fiber of my being.

"Fucking bitch," the man growls.

He lets go of Mom and grabs hold of my arm, trying to shake me off. I have no idea how I'm able to function during the terrifying situation, but I repeatedly slam my fist against the side of his face and neck.

My breathing becomes harsher, and I'm unable to get a word out, only managing snarls. It's as if I've been reduced to my most basic animal form and I've gone into pure survival mode.

The man ducks forward, and he manages to throw me off. I slam hard into the wall, pain shooting through my right shoulder.

I'm grabbed by my hair and yanked backward. The next instant, a fist connects with my nose. My face erupts with a pain so intense, I can't think. My eyes instantly tear up, blood spills from my nose, and my ears ring.

"Kelcie!" Mom cries, her voice raw with panic.

Another blow hits my left cheek and eye, causing everything around me to darken and my legs to go numb.

"No!" It sounds like Mom's screaming down a dark tunnel.

I'm pushed hard, and as I stumble backward, the ground suddenly gives way beneath me, and I tumble down the stairs. Somewhere in my stunned mind, unbearable terror registers, and I realize there's an attacker in the house and we're in grave danger.

I come to a groaning stop in the space between the kitchen and the living room, and as my sight focuses for a few seconds, I see Mom fighting the man. He has her pinned against the wall, one hand clamped around her throat while he tries to dig something out of his pocket. She hits and claws at the black fabric covering his face.

I force myself up into a sitting position. My body aches all over, and it feels like there are hammers slamming against my skull. When I try to call Mom, my voice comes out weak.

Dad lets out an agonizing roar, and my gaze snaps to the living room on my right.

As if I'm stuck in slow motion, I take in every single detail around me. The couch that's askew. The overturned lamp. The shattered glass by the doors that lead to the backyard.

Another masked man is on top of Dad, stabbing him over and over, the sight of the blood-coated blade filling me with terror. Dad's bruised face is twisted with pain and desperation.

A third man is kicking Sage, and she seems to be unconscious. There's a deep gash on the side of her head, and her skin is deathly pale.

A garbled sound draws my attention back to Mom, and seeing blood gush from where her neck has been sliced open, I'm filled with unbearable devastation. It shreds through me until all that remains are the unrecognizable pieces of my once-happy life.

My emotions spiral into a turbulent mess, making it impossible for me to form a coherent thought.

When the man lets go of Mom, her body sags down until she's sitting on the floor, lifting a limp hand to her neck while her eyes widen with horror.

Mom!

"Kelcie," Dad groans, "run!"

The urgency in his tone has me shooting to my feet and running past the dining room and formal sitting room to get to the front door. Before I can reach for the doorknob, a gunshot rings through the open-plan living space, and pain slams into my back.

Shock ravages me once again, my entire torso consumed by severe pain. Somehow, I'm able to get the front door open, and I stagger out onto the porch.

Blue and red lights flash over me as my legs give way, and I sink down to my knees.

"Kelcie!" I hear Sheriff Williams shout. "Jesus."

I slump to my side, and my vision goes in and out of focus. Here and there, I make out the sounds of the sheriff's department moving into the house.

I hear two gunshots and a lot of shouting.

Slowly, everything fades away, and the last thing I see are the peonies Mom planted a week ago. Even though they always die, she keeps buying a bunch every year in the hopes that she can get them to grow.

"Hang in there." I hear a woman's voice beside me.

"Kelcie!"

Is that Colby?

"Keep everyone back," Sheriff Wilson orders, his tone grim, then he asks someone, "How's she doing?"

"We have to get her to the hospital," the woman beside me replies.

Their voices are swallowed by a thick darkness, and I'm bombarded with flashes of Mom, Dad, and Sage being attacked.

The blood. The devastation. The brutality.

I fight to open my eyes, but all I see are blurring bright lights.

Then everything fades to black.

A few days later . . .

Sluggish and disoriented, it takes a few seconds before my sight focuses on a machine, and I watch as my heartbeat and vitals reflect on the screen.

"Kelcie." I hear Jordan's voice, then I feel his hand as he grips mine tightly.

I become aware of a dull pain in my back and midsection, and I feel too hot. My mind is a jumbled mess, and I struggle to focus on a single thought.

A cool hand settles against my cheek, and only then do I see my brother as he leans over me. His eyes are rimmed red, and he looks haggard. His skin is grayish, and his hair's a mess.

"Jordan?" I whisper, my voice hoarse as if I haven't used it for a while.

A trembling smile forms on his face, and a tear escapes. "Hi." He clears his throat, then asks, "How are you feeling?"

"Sore." My tongue darts out to wet my lips, and I taste something bitter. *Antiseptic fluid?* My mouth feels impossibly dry, and I add, "Thirsty."

Jordan lets go of my hand, and I watch as he picks up a glass from the cabinet beside the bed. When he brings it to my mouth, I'm able to lift my head and take a few sips before dropping back against the pillows.

As the water hits my stomach, I begin to feel queasy, and a second later, I'm hit with one horrible memory after another.

"Mom! Dad!" My eyes fly to Jordan's. "Sage?"

He sits down on the side of the bed and leans over me while gripping my hand in one of his. "Sheriff Williams told me three men broke into the house."

My lips part, but no sound comes out as the flashes of the nightmarish memories begin to torture me.

Mom's fingers fumbling in the blood spilling from her neck. Dad being stabbed. Sage's body jerking with every kick.

"You're the only one who survived," Jordan groans, his tone thick with sorrow. He brushes his other hand over the side of my head. "Mom, Dad, and Sage didn't make it."

"What?" Even though I hear what he's saying, my mind refuses to process the words. "Where are they?"

My gaze darts to the door, and instead of accepting what Jordan's telling me, I take in the fact that I'm in the hospital.

"Kelcie," Jordan says, his voice breaking from the heavy weight of grief. He waits for me to look at him before repeating, "They were killed. Only you survived."

Heartache begins to creep into my bones, and I shake my head. "No."

The sad emotion filling every inch of me begins to grow until it morphs into harrowing anguish. A sob bursts from me, making the dull ache in my torso turn into something so sharp, and I struggle to breathe.

"They're gone," Jordan says again as he leans closer to me, more tears rolling down his cheeks and dripping onto the white sheet covering me.

His palm repeatedly brushes over my forehead and hair.

The horrendous events of the attack assault me, and as the excruciating fact that my parents and Sage were killed shudders through me, I begin to weep uncontrollably.

I can't handle the hell that's my new reality, and at some point, a nurse enters the room and injects something into my IV.

With Jordan gripping my hand tightly and brushing his other palm over my hair, a medicated drowsiness drags me into an empty darkness.

Chapter 3

LEVI

Sitting in front of my laptop, I stare at the title I just typed on the first page.

The Edge of Rationality.

My agent is expecting this book in a year, and I can't think of a single plot. It took me a week to come up with the damn title.

Since my book *The Elimination Project* was made into a movie, which received critical acclaim, I've been stuck.

Writer's block is a real bitch.

At first, I was riding the high of signing a film deal, then I was beside myself with happiness when I heard Easton Rowe, the best action star, would be the leading actor. After that, everything became too much. All the attention. The reporters. The fucking messages on my Instagram account from the worthless woman who calls herself my mother. I keep blocking every account she opens, but she doesn't seem to get the message that I don't want to talk to her.

Unable to deal with the fame that came from having a bestselling book turn into an award-winning movie, I've been hiding from the world, refusing to leave my house here in Grand Rapids.

Thank God for DoorDash.

As I keep staring at the flashing cursor, my thoughts turn to my mother again. All the neglect and pain I suffered because of her and the bastard she married when I was five shudders through me for the millionth time.

My abusive past has shaped my life. I tried the marriage thing, but it didn't even last a year. I never loved my ex-wife. Honestly, I think I'm incapable of loving another person. She wanted affection, and it's something I struggle with. When she asked for a divorce, I didn't put up a fight. I signed the papers and walked away, feeling relieved to put an end to trying to act as if I'm a normal person.

Besides talking to my agent and interacting with some of my readers and fellow authors on social media, I avoid people as much as possible. I'm filled with repulsion from the simplest touch and get annoyed by the slightest thing.

In short, I'm as fucked up as they come.

I push my chair backward and climb to my feet. Patting against my leg, I indicate for Lick, my border collie, to follow me.

I found her as a puppy when she darted into the middle of the road in front of my car. It took me a week to get her comfortable with me, and then she licked the shit out of me and every damn surface she could find. I felt the name was fitting.

Walking into the kitchen, I open the fridge and grab a bottle of water before I open the back door so Lick can take a toilet break.

I sit down on the top step and watch as she sniffs random patches of grass before finally finding the perfect spot to pee.

Because I don't like to talk, I taught Lick our own form of sign language, which she responds to very well. I once verbally instructed her to follow me, but she ignored me and remained lying down until I indicated for her to come. Only then did she get up to carry out the order.

Lick comes over to me, and when her left ear keeps twitching, I give her scratches. She leans into my hand, letting out little moans of pleasure.

It's weird. I have no problem touching animals, but when it comes to people, it makes me want to crawl out of my skin. I always have to take a scorching hot shower and scrub my skin raw to get rid of the sickening disgust.

Looking into Lick's pretty blue eyes, warmth spreads through my chest. The vet says she's one-quarter Australian shepherd, and that's where she got her blue eyes from.

"Hi, Levi," I hear one of my neighbors call. I only spare the woman a quick look.

I've never bothered to remember her name, and as she starts to walk in my direction, I get up and go inside. I shut the back door and lock it, then head to my office.

I don't care if people think I'm an asshole. It takes way too much energy to pretend to be social.

When I sit down on my chair, it creaks. Lick lies down on the couch I've placed beside my desk and rests her head on her pillow. Sometimes she's more human than I am.

Looking at the screen again, I let out a sigh.

What the hell am I going to write?

Forcing myself to focus, I begin to play around with ideas, but nothing sticks. Two hours later, I give up and open my internet browser. I read through the latest news until a specific article grabs my attention.

The three men who've been arrested for the brutal murder of the mayor of Verona, WI, have been identified as Trent Crawford, Wesley Porter, and Dustin Baker.

Holy fuck.

Shock shudders through me as I stare at the names before I read the rest of the article. As I learn about the deaths of the mayor, his wife, and their daughter, an unsettling emotion takes root in my chest. Something akin to guilt.

It says one person survived the brutal attack, and then my eyes lock on a photo of the survivor. Her name is Kelcie Woodruff, and she's only twenty-four. I take in the beautiful face and the happiness shining from her eyes.

Never again will she look happy like she does in the photo. Not after suffering through such a brutal attack and losing her family.

I begin searching for every bit of news I can find regarding the murders and Kelcie, and by the time the room starts growing dark around me as the sun sets, I feel sick to my stomach.

Wiping my palm over my face, I close my eyes while I try to process what I've just learned.

Lick gets up from her bed and comes to rest her head on my thigh. I place my hand on her soft fur, and letting out a sigh, I climb to my feet so I can feed her.

While I go through the motions of warming up her dinner, which consists of chicken liver, veggies, and rice, I blankly stare at the timer on the microwave.

The guilt I've been feeling since I read the initial article keeps growing.

It's none of your business. You left that life behind when you ran away.

The microwave beeps, and I remove the container so I can stir the food and make sure it's not too hot. I mix it in with some dry dog food before setting Lick's bowl down so she can eat.

I should make myself something to eat as well, but I have zero appetite.

I keep seeing Kelcie Woodruff's happy face in my mind's eye, and as I watch Lick devour her dinner, I feel more and more guilty about what happened to her family.

It's tragic, but it has nothing to do with you.

Chapter 4

KELCIE

A year later . . .

With my back resting against the tree and sitting cross-legged on the grass, I stare at the three headstones.

I can't believe it's been a year since I lost them.

When I think back over the past twelve months, I don't remember much. It's as if time has gone by too fast and super slow all at once.

Some days are a blur, and then there are moments where the trauma is too much to handle. Unbearable grief digs its claws deeper into my soul and drags me down into a pit of despair.

It feels like I'm dying a slow and agonizing death. I haven't cried since Jordan initially told me our parents and Sage were killed.

The sound of a phone ringing gets through to me and pulls me out of my morbid thoughts. I glance around the cemetery, and realizing it's my phone, I dig the device out of my pocket.

Jordan's name shows on the screen, and for a moment, I hesitate before answering, "Hey."

"I'm at your house. Where are you?"

Crap, I only expected him this afternoon. I climb to my feet and dust off my backside while I keep looking at Mom, Dad, and Sage's final resting place.

"Sorry, I felt like taking a walk. I'm at the cemetery."

"I thought we were going together," Jordan grumbles. "I'm coming. Wait there for me."

I end the call and exhale a heavy breath. I thought I could visit on my own this morning before coming again later with Jordan.

Jordan will lose his shit if he finds out I spend every morning here. The mere thought of skipping a day always makes me spiral until I'm overcome by a severe panic attack. I just can't bring myself to let go of them.

I lose track of time as I stare at the words carved into the granite headstones.

A hand falls on my shoulder, making my body jerk. When my head snaps to the side and I see Jordan, I relax.

"You can't stand here so deep in thought. I could've been some random person," he chastises me, an angry expression on his face. "Why didn't you wait for me?"

"I'm sorry," I mumble half-heartedly.

When Jordan keeps staring at me, I take a deep breath before meeting his upset gaze.

"It's been a year, Kelcie. I've tried to be patient, but this has gone on long enough. I want you to move to Naperville. The guest room is ready for you." Looking at the three graves again, I shake my head while Jordan keeps talking. "Goddamn it, you can't stay here. We have to sell the house."

"No!" My breaths begin to speed up so fast, and before I know it, a panic attack hits hard. "No," I whimper while desperately trying to get air into my lungs.

"Shit. It's okay," Jordan says, his tone no longer angry but instead filled with worry. He takes hold of my shoulders and leans down until we're eye level with each other. "Hold your breath for five . . . four . . .

three . . . two . . . one." I try my best to focus on my brother while doing the exercise Dr. Swafford gave me for moments like this.

I have medication to help, but I forgot it at home.

It takes a little too long, but when my breathing finally begins to return to normal, Jordan pulls me into a hug and brushes his hand up and down my back. "I'm sorry," he murmurs. "I just want you out of this damn town and living with me, where I know you'll be safe. Staying in that shitty rental that isn't even properly decorated is stupid. I never should've let you move back here."

During the first three months after the attack, I stayed with Jordan, Natalie, and Brady, but I could see my mental state, nightmares, and panic attacks were taking a toll on them, so I came back to Verona. It led to the biggest fight Jordan and I have ever had.

I can't bring myself to go into my parents' house, so I haven't been to my workshop either. I've put a notice on my website that I'm not taking orders. The interest I receive from my share of the inheritance Jordan helped me to invest is enough for me to live on. Luckily, I don't have to worry about money while I try to pick up the pieces of my destroyed life.

If that's even possible.

Instead of going home, I moved in across the street from Colby's parents, Mr. and Mrs. Adams, because Colby told me the house was available. It's a fixer-upper, and I thought the work would keep me busy. But I keep postponing things because I just can't gather enough strength to get started with the repairs.

Not long after I moved in, the Richardsons, my neighbors on my left, sold their house and left Verona. Sometimes I think it's because they didn't want to live next to a woman who screams her head off every other day when she's woken by nightmares.

At first, my neighbors came to check if I was okay, but when they realized it was just bad dreams, they stopped coming over.

It only took a couple of months for the Richardsons' house to sell, and I got a new neighbor who keeps to himself and doesn't seem bothered by me. I haven't even seen the man up close, which suits me just fine.

My other neighbors, Jill and her daughter, Holly, are amazing. From what I understand, she's a single mother and not interested in dating after she lost her boyfriend in a car accident a month before Holly was born.

I lift my hand and grip Jordan's shoulder while I rest my cheek against his chest. My eyes burn with tears, but there's no relief because they refuse to fall.

"I'm sorry," I whisper again. I've lost count of the number of times I've said those words to my brother. "I can't leave. I can't . . ."

When my breathing begins to speed up again, he quickly pushes me back and locks eyes with me. "Shh . . . take deep breaths."

My face crumples, but still no tears fall, and I close my burning eyes. "Today is extra bad."

"I know." Jordan places an arm around my shoulders and leads me to where his SUV is parked. "Let's go to your place. I don't think it's doing you any good being at the cemetery."

The drive to my house is filled with silence, and even though I stare out the window, I don't take in any of my surroundings.

"How's your new neighbor?" Jordan asks as he pulls up my driveway.

I glance at my brother and notice he's looking at the man who's busy throwing a ball for his dog on the stretch of grass between our houses.

"He's quiet. Jill says he's very antisocial. Apparently, he doesn't speak to anybody and keeps to himself," I reply as I push the passenger door open and climb out.

When Jordan walks toward my neighbor, I let out a sigh and wait by the front of the car.

"Hi," my brother says, holding out his hand. "I'm Jordan Woodruff."

"Hi," the man replies, his eyes flicking to me before returning to my brother. "Levi Graye. Sorry, but I don't touch people."

Jordan hesitates for a couple of seconds before he lowers his hand. "My sister told me she got a new neighbor, and I thought I'd introduce myself."

It's the longest I've looked at Levi, and I notice he's taller and more muscled than Jordan. I can't make out his eye color, but he has black hair that's ruffled, some of the strands hanging over his forehead.

No wonder Jill always mentions our new neighbor. He's really attractive in a rugged way. I take in the white T-shirt and faded black jeans he's wearing. His brown boots look as worn as I feel.

When the dog starts sniffing around Jordan's legs, Levi murmurs, "Excuse me." He pats against the side of his thigh, and the dog quickly follows him as they walk away.

Jordan keeps glancing at Levi's house while he heads toward me, then says, "You weren't lying when you said he's quiet."

I don't comment and go to the front door. When we step inside the sparsely decorated space, my brother scowls at the single couch that doubles as my bed. I only go upstairs when I bathe or shower, and pretty much live on the couch.

"How are the security cameras?" Jordan asks as I go to the kitchen to make us some tea.

"They're fine."

"Do you even check that they're still working? When did you last test the alarm?"

I glance at my brother. "Trust me, it's the one thing I check religiously." I drive the security company insane because I test it every two weeks. Luckily for me, they're patient and put up with my obsessive behavior.

Jordan leans back against a counter and crosses his arms over his chest. "Do you still take your medication for the panic attacks?"

I let out a heavy breath before answering, "I'm trying to use it less. I can't keep taking the pills forever."

"What does Dr. Swafford have to say about it?"

"It doesn't matter what he thinks," I mutter as I begin to get annoyed.

"Kelcie—"

I turn to face Jordan and shake my head hard. "I get that you're worried about me, but you have to stop. I'm fine. The security cameras and alarm work. I eat regular meals, and I take the medication when things become unbearable. But that's as good as it's going to get." A breath shudders from me.

Jordan comes closer and places a hand on my shoulder. His features are torn with heartache. "You can't heal here, Kelcie."

My eyebrows draw together, and my eyes begin to burn again. "I'll never heal. No matter where I go, it won't help because I can't move away from the memories."

He lets out a sigh while pulling me into a hug and presses a kiss to the top of my head. "If you come to Naperville and you put some distance between yourself and this town, you'll start getting better."

I close my eyes, and not responding to what he says, I just stand still in his embrace.

Jordan will never understand.

After a few minutes, he lets go of me, and I finish preparing our tea before handing him a cup.

"Chamomile?" he asks as he follows me to the living room.

"Yes."

Mom's favorite.

I move the blanket and pillow to the side and sit down on the couch. Jordan takes a seat beside me, and we stare at the black TV screen and the window that looks out onto the front yard.

"The grass is getting long," Jordan mentions.

"I'll cut it tomorrow."

"Want me to do it?" he asks, his tone soft as if the fight has left him.

It always happens when he spends time with me. My depression rubs off on him, and I hate it.

"No," I reply, my tone hollow. "It's something to do to keep me busy."

Everything feels devastatingly empty around us. It's as if I stopped living the night our parents and Sage died. I barely manage to exist.

At least Jordan still has Natalie and Brady to live for.

"You don't have to drive out here anymore," I whisper.

"Don't start," he grumbles.

"The phone calls are fine." My fingertip traces the rim of the cup.

"Drop it, Kelcie. Driving from Naperville to Verona once a month won't kill me."

The moment the word leaves his mouth, my body jerks, and I squeeze my eyes shut.

"Shit. I'm sorry." He lifts his arm and wraps it around my shoulders. "I like the drive. It gives me some time alone."

"Okay."

"Talking about driving. Have you taken your car for its yearly service?"

I give him a sheepish look. "I haven't driven in a long while. It probably won't even start."

Jordan lets out a sigh as he climbs to his feet. "Come on. Let me take a look."

"You don't have to. I can ask Malakai or Asher to check the battery." The brothers took over the gas station and auto repair shop from their father when Mr. Woods retired.

Ignoring me, Jordan asks, "Where are the keys?"

I walk to the kitchen and pull open a drawer I use as storage for random things. I dig around, and finding the keys, I hand them to him before reluctantly following him to the garage.

While watching Jordan tinker with the battery, I stifle a yawn. I usually sleep between twelve and six in the afternoon. Since the attack, I sit up every night as if I'm waiting for the killers to come back, even though I know they're locked away.

When my thoughts threaten to go down the dark path that leads to the worst night of my life, I shake my head and force myself to focus on Jordan.

"Yeah, the battery's dead," he mutters. "I'll go get a new one quickly."

"You don't have to. I don't use the car much. I'll get it done when I need to drive somewhere. Getting a new one will be a waste of money."

I can see Jordan isn't happy with leaving the car like this, but he doesn't say anything.

The doorbell rings, and my head snaps up.

"Are you expecting anyone?" Jordan asks.

"No. It's probably Jill or Holly." We leave the garage, and when I open the front door, Maggie Johnson smiles at me. She's in her late sixties, her gray hair caught in a neat bun. She's one of the sweetest people I know.

Holding up a pie, she says, "It's cherry. I made too many for the inn and thought you'd like one."

Maggie owns Sugar River Inn, and since the actor Easton Rowe stayed there and signed her wall, the place has become a favorite destination for his fans. I know she's made time in her busy day to check in on me because it's the one-year anniversary, and it warms my heart.

"Hi, Maggie," Jordan greets her from behind me.

"Hi, Jordan. It's so good to see you."

I take the pie and smile. "Thanks, Maggie. It's really kind of you."

She gives us a compassionate look. "How are you both holding up?"

I turn sideways so Jordan can move closer, and let him answer, "We're doing okay. Thanks for the pie. How's business?"

"I don't know if I'm coming or going. I have to hire more staff, but that's a problem for tomorrow."

Old me would've offered to help, but I can't bring myself to say the words. Instead, I stand with the pie in my hands and a strained smile around my lips.

"I have to get back to the inn," Maggie says, her eyes softening even more when she looks at me. "Don't hesitate to call on me if you need anything."

I nod. "Thanks, Maggie."

"Don't be a stranger around these parts," she tells Jordan before walking to her car.

While Jordan shuts the front door, I go to the kitchen and place the pie on the counter. "You should take it with you."

"You don't want any?" he asks.

"I had a slice of apple pie at the diner yesterday," I lie because I have no appetite. It will also make Jordan think that I'm not holed up in this house and at least going into town.

"Do you want to go grab some lunch?" he asks.

I shake my head. "With it being the anniversary, half the town is probably going to stop by to drop off food."

"True. At least you won't have to worry about making meals for the next week." Jordan's eyes meet mine, and for a long moment, we stare at each other before he murmurs, "I wish I could make things better for you."

I wish we could visit without me dragging you back down with my grief and trauma.

"You do." I force a smile to my face so it will ease his worry. "I'm okay. Don't worry about me."

Jordan closes the distance between us and envelops me in a tight hug. "I love you, Kelcie."

My chin begins to quiver, and my sight blurs with unshed tears. "I love you too."

Chapter 5

LEVI

Hearing a car's engine, I peek through the curtains and let out a breath of relief when I see Jordan drive away.

I doubt my sanity, once again, as I let the fabric fall back into place. After I learned about the horrific events that transpired in this small town, I couldn't stop thinking about Kelcie and Jordan. The guilt kept eating away at me even though I knew it was unreasonable.

The first time I came to Verona after the attack, it was under the guise of being on vacation. The few times I saw Jordan, he seemed to be doing okay, but Kelcie was spiraling.

I know what happened to the Woodruffs isn't on me, yet I couldn't stop feeling bad for them, and like the fucked-up, crazy person I am, I moved to Verona and bought the house right next door to Kelcie.

Over the past two months, I've watched her like a fucking stalker. I've learned her routine and matched mine with hers.

Yep, I'm fucking insane.

I try to write at night, but I haven't gotten much done the past year and had to ask for an extension on the book, which the publishers agreed to.

In the mornings, Kelcie leaves for two to three hours to visit the cemetery, and I use that time to go for a jog and play catch with Lick so we can get some exercise. Afterward, I manage to get roughly four hours' sleep before Kelcie's screams wake me.

I've been trying to think of a way to help her, but I can't come up with anything.

Lick nudges her snout against my hand to get my attention, and I walk to the back door to let her out. Like always, I take a seat on the top step, and while Lick sniffs for the perfect spot, I glance at the house next door.

When I see Kelcie come outside with a glass of wine, my eyes follow her as she walks to the old wrought-iron table and plastic chairs.

She sits down and stares at the trees behind our properties. I once took a walk out there with Lick to explore the area and found a stream. Since then, it's the trail I use for my morning jogs.

With my gaze on Kelcie, I think back to earlier today when Jordan introduced himself to me. She kept her distance, though. Honestly, she looked so fucking lost and broken as she stood by the SUV, it took a swing at my heart.

A breeze picks up, and it plays with her caramel brown hair, which hangs past her shoulders. Lick looks at Kelcie, then at me as if she's silently asking permission. Gesturing for my dog to go, I watch as she slowly jogs to Kelcie.

Lick stops beside the chair and sits down, happily panting, which gets my neighbor's attention.

"Oh, hey there," Kelcie says. She sets the wineglass down on the table, then holds her hand out for Lick to sniff.

My dog takes the chance and licks Kelcie's hand. Her mouth curves into a slight smile that looks more sad than happy, and I can't tear my eyes away from her beautiful face.

I read that she was beaten and shot during the attack. She almost didn't make it. As I get a good look at the petite woman who's been on my mind twenty-four seven since I read the article, it's hard to believe someone could hurt her.

Yet they did. In the most unimaginable way.

"You're very friendly." Kelcie scratches Lick's head and ears before she glances at me and calls out, "What's his name?"

"Her name is Lick," I answer, and not letting the moment slip through my fingers, I get up and walk closer to them.

"Good name." She lets out a soft chuckle when Lick's tongue takes another swipe at her hand. "You're such a pretty girl," Kelcie murmurs, clearly falling in love with my dog before she looks at me again. "She's so well behaved."

"Thanks." I stop a few feet away from the table. "I'm Levi."

Up close, she's even more striking, and for the first time in a really long while, I feel a pull of attraction.

"Kelcie." Her gaze gets stuck on my face for a moment, then a faint blush creeps up her neck. "I'm sorry for being such a bad neighbor. I should've introduced myself when you moved in."

Her brown irises are dark with grief, and it makes something shift in my chest. Wanting to make her feel better, a rare smile tugs at the corner of my mouth. "That's okay. I should've made an effort to come over sooner."

She shakes her head and turns her attention back to Lick. "How old is she?"

"She's about four years old."

"She's beautiful." Kelcie pets Lick, then mentions, "Her coat is nice and shiny. You take good care of her."

"You know about dogs?" I ask.

"My brother dated a girl who wanted to become a veterinarian, and it's the only thing she ever talked about. But she ended up opening a doggy parlor. I can give you her number if you want to take Lick to get groomed."

"It's okay. I like bathing her."

Lick jumps up, and placing her front paws on Kelcie's thigh, she tries to move closer. Instead of telling my dog to get down, Kelcie places her arms around Lick and gives her a hug.

I take a few steps to the side so my border collie will see me and gesture for her to stay before I say, "I'll catch you later, Kelcie."

When I walk away, she calls out, "What about Lick?"

"She can visit with you until it's time for dinner."

I don't give her time to reply as I step into my house. Leaving the back door open, I watch her through the kitchen window. She climbs off the chair and sits down cross-legged on the lawn. It looks like she's talking to Lick, and knowing my dog will do her more good than I ever could, I head to my office and take a seat at the desk.

It's the one-year anniversary of the attack, and I assume Kelcie won't be getting much sleep today, which means I won't get any either. I might as well try to knock out some words.

I open my laptop and type in the password. I have two documents open, one with the meager plot I've managed to think up and the other for the manuscript, which only has eleven thousand, two hundred and thirty-six words.

At this deplorable pace, I'm never going to get the book done in time, and I doubt the publishers will give me another extension.

Luckily, I didn't spend the advance they paid me, and I'll be able to give it back should the worst happen and I'm unable to write.

I used to dream about being a successful writer. It was all that mattered to me, and I worked my ass off. But after the dust from the instant success settled, my life felt meaningless. I made millions from my royalties, but I can't think of a single thing I'd like to spend it on.

I'd give every cent I have if it would erase the past year and give Kelcie and Jordan their parents and sister back.

If only money had that kind of power.

I lean back in my chair and cross my arms over my chest while I try to focus on the book.

"Hello?" I hear Kelcie's voice, followed by the sounds of Lick's paws on the wooden floor.

It's only then I realize I zoned out, and it's dinnertime for Lick. Getting up, I hurry out of my office, but when I dart into the kitchen, Kelcie is already gone, and the back door is shut.

I yank it open, and when I take the steps down to the lawn, I see her walking toward her house.

"Kelcie," I call out to get her attention.

She spins around, and I feel like shit when I see her eyes widen and a startled expression tighten her features. I need to tone down my assholishness around her.

"Sorry, I didn't mean to bother you," she says.

"You didn't." I come to a stop a safe distance from her, and when she gives me a questioning look, my mind races to come up with a reason for why I stopped her.

Fuck. Think faster, Levi.

"Ahh . . ." I have zero brain activity while I stare at her like a creep.

Frustrated that I'm so antisocial, I rub my fingers over the week-old stubble on my jaw.

"You look like you could use a glass of wine," she says. "It's just sad when I sit outside and drink by myself, and I can't be inside right now. We don't have to talk."

I don't like wine, but I'm not letting this chance pass me by. "Sure."

While I walk to the table, Kelcie heads into the house to get the bottle of wine and another glass. When she comes out again, she asks, "Don't you have to feed Lick?"

"Shit. Right." I jog back to my place and hope Kelcie doesn't pull a disappearing act while I warm Lick's food. Looking down at my dog, I mumble, "Sorry." I crouch down and press kisses to the white fur between her eyes. "Your dad's a little out of his depth right now. If you notice I'm making a fool of myself, feel free to jump in and stop me."

Lick just pants, the excited look on her face for the smell of beef and kidney with vegetables filling the air.

"Your food stinks," I add before I straighten up. When the microwave dings, I quickly mix the meal with dry food and scoop it all into Lick's bowl before setting it down.

Knowing Lick will come outside once she's done eating, I leave the house. As I walk toward the table where Kelcie is sitting, I notice she's already poured wine into the glasses.

I sit down in the only available chair that's near Kelcie's. Usually, I'd feel bothered about being so close to another person, but there's no discomfort as I give her a quick smile. "Thanks."

She nods, her eyes tracking my movements as I pick up the glass and take a sip of the wine.

At least it's sweet. The last time I had wine during a dinner with my agent, it was dry and hard to swallow.

"How do you like Verona?" she asks.

"It's okay."

Kelcie nods, then glances at the trees.

We sit in silence for a few minutes before I realize I need to ask her questions, or she might get suspicious of me because I'm not supposed to know much about her.

"Have you lived in Verona all your life?"

Her attention turns back to me, and she nods. "Born and raised."

I suck in a deep breath, and my heart clenches when I ask the next question. "Does Jordan also live here?"

Her beautiful features tighten with grief as she shakes her head. "No. He lives in Naperville."

When she doesn't mention her parents and sister, I just don't have the heart to ask any more questions and stare at the glass of wine.

What the fuck am I doing inserting myself into her life like this?

"And your family?" she asks.

My eyes lift to hers, and I shake my head. "No contact."

She looks at me for a little while before she glances at the trees again.

Shit, I suck at being social. I wish I was an extrovert and I could say something to cheer her up, but instead, we sit in silence.

Lick comes out of the house and goes about her routine of finding a spot to pee. When she's done, she picks up her ball and comes over.

I indicate to her that we won't be playing, seeing as she's just eaten, and she drops the ball. I pat my leg, and she comes to sit between the chairs.

Kelcie glances at me and Lick, then asks, "You taught her sign language?"

"Our own kind." I pause before adding, "I'm not much of a talker."

"I'm not much of a talker myself these days."

"It's overrated."

We both watch as Lick cleans her paws, and when someone suddenly comes around the side of the house, my eyes instantly snap to the man.

In a split second, I take in his dark blond hair and blue eyes. I notice the possessive expression on his face as he glances between Kelcie and me.

"What's going on here?" he asks.

When Kelcie startles, I'm hit with regret for not warning her about the unexpected visitor.

"Oh, hi, Colby," she greets the man.

He comes to stand beside her chair and places his hand on her shoulder. Leaning down, he kisses the side of her head as if he's trying to show me she belongs to him.

I've seen him around. I think the couple across the street are his parents, but I don't know for sure.

Kelcie gestures at me. "This is Levi. He's my neighbor." She waves at Colby. "This is Colby. He's a friend from school."

I might be mistaken, but it sounds like she's putting emphasis on *friend*.

Like always, my tone is brisk. "Hi."

Colby gives me a chin lift, then he turns his attention to Kelcie. "Want to have dinner with my folks and me?"

She starts shaking her head before he's even done asking. "No, thanks. It's been a long day, and I want to relax out here." When it looks like he is going to argue, she adds, "Besides, people brought food over, and I have enough to last me a week."

She glances at his hand on her shoulder, giving me the impression that it bothers her.

My skin begins to crawl on her behalf, and I have to bite back the words when the urge to tell him to get his hand off her surges through me.

Kelcie turns her head to me, giving me a pleading look. "You're staying for dinner, right?"

Without thinking twice, I nod.

She glances at Colby again. "Say hi to your parents for me."

He reluctantly pulls his hand away from her, and with a scowl on his face, he mutters, "I'll come by to check on you tomorrow when you're not busy."

"Jill is coming over tomorrow." The words burst from Kelcie as she gives him an apologetic look. "You don't have to check on me. I'm fine."

A tense smile forms on his face. "I just want to make sure my favorite girl is okay. I know it's a difficult time for you."

Anguish flashes over Kelcie's features, and I grind my molars to keep from telling Colby to take a hike.

Having had enough, I signal to Lick to take an attacking stance, and my dog doesn't let me down. She darts to her feet and begins to growl threateningly.

Colby glares at her, then mutters, "You should put a leash on that dog."

"Usually, she loves people. It's the first time she's reacting like this." Knowing she won't listen, I say, "Down, Lick." She intensifies her growling, and I lean over to take hold of the thick fur around her neck before glancing at Colby again. "You better go."

"I'll call you later when you don't have company, Kelcie," Colby spits out before finally walking away.

I pat Lick's head and gesture for her to sit. She instantly obeys and pants happily.

Kelcie leans over and brushes her hand over Lick's head and neck. "I wonder why she reacted like that to Colby."

"She probably senses he was agitated with my being here."

Kelcie lets out a sigh. "He means well."

Right.

Keeping her gaze locked on my dog, she continues, "Colby had a crush on me in school, and he's been trying to get me to go out with him the past six years." Her shoulders slump, making me think she's exhausted with his advances. "He's a good guy, and he has been there for me . . . during hard times."

"Doesn't mean you owe him a date." I give my opinion.

"Yeah." She lets out a half-hearted chuckle. "I still feel bad, though."

Wanting to divert her attention away from Colby, I say, "You mentioned dinner?"

She glances over her shoulder at the house. "The townsfolk dropped off enough food to feed a small army. Want to see what there is, then you can choose what you'd like to eat?"

"Sure."

She looks at the half-empty bottle of wine and our glasses. "You don't have to drink it. I have sweet tea and sodas."

"Sweet tea would be great." I smile as I climb to my feet and pick up the glasses. "I'm not much of a wine drinker."

"Me too. Jill left the bottle here." When she sees I don't recognize the name, she explains, "Jill and her daughter, Holly, live over there." She points to the light blue painted house to our right.

"I've seen them around," I mention.

When we walk to the back door, I begin to feel a little antsy. Everything I've done today is far out of my comfort zone.

We step into the kitchen, and I place the glasses in the sink before looking at Kelcie.

She waves her hand over six dishes sitting on the counter. "Pick one."

I move closer, and when I'm standing beside her, I realize she's much shorter than me. The top of her head barely reaches the middle of my chest.

She smells like flowers.

She opens all the containers, and I gesture at the cheesy chicken casserole.

"Good choice," she says. "I love cheese."

Suddenly, there's a flash of extreme pain on her face, and when her breath hitches and speeds up, I don't hesitate and place my hand on her lower back.

I keep my tone as gentle as possible as I murmur, "Just breathe through it."

She closes her eyes, and while a thin layer of sweat beads over her forehead, her lips move as she silently counts until the wave of grief passes.

As soon as she's regained control over her breathing, she whispers, "Sorry."

"No need to apologize."

She moves away from me and takes two plates from one of the cupboards.

Only then do I realize I touched her and felt no disgust. Shock ripples through me, and I look down at my palm and fingers, thinking how warm and fragile she felt.

When I met my ex-wife, touching her didn't fill me with disgust but instead only made me uncomfortable. It was something I could live with.

But that's not the case with Kelcie.

My palm itches with a need to touch her again, to see if it will feel the same. It's unnerving as fuck for reasons I can't quite fathom.

"Shoot. You touched me," Kelcie says. My gaze flicks to hers. "I overheard you telling Jordan you don't touch people. I'm sorry. Are you okay?"

She just had a panic attack, and not even seconds later, she's more worried about me than herself?

When I keep staring at the woman who's having the weirdest effect on me, her features tense with more concern.

"Levi?"

I shake my head and clear my throat before I reply, "I'm okay."

"I won't take offense if you need to wash your hands."

God, she's so sweet.

The corner of my mouth lifts. "I don't need to do that."

"Okay." She grabs a serving spoon, and while she dishes some of the casserole onto the two plates, I take in every movement she makes.

There's no urge to run back to my house. There's no annoyance of being overstimulated. There's zero disgust.

Instead, the attraction I felt earlier has grown, and it makes me curious to know everything about Kelcie.

But even if she felt attracted to me, there could never be anything romantic between us. I just plan to hang around until I'm sure she's okay, then I'm heading back to Grand Rapids.

There's no way she'll tolerate having me in her life when she finds out who I really am.

Chapter 6

KELCIE

Sitting at the table outside, I try to focus on the food I'm eating, but I still don't have an appetite. Eventually, I give up and drink some of the sweet tea.

My eyes wander to Levi, and I watch how he holds the plate with his right hand, his body seemingly relaxed. When he takes a bite, I feel a strong pull of attraction, finding it hot how his jaw moves.

The man is next-level handsome, but I'm more surprised by how nice he's been to me since we started talking. After hearing how grumpy and rude he's been to people in town, it was unexpected, to say the least.

If someone told me this morning I'd be spending my evening with Levi, I would've told them they're crazy.

But here we are.

He actually makes me feel comfortable and isn't pushy in any way. Unlike the rest of the town, he hasn't bombarded me with questions or condolences. There's no pity in his eyes when he looks at me.

I had a panic attack in front of him, and he didn't make me feel weird about it at all. Instead, he was supportive, as if he's done it a million times before.

Earlier, when he approached me, he seemed troubled, but with time, he's relaxed. I wonder if he has always been like this. So quiet and withdrawn. Or did something bad happen to make him this way?

Levi's gaze lifts and connects with mine, and when he catches me staring at him, he asks, "What?"

I shake my head and turn my attention to the trees lining the back of our properties.

"You can ask me questions."

I hesitate before I reply, "That means you'll ask me questions in turn. I'd rather pass."

"I won't."

I glance at Levi again, and as the sun begins to set, it strikes me once more how attractive he is. The dark stubble on his face gives him a rugged look. I think he's in his early or mid-thirties.

He has hazel eyes. The green lines around his irises are so dark that they make the brown appear golden.

At first glimpse, the permanent frown on his forehead and dip of his eyebrows give the impression he's grumpy, but the longer I look at him, the more I see the expression for what it is.

This man has suffered.

With my gaze still glued to his, I whisper, "Why don't you touch people?"

He clenches his jaw and looks down at where Lick is sleeping like the dead. "Bad childhood."

My heart squeezes with empathy. Whatever happened in Levi's childhood must've been traumatizing for him to hate touching people.

"I'm sorry," I say, my tone soft and filled with compassion.

When he inhales a deep breath, his chest strains against the fabric of his shirt to the point that I can make out his muscles. The sight has my stomach buzzing with a nervous energy I haven't felt before.

Lick wakes up from her nap and goes to get her ball. She drops it near my chair and stares obsessively at it.

"She wants you to throw it for her," Levi says, the tension gone from his voice.

I lean over, and picking up the ball, I throw it as hard as I can. Lick sets off at a crazy speed, then jumps into the air and catches the ball.

For the next hour, I play catch with Lick, a comfortable silence falling between Levi and me. The dog has an endless supply of energy, and I begin to work up a sweat.

Besides the times people pop in to check on me and Jill comes over to visit, I've tried to avoid everyone in town as much as possible. That's not the case with Levi. I assume it's because he's so quiet, and I love playing with his dog, so I don't read too much into it.

Finally, Lick calls it quits and lies on the grass, panting so hard, her tongue is hanging out the side of her mouth.

I look at Levi again, and when I see the relaxed smile on his face, I'm hit with an intense wave of attraction.

No, Kelcie. Stop it. You're too broken. Don't go getting a crush on him.

Clearing my throat, I ask, "I'm not sure what the time is, but would you like some tea or coffee?"

"I'd love coffee."

We gather our dishes and walk back to the house. While I get everything ready for our beverages, Levi clears our plates and places them in the dishwasher.

My phone rings, and I suppress a sigh as I walk to the couch where I left the device.

When I see Colby's name, the sigh escapes before I answer, "Hi."

"Is that man still there?"

"Yes."

"I don't like this one bit, Kelcie. He looks like trouble. I'm coming over."

"No, you're not." I move a little farther away from Levi. "I'm actually having a nice evening."

"You couldn't have a nice evening with me?"

Instantly, I feel tired, as if the meager energy I've managed to scrape together just ups and vanishes.

When I remain quiet, Colby says, "I'm sorry. I'm glad you're feeling better. I just wish it were with me and not some stranger who only moved to town two months ago."

"I have to go." I glance over my shoulder and see that Levi is busy pouring water into my teacup and his mug. "We'll talk another time."

"Be careful and call if you need me."

"Good night."

I end the call and notice there are many missed calls. Checking them, it shows they're all from Colby, and I shake my head.

I really appreciate his friendship, but I know he's only hanging around in the hopes of having a romantic relationship with me.

"Everything okay?" Levi asks.

I force a smile to my face as I turn around. "Yes." Setting the phone down on the couch again, I notice the time showing on the screen.

Crap. It's already ten p.m.

My gaze darts to Levi. "I didn't realize how late it is."

He picks up the mug and takes a sip of the coffee before he asks, "Do you want me to go?"

"No." My honest answer catches me completely by surprise, and I feel my cheeks flush with heat.

He gestures at my tea. "I didn't know if you wanted sugar or milk."

"Neither." I pick up the cup and take a sip. "It's perfect."

We stand in silence for a few seconds, then I glance at the sparsely decorated living room. "Do you want to sit inside or outside?"

"Outside."

I follow him back out into the yard and place my cup on the table as I take a seat.

I tug my bottom lip between my teeth, then say, "You're probably wondering why people dropped off food here today."

He shakes his head. "I know what happened to you and your family. You don't have to talk about it if you don't want to."

I look down at my hands and twist my fingers together. "That's the bad thing about living in a small town. Everyone knows your business."

We're quiet for a little while, then I lift my head and force a smile to my face. "What do you do for a living that allows you to stay at home all day?"

His features grow tense. "I'm a writer."

The memory of Mom lost in a book flashes through my mind, and it sends a crippling wave of pain through me.

I inhale deeply before letting the air out slowly, taking a moment so the grief will lessen.

Wanting to keep the topic on him, I say, "I've never met an author before. What kind of books do you write?"

"Fiction. Mostly action and thrillers."

There's a pause in the conversation before I ask, "Do you love it?"

Levi lets out a heavy breath, his eyebrows drawing together. "I used to."

I tilt my head. "Why past tense?"

His gaze lifts to mine, and I feel a zap through my stomach and abdomen from the intense look in his eyes.

"I had a book that got picked up for film. It was a huge success, and when the movie aired, all my books featured in the top hundred of all the bestseller lists."

"Oh wow. So you're famous?" As soon as the words leave me, I feel awkward for saying them.

"Only by name." Levi shakes his head and glances over the dark backyard. "Few people know what I look like." His thumb brushes along the handle of the empty mug in his hands. "Since the instant success, I don't know what to do with myself, and I have writer's block."

"Can't you take a break?"

His eyes find mine again. "I signed a contract with a publisher, and they already gave me an extension. I'll just have to power through."

"I'd offer my help, but I know nothing about writing a book."

He stares at me until it feels as if we're being enclosed in our own private bubble, then he murmurs, "Talking to you helps. In a way, I'm letting go of some of the stress."

"Yeah?"

Levi nods. "Sometimes you just have to find the right person to talk to. Someone who will listen and not tell you to heal and move on."

My eyes begin to burn with unshed tears because his words hit me hard.

"Everyone just wants me to heal," I whisper. "They don't realize they're asking for the impossible."

Levi tilts his head, his face filled with understanding. "You can't heal something that's destroyed."

My chin quivers, and I lower my head. "What do you do when you're destroyed?"

"You have to create a new version of yourself. A version you can live with." I'm surprised when he reaches over and his hand covers both of mine. "And that will take time. Don't let anyone rush you, Kelcie."

I take in the veins snaking beneath his skin, thinking his hand looks really strong.

"I miss the old version of me," I admit softly. "I was so happy." My vision blurs, and I close my eyes to ease the sting from not being able to cry. "My life was perfect."

Levi's fingers tighten around mine, and Lick comes to rest her head on my thigh.

Sitting in the dark, I get more comfort from a dog and this man I hardly know than I've gotten from anyone else since the attack. Everyone's tried to be supportive, but they're always uncomfortable around me. They don't know how to deal with my grief and trauma and eventually give up.

Because Jordan's been able to deal with the loss he suffered, he expects me to do the same. Only, he wasn't there. He didn't hear their screams. He didn't see the violence.

Suddenly, I'm hit with the memory of Sage's pale face, Dad being stabbed, and Mom clutching her neck.

The next breath I try to take slams into my throat and refuses to fill my lungs.

Knowing it's going to be a severe panic attack, I jump up and run to the kitchen. Horrible sounds come from me as I begin to hyperventilate, and I yank open the cupboard where I keep my medicine.

When I take hold of the box, it slips from my hands and falls by my feet.

Levi appears and quickly picks it up. He reads the label, then takes a pill from the foil before pushing it past my lips. He grabs water from the fridge, and placing one of his hands behind my head, he brings the bottle to my mouth so I can drink some and get the pill down.

I'm trembling something fierce and still struggling to breathe. Desperately needing comfort, I slam into Levi's chest and tightly hold on to him.

He curls one hand around the back of my neck while his other grips my bicep. He's not caging me in his arms but is trying to offer me comfort.

"Just breathe," he says with a gentle tone that gets through to me. "You're safe."

Why does it feel like this man knows exactly what I'm going through?

The pill begins to take effect, and my breathing slows down until I become aware that my cheek is pressed against his muscled chest and my hands are gripping his shirt.

Usually, I'd pull back as quickly as possible, but instead, I take a deep breath of his scent, which smells like cedarwood and citrus. It reminds me of my workshop.

God, I miss the smell of wood as I carved it into any shape I wanted.

"Better?" Levi asks.

"Yeah." Pulling back, I lift my head and lock eyes with him. "Thank you." I gesture at his chest. "Sorry for touching you."

"Don't apologize." He tilts his head slightly. "I'm okay with you touching me." He glances at the box. "Do you need to take them often?"

"I'm trying not to depend on them too much." I put the medicine back in the cupboard, then say, "We should call it a night."

"Okay." Levi's eyes drift slowly over my face. "Try to get some rest, Kelcie."

I nod, and once he leaves, I retrieve the mug and teacup from outside and load them into the dishwasher before switching on the machine.

After I shut the back door and make sure to lock it, I head to the couch and drop down with a huff. I pull up my legs and wrap my arms around them, resting my chin on my knees.

Today turned out to be much better than I expected. Besides the panic attacks, I actually had a pleasant evening with Levi. It feels like we're similar, and I don't have to pretend around him.

Curious about Levi, I pick up my phone and google his name.

When I see the title of the book that was made into a movie, my eyes go wide as saucers.

The Elimination Project. Oh my God! Easton Rowe acted in that movie.

Levi even has a Wikipedia page and hundreds of articles about his books. He was named as one of the hundred most influential people by a popular magazine.

Holy crap, the man is much more famous than he lets on.

He uses a logo for his brand, and I can't find any photos of him online. There's also no personal information about him.

Wanting to see what Levi's book was about, I switch on the TV and purchase the movie.

I pull my blanket over me and lie down, snuggling into my pillow.

Not even ten minutes into the movie, I'm so engrossed with what's happening that a bomb could drop beside me and I wouldn't notice.

Chapter 7

LEVI

After spending time with Kelcie, it's become more difficult to keep my distance.

It's been four days, and every time I catch a glimpse of her, I have to suppress the urge to go over and check on her.

I hold the car's back door open for Lick to jump up onto the seat before I shut it. When I climb in behind the steering wheel, I glance at the house beside mine, wondering whether Kelcie is home from her morning visit to the cemetery.

Probably not.

I start the engine, and as I drive to the vet for Lick's yearly checkup, my thoughts return to the other night. I can't remember when I last talked so much. I figured I needed to open up so Kelcie would feel comfortable with me.

Then she had a panic attack, and when she slammed into my chest, I was stunned out of my mind. I was overcome with an intense need to hold and comfort her.

Touching her neck and arm was . . . Jesus, it was downright incredible. Feeling her pressed against my chest made a protective emotion flood my heart.

The entire episode was mind boggling, to say the least. I've never experienced anything like it before.

During the drive to the vet, I find myself searching the sidewalks for Kelcie, and by the time I park the car, I'm low-key annoyed with myself.

I should pack up and go back to Grand Rapids. I'm looking for trouble, staying here.

After getting out of the car, I keep a tight hold of Lick's leash and enter the building. Luckily, there aren't any other animals, and the appointment goes smoothly. I buy her a few treats, and after leaving the veterinary clinic, I pause on the sidewalk to let her eat one of them as a reward for being so well behaved.

I glance up and down Main Street, and once Lick is done wolfing down her treat, we walk to the general store. I grab a basket and get the few items I need, and as I go to pay, there are two women ahead of me at the counter.

"I hear Kelcie is still hiding in that house," the brunette with a ponytail says.

The second I hear Kelcie's name, I shamelessly eavesdrop.

The elderly woman who's loading her groceries onto the counter replies, "It's such a shame that the Woodruffs' old house is just standing empty. They don't even take care of the garden. The sheriff's department has to send someone out to mow the lawn." She makes a *tsk*ing sound. "Libbie told me Jordan wants to sell, but Kelcie is being stubborn."

"You know it's bad when the sheriff's department has to get involved," the cashier gasps. "It was a terrible thing that happened to her family, but it's been a year, and sitting around wallowing in grief all day long isn't doing anyone any favors." She gives her two cents. "Jeez, get over it and move on already."

Anger pours into my chest, and I clench my jaw to keep my mouth shut.

The brunette glances over her shoulder, and when she sees me and a wide smile spreads over her face, I groan internally.

"Aren't you the guy who moved into town two months ago?" She thinks hard. "Levi . . . something."

"Levi Graye," the elderly woman informs her friend, all three women now openly looking me up and down with way too much interest.

I'm immediately uncomfortable and contemplate leaving the basket and getting my ass out of the store, when the brunette reaches out and places her hand on my arm.

Disgust creeps over my skin until it feels as if something's crawling beneath the surface.

"Welcome to Verona. I'm Ellie. My husband and I own The Black Door. You probably saw our bar when you drove into town. You can't miss it. If you're in the mood for a drink after a hard day of work, don't hesitate to stop by."

Repulsed, I rip my arm free from her hold and take three steps backward, a sheen of sweat breaking out over my body. Lick instantly moves in front of me to act as a barrier between the woman and me.

Ellie's features tense with confusion, and when I just glance away and don't bother to talk to her, I can feel the air stiffen.

"Well, I never," the elderly woman mutters. "So the rumors are true. He is nothing but a rude thug. Doesn't he live next door to Kelcie? We should tell Sheriff Williams to do a welfare check on her."

Fuck this shit. I don't need the groceries. I'll call the order in later and have them deliver. Setting the basket down, I stalk out of the store and head straight for my car. My breaths become shallow, and the trembling in my body keeps growing.

On my way home, I see Kelcie walking up ahead. Earlier, I would've stopped to offer her a ride, but needing to be alone, I drive by her without a second glance.

After I pull the car into the garage, I switch off the engine and sit for a moment while I breathe through the disgust creeping all over my body.

Lick barks to remind me we have to get out, and I automatically go through the actions. Once we're inside the house, I set the pack of treats down on the counter in the kitchen before walking through the house and closing all the curtains.

I leave the door to the bathroom open so Lick can come and go as she pleases, and switch on the faucets in the shower. Once I'm undressed, I step beneath the hot spray and let it burn over my skin.

Memories skirt around the edges of my mind, and my breaths turn harsh as I fight to keep them from overwhelming me.

It's been seventeen years since I ran away from home, and there are still moments when the hell I went through as a kid haunts me.

I don't think I'll ever fully heal from it.

I glance down at my chest, and lifting my hand, I brush my fingertips over the old scars that are hidden beneath a tattoo. It looks like black ink has been splattered all over my chest, and a phoenix is visible with red and orange ink, giving the impression that the creature is on fire.

My back is covered in black, dead branches, with a single orange flower on my left shoulder blade.

Grabbing the bodywash, I begin to scrub myself, and only when I'm finally rid of the disgust crawling all over me do I switch off the faucets.

I dry myself and put on sweatpants before I drop down on my bed. Lick jumps up and comes to lie beside me, resting her head on my chest.

With my own trauma retreating, I remember what the women said about Kelcie.

I'll keep an eye on her parents' house and take care of the garden so she doesn't get in trouble and people stop gossiping about it.

It's a way for me to help her and Jordan.

My thoughts turn to Kelcie and how she looked for comfort in my arms when she was suffering from a panic attack. I didn't feel any disgust. Instead, the urge to hold her and never let go was intense.

She's beautiful, kind, and so unbelievably strong, and now that I know I can touch her without being overcome with revulsion, it makes the attraction I feel for her grow in leaps and bounds.

Closing my eyes, I exhale a sigh.

Don't, Levi. Nothing romantic can ever happen between the two of you.

KELCIE

I'm abruptly woken by someone knocking, and half asleep, I stumble to the front door. I peek through the peephole, and seeing Jill, I open it for her.

She takes one look at my messy hair, then asks, "Dang, did I wake you? I'm sorry."

"It's okay. It's time for me to get up." I let Jill come in before I shut the door behind her.

"Ooh boy, do I have news for you," she says as we walk to the kitchen.

Stifling a yawn, I ask, "Would you like something to drink?"

"I'm good. I just had a soda at home." While I prepare tea for myself, she comes to lean back against the counter. "Our grumpy neighbor has the whole town up in arms."

My head snaps toward Jill. "What? Why?"

"Ellie and Miss Juniper were at Jim's convenience store, and Levi was behind them in line. Ellie introduced herself to him, and he ignored her flat out." Jill's eyes are wide, her tone excited. "According to her, she touched his arm, and he shook her hand off as if he was disgusted by her. Can you believe that?" Jill gasps. "Anyway, when Miss Juniper laid into him, he set his basket down and left abruptly." She lets out a sigh and gives me a knowing look. "Apparently, Miss Juniper went straight to the sheriff's department and told Libby to send one of the men out to do a welfare check on you because she's worried that you're living next door to a 'rude thug.'" She makes air quotes with her pointer fingers.

"That's insane!" My words aren't even cold when the doorbell rings.

My shoulders slump as I walk to the front door and open it.

Sheriff Williams smiles at me while tipping his hat. "Hi, Kelcie. I just wanted to check in on you and make sure you're okay."

"Hi, Sheriff." Annoyed by everything Jill told me and being forced to interact with people before I've even had a chance to wake up properly, I get right down to business. "Thank you for coming by, but I'm okay. Don't believe any of the rumors you hear about Levi."

"He was pretty rude to Ellie and Juniper," the sheriff informs me. "Tamara was working and backed their complaint."

I'm sure she did. Tamara is one of the biggest gossips in town.

"Levi is an introvert who doesn't like people touching him," I explain. "You should tell Ellie to keep her hands to herself."

Sheriff Williams seems to relax. "So he hasn't given you any trouble?"

"Not at all." My smile turns natural. "Levi has been very supportive and kind. I'm lucky to have him for a neighbor."

"Well then, my job here is done." Tipping his hat again, he begins to turn away from me. "You have a good day now."

"You too. Thanks for stopping by."

When I close the door, a scowl forms on my forehead, and I march through the house while muttering, "Just give me a minute, Jill."

I stalk out the back and cross the lawn between the two houses. Before I reach Levi's door, it opens, and Lick comes darting out. A few seconds later, Levi comes into view, and my eyebrows fly into my hairline.

Oh. My. God.

He's only wearing sweatpants, and I can't stop myself from drinking in the sight of his chest and the ink covering most of his skin. After getting a good look at the phoenix tattoo, my gaze lowers to his six perfectly carved abs and the V-shaped muscular grooves running alongside his hips.

"Kelcie?" Levi asks, sounding a little taken aback by my sudden appearance.

I blink like an idiot and quickly glance to where Lick is sniffing the grass. "I heard about what happened in town and wanted to check on you." Turning my gaze back to Levi, I notice the grim lines on his face. "Are you okay?"

I haven't seen him in the past few days and thought he just needed some space, but after learning about how he reacted to Ellie touching him, I wonder if I was too much when I had my panic attack.

"I'm fine," he replies. When Lick comes toward me for pets, Levi pats against his thigh, and she quickly goes back into the house. "See you around."

Levi shuts the door, and with a sinking feeling, I turn around and walk back to my place.

Crap, maybe I did upset him the other night with all the touching and asking him to stay for dinner, and he was just too overwhelmed to put me in my place.

The instant I step into the kitchen, Jill says, "What's going on with you and our hot, grumpy neighbor?"

I shake my head. "Nothing is going on." I finish making my tea and manage to take a couple of sips before my doorbell rings again. "What now?" I mutter, refusing to admit that I'm a little hurt by Levi being so brisk with me.

When I open the door and see Colby, my shoulders slump.

"I heard Sheriff Williams was here because of the bastard next door. I told you he was nothing but trouble."

Completely overstimulated by all the activity, I can't stop myself from snapping, "Levi isn't a bastard! I wish everyone would mind their own business." When Colby tries to come in, I don't step out of his way. "Look, I just woke up from a nap, and Jill is here. Thanks for stopping by."

I shut the door in his face and rest my forehead against it.

Dang, this afternoon is getting the better of me. I'm used to being alone ninety percent of the time and feel completely rattled.

When I finally turn around, it's to see Jill carry my teacup to me. "Sit down on the couch and drink your tea."

"Thanks." I don't even bother moving my blanket and plop down on top of it.

As I take a sip, I glance through the window and see Colby crossing the road to his parents' house.

"So Colby still isn't taking the hint?" Jill asks, sitting down beside me.

"I've been super clear with him, but he refuses to hear that there will never be anything between us." Even though I got five hours of sleep, I let out a tired sigh. "I just wish he'd give up and set his sights on someone else."

We're quiet for a moment, then Jill turns her body so she's facing me. "There's a brave boy from school who knocked on my door last night. He asked me whether he could take Holly out on a date."

My eyes widen. "Oh my gosh. And? What did you say?"

"I told him I'd think about it." She scrunches her nose. "Holly is only fourteen. I feel she's too young to start dating, but if I say no, she might do things behind my back." Worry fills her eyes. "What do you think I should do?"

"Gosh, I don't know. I have zero parenting experience." I think for a moment. "Maybe you could say yes on condition that you go with them. If they go watch a movie, you could sit a few rows away?"

Jill's face lights up. "That's a great idea!" Climbing to her feet, she hurries toward the front door. "I'm going to give Holly the good news and let you wake up in peace and quiet. See you later."

"Bye."

When she pulls the door shut behind her, I continue to drink my tea while trying to make sense of the last hour.

What a crappy way to wake up.

Rising to my feet, I walk to the kitchen to make myself another cup of tea. With the steaming beverage in hand, I head outside and take a seat at the table.

I stare at the trees while my thoughts revolve around Levi.

He was so patient and kind when we had dinner, but today he was cold and standoffish.

Suddenly, Lick's snout nudges against my thigh, and it takes all my strength not to look at Levi's house to see if he's coming outside as well.

"Hey, girl," I murmur while brushing my palm over her soft fur. "I heard you had a rough day."

"I'm sorry." Levi's voice sounds rough and deep, and it sends a wave of goose bumps spreading through my body. When he sits down in the other chair, I glance at him.

He's dressed in a pair of jeans and a sweater that looks as soft as Lick's fur.

Feeling relieved that I get to interact with him again, my tone is gentle as I reply, "It's okay."

He shakes his head and glances over the yard. "I ran away from home when I was sixteen. I got married when I was young and stupid, but it didn't even last a year. Since then, I've been on my own. It's become very difficult to interact with people."

My eyebrows draw together, and there's an intense pang of sadness in my heart, learning that he's been alone for such a long time.

"How old are you?"

His gaze turns back to me. "Thirty-three."

We're quiet for a little while before I say, "Well, if you're looking for a friend, it just so happens I have a spot open."

The corner of his mouth lifts. "Yeah? You don't mind being friends with a grumpy asshole?"

"Not at all." I let out a sigh. "In case you haven't noticed, I'm not the most social person in town. We're two peas in a pod."

Silence falls between us while Lick soaks up all the attention I'm giving her. "Where's your ball?"

She darts away like a bat out of hell to fetch her toy inside the house before coming back. She drops the ball near my chair, then stares at it, her tongue already hanging out.

I throw as hard as I can, and Lick tears across the yard to fetch it.

"I have a couple of steaks and was thinking of firing up the grill," Levi says, his tone much kinder. "Want to join me?"

Keeping my attention on Lick, I answer, "That sounds nice. I can make corn on the cob."

"Sounds good." He gets up, and when he walks back to his house, I steal a glance at him.

His broad shoulders and trim waist have my stomach fluttering, and I frown at myself.

You have to kill the attraction before it gets out of hand. Levi is clearly not interested in anything romantic, and you shouldn't be either.

Chapter 8

KELCIE

While I make sure the corn on the cob doesn't burn, Levi keeps an eye on the steaks.

He cuts off a piece and sets it aside. When he notices I'm looking, he explains, "I'm letting it cool down for Lick."

"Why did you name her Lick?"

"Because as a puppy, she used to lick every damn thing she could get her tongue on."

I let out a chuckle and remove the corn on the cob, then head into Levi's kitchen to set them down on our plates. Seconds later, he joins me with the steaks.

I glance around, and spotting drawers, I try the top one. "Bingo." I grab knives and forks for us before asking, "Where do you want to eat?"

He gestures at the kitchen table. "We can sit here."

While I set the silverware down, Levi brings our plates before heading to the fridge. "I have beer and water."

"A beer will be great."

Sitting down, I try to ignore the burst of happiness I feel because I'm getting to hang out with Levi. It's the first time in a really long while since I've felt something positive.

I take a bite of the steak, and when it melts in my mouth, a satisfied groan escapes me. "So good."

Levi stares at me until I begin to feel awkward, then he looks down at his food and cuts into the meat.

We enjoy our meal in silence with Lick sleeping beside the table. Once we're done, I carry the dishes to the sink and rinse everything off before placing them in the dishwasher.

Picking up my beer, I take a sip and try to come up with a reason to visit a bit longer.

When I glance at the back door, Levi asks, "Do you want to go home?"

I shake my head.

"Let's go sit in the living room," he suggests.

I try to suppress a smile as I follow him out of the kitchen. When we step into the living room, I take in the TV mounted on the wall, the light gray couches, and the shelf with books.

Moving closer, I read the titles and look at the framed pictures of his movie and publishing deals. There are also images of his book covers and them ranking number one on various lists.

The last frame contains a photo of Levi standing beside Easton Rowe.

"It's so cool that Easton starred in the movie. Did you know he's from Verona?"

I glance over my shoulder in time to see Levi nod. "I read about it in an article."

"He's much older than me, so I never spoke to him, but whenever one of his movies is released, the town usually sets up a big screen on the football field, where everyone can watch. They make a big fuss about it." Levi takes a seat on a couch, and noticing worry creeping into his hazel gaze, I add, "I don't think anyone in town knows who you are. But you better keep it a secret or they'll wear out your welcome mat."

"I don't have a welcome mat."

A burst of laughter escapes me. "Figuratively speaking."

I pick the other couch and sit down. When I look at Levi again, our eyes lock, and it feels as if an invisible current passes between us.

"So I'm the talk of the town?" he asks as he starts to peel off the label around his beer bottle.

I shrug. "Don't worry about it. Tomorrow they'll have something new to gossip about."

Leaning forward, he rests his forearms on his thighs, and it makes the veins look ridiculously hot as they snake beneath his skin.

"They were talking shit about you before Ellie noticed me and placed her hand on my arm." His features tighten with disgust, and he clears his throat. "It makes my skin crawl when people touch me."

"I'm sorry that happened," I murmur, my tone soft. "And I'm sorry for all the touching the other night."

He shakes his head, lifting his eyes to meet mine. "For some reason, I'm okay with you."

His words make more happiness trickle into my heart. "I'm glad to hear that."

"You're not curious to know what they said about you?" he asks.

"It's probably nothing I haven't heard before." I make air quotes. "I have to deal with everything and move on. I'm stubborn for not selling . . ." My voice disappears, and I'm unable to finish the sentence.

His tone is gentle when he says, "Don't let them get to you. You do what's right for you."

I nod, a weak smile tugging at my mouth. "It just sucks, you know?"

"I do. They're insensitive and don't understand. They haven't been through something so traumatic."

Slowly, I lift my gaze to his. "It doesn't get any better, does it?"

Levi stares at me for a long while before he shakes his head. "At least, it hasn't gotten any easier for me."

I let my eyes trail down his arm again, and a scar grabs my attention. It looks like a burn mark.

Then I see another one, and my heart constricts.

He said he had a bad childhood. Did his parents abuse him? Did they leave those marks on him?

Levi notices what I'm looking at, and when his fingers brush over the scars, my cheeks warm with shame for staring at him, and I quickly whisper, "I'm sorry."

He leans back against the couch and lets out a sigh. "My stepfather liked to use me for an ashtray."

I suck in a sharp breath as shock shudders through me. My hand flies up to cover my mouth. "God, Levi."

When his gaze captures mine, I see the endless trauma darkening the green ring around his irises. "I'm telling you in the hopes that you'll open up to me. Everyone needs someone to talk to."

"Have you talked to anyone about what happened to you?" I ask.

"Never." He shakes his head. "Not until you."

"Why me?"

"Because you'll understand." His attention returns to the half-destroyed label around his beer. "Like you said, we seem to be two peas in a pod."

We're quiet for a few minutes while we sip on our beers, and when my bottle is empty, I ask, "Do you have any happy memories of your childhood?"

Levi just shakes his head.

I don't know if I'll be able to talk about my family, but I can't stop myself from asking, "Want me to share some of mine with you?"

The corner of his mouth lifts. "I'd love that."

I lean forward and set the empty bottle on the coffee table while I let myself willingly think of my childhood for the first time in a really long while.

Memories flood me, and a sad smile pulls at my mouth when I think of something I can share. "Before Jordan and . . ." Pain slices through my heart, and I squeeze my eyes shut. ". . . Sage moved out, we used to have little treasure hunts for our birthdays. We'd hide twelve pieces of candy all over the house and garden, and whoever's birthday it was had an hour to find them all." My nose tingles as the urge to cry builds in me. "It was just candy, but we had so much fun. We'd blow those birthday whistles . . ." I open my eyes to look at Levi. "You know the ones that roll out?" When he nods, I continue, "Anyway, we'd blow them if the person was heading in the wrong direction." My smile widens. "The one time, Dad started laughing. I can't remember why, but his whistle kept squawking like a duck. I laughed so hard, I almost wet myself that day."

When I blink, a tear slips free and rolls over my cheek. I brush it away, and when I see the wetness on my fingertips, a weird mixture of a sob and laughter bursts from me.

My voice is hoarse as I admit, "I haven't cried since I left the hospital."

After a while, Levi whispers, "Thank you for sharing your happy memory with me."

Even though it's growing dark in the room, Levi doesn't move to switch on a light.

Lick snores, and it pulls my attention to her. "She lies like a human when she sleeps. It's so cute."

"Yeah."

I keep looking at the beautiful dog as I ask, "Do you want to share a memory with me?"

"You want us to make a memory-for-a-memory deal?" he asks.

My eyes dart to him, and I don't even think twice. "Yes."

His expression grows tense again. "Just tell me if any of mine are too much for you, and we can stop."

Dear God.

I straighten up and square my shoulders to ready myself for whatever he's going to share with me.

"I was five when my mother remarried. I never knew my biological father, and I was excited that I finally had a dad." Levi pauses, and I see the moment he slips into his past, his expression tightening until he looks tormented.

I'm overcome with the urge to go to him and hug him tightly, but I sit still and listen.

"At first, he was only verbally abusive. My mother was already pregnant when they got married, and not long after, my half brother was born. That's when things changed drastically. If my brother cried, my stepfather would beat me, so I spent every waking moment trying to soothe him. I would push his stroller for hours." Levi seems to come out of the daze and exhales a heavy breath. "To this day, the sound of a crying baby puts me on edge."

Unable to keep my distance, I get up and walk over to Levi. Sitting down beside him, I ask, "May I hug you?"

He turns his head slightly toward me, then nods.

I scoot closer until our bodies touch and wrap my arms around his neck. When he leans into me and places his left hand on my back, I don't think and press a kiss to his hair. "I'm so sorry you had to experience that."

His other arm comes around me, and he grips me tightly to him.

After a few minutes, he whispers near my ear, "Your turn."

"When I was sixteen, we all had to take lifelike baby dolls home for a weekend. It was to teach us how difficult it is to have a baby. At night, my family took shifts to take care of the doll, and during the day, they all helped with the diapers and feedings. When I asked my parents why, they said that's what it would be like if I came home with a baby. Everyone would pitch in to help and make things easier for me." Laughter sputters from me. "Then they gave me the talk about using protection, and I almost died from embarrassment."

Levi lets out a chuckle, the sound deep as it rumbles from his chest, and it makes me feel like I did something good.

When it sinks in that he isn't going to pull back first, I slowly let go until I'm able to meet his gaze. "Thank you, Levi."

"For?"

"Doing what no one else could do the past year."

His eyes soften as they drift over my face. "What's that?"

"Helping me to remember the happy times I shared with them." I lower my arms as I admit, "I don't want to forget them."

"You won't." He brings his hand to my face and carefully cups my cheek. "One memory at a time. Okay?"

It feels like something bigger than us fills the air between us as I reply, "Okay."

Suddenly, he pulls back and climbs to his feet. "Tea?"

"Sure." I get up, and as we walk to the kitchen, I ask, "What's the time?"

Levi gestures to a clock on the wall, and when I see it's already past midnight, I gasp. "Oh my God. I'm keeping you up."

"You're not. I don't sleep at night."

Shocked, my gaze swings to him. "Really? Me too. When do you sleep?"

"I catch a few hours during the day." He opens a cupboard, then says, "I only have black tea. Is that okay?"

"Yes."

While he prepares coffee for himself and tea for me, he asks, "Can you open the back door for Lick?"

As soon as I pull the door open, Lick darts out of the house. I watch as she goes about her business until Levi brings me the cup. "Thanks." I take a sip, then smile at him. "It's good."

He drinks his coffee while he looks at his dog. "When we moved in with my stepfather, he tied my dog to a pole in the backyard of our old home and said I had to leave him behind. I spent the week after we moved worrying about Dodger, then I overheard a call between my mother and our landlord. Luckily, he found and adopted Dodger, but he let my mother have an earful and refused to return her deposit."

What kind of monsters force a little boy to give up his dog like that?

"We need to make a new deal," I say.

Levi's face fills with worry. "Too much?"

"No, but I get the feeling I'm going to want to hug you after every bad memory. Is that okay?"

His mouth curves up. "You have a deal."

I give him a sideways hug before I move out of the way so Lick can come back into the house.

Chapter 9

LEVI

I spent the entire morning at the Woodruffs' house, getting rid of weeds and gathering all the dead leaves, which Lick had a blast playing in. A few of the neighbors gave me weird looks, but I just ignored them.

After I pull up to my house, I unload the trash bags and place them in the garage, thinking I'll move them out onto the sidewalk when they come to collect the trash.

Lick and I head straight for the bathroom, and while I shower, she makes herself comfortable on the mat and sleeps like the dead.

It actually felt good doing all that yard work. I'll go twice a month to keep an eye on the place.

Once I'm clean and dressed, I walk to the kitchen and grab a bottle of water before I go to my office to see if I can get some writing done. I should sleep, but when I open my laptop, I'm struck with an idea and start typing.

For the first time in a long while, the words come easily, and it feels so damn good, a smile settles on my face.

One chapter becomes two, and a few hours later, I take a break to stretch my muscles and let Lick go outside.

I roll my shoulders and make sure to drink some water while I watch Lick. Glancing at Kelcie's house, I notice her yard needs some tending to. I'll take care of it tomorrow for her. There's also the added bonus that manual labor seems to be good for my writing.

Or is it hanging out with Kelcie and talking to her that's making all the difference?

For someone who thought he was unable to feel love for another human being, I find myself fighting the emotion more and more. Whenever I'm around Kelcie and she shares one of her happy memories, I fall a little harder.

I know I'm playing with fire and this situation is bound to explode in my face, but I can't stay away from her.

You have to think of Kelcie, asshole. What will it do to her when she finds out who you are?

Guilt rears up in my chest, but the next second, I hear an agonizing cry from Kelcie's place.

Dropping the bottle of water, I shoot forward and run to her back door, which is locked. I look through the kitchen window, and not seeing Kelcie, I pound my fist against the wooden door.

"Mom!" she screams, the terror in her voice breaking my fucking heart.

I continue hitting the door hard while I keep looking through the window, and when I catch sight of Kelcie getting up from the couch, I let out a breath of relief. She looks completely out of it as she staggers to the door, and the second she opens it for me, I move forward and wrap my arms around her.

I've heard her screams before, but since I've begun to develop feelings for her, they take brutal swings at my heart.

Her breathing is harsh as she clings to me, her body trembling.

I hesitate for a moment before I press a kiss to the top of her head, and as I hold her, I slip closer to the edge, knowing that once I tip over, there will be no turning back.

Kelcie is the one person I can touch. She's the only one I can talk to.

My arms tighten even more around her, and I lean my head down, pressing another kiss to her temple.

The air around us tenses, and when she lifts her arms and wraps them around my neck, alarm bells go off in my mind.

Don't go there with her.

Kelcie tilts her head slightly back, and I feel her breath on my throat.

Fuck.

I try to fight it, but when my eyes lock with her brown ones, and I see the desire on her face, my self-control is pushed to its limits.

For the first time in my life, I'm hit with an intense urge to kiss a woman. It turns my breathing ragged, and every muscle in my body coils tightly. It used to take effort to get hard so I could have sex with my ex-wife, but with Kelcie, it comes naturally.

FuckFuckFuck.

I have no idea where the strength comes from, but I let go of her and move backward until I'm standing on the lawn. "Ahh . . ." My tongue flicks out to wet my lips, my hands fisting at my sides. "I heard you scream and thought I should wake you."

Looking rattled, Kelcie places her hand on her neck but then lifts it higher and wipes over her forehead. "Um. Thanks."

Lick sniffs at the steps before going into the kitchen and wagging her whole damn body with the excitement of seeing Kelcie.

Yeah, I know the feeling.

Needing to get away from Kelcie before she notices my hard-on, I indicate for Lick to stay while I turn away and walk toward my house.

When I reach the safety of my kitchen, I brace both my hands on the table and lean forward while breathing through the intense desire I'm experiencing.

I'm used to living a quiet life where the most excitement I get is writing an action scene. But whatever this is that's developing between Kelcie and me is so unnerving, and I don't know how to handle it.

You're not going to act on it. That's how you'll handle it.

She's already doing better. You should leave before one of you gets hurt.

Even as I chastise myself, I know I'm not going to listen.

I enjoy spending time with her. I'm starting to live for her smiles and the sound of her chuckles and laughter.

I'm finally writing again.

Maybe I can hide who I really am from her forever?

I've been able to keep the information from the press, so it should be easy with Kelcie.

I've been lucky so far, and my fucked-up family hasn't spoken publicly about me.

But what if I run out of luck?

Straightening up, I lift my hand and rub the back of my neck as I walk to my office. When I take a seat on the chair at my desk, I pause and stare at the bottom left drawer. Opening it, I pull out the envelope I've reluctantly carried around with me. It contains all my personal documents, and I haven't looked inside since I had to apply for a visa to visit China.

Wow, that was four years ago.

Opening the envelope, I slide the documents out onto my desk. There's an unabridged birth certificate, which I applied for when I turned eighteen. I thought I might need it at some point. It only contains Rene's details under the section for mother. I hate to think of her as my mother because she was never one to me. The space for my father is blank.

I look at the aged marriage certificate and divorce decree, shaking my head because I was so fucking stupid to marry a woman I didn't love.

Margo deserved so much better than me.

The last time she called to check on me, she told me she was getting married again. I was really happy for her, and it gave me some measure of peace, knowing another man would give her what I couldn't.

Lick comes trotting into the office, drawing me out of my thoughts, and I quickly put all the documents back in the envelope. Just as I slip it into the drawer and push it shut, Kelcie appears in the doorway.

There's an unsure expression on her face, and her voice is filled with vulnerability as she says, "Hey. Want to have dinner with me?"

I hate that she isn't comfortable around me any longer.

Climbing to my feet, I smile to set her at ease. "Sure. What are we having?"

She lets out an awkward chuckle. "I haven't thought that far ahead."

"How about ordering in? I haven't had pizza in a while."

Her features tighten with pain, and I take an involuntary step closer to her. "You okay?"

She glances over her shoulder at the living room. "I haven't had pizza since . . ."

"We can have something else. Tacos. Burgers and fries. You pick."

For a long moment, she keeps staring at something, then she shakes her head. "No. Let's have pizza. Want to play rock, paper, scissors to see who has to call and place the order?"

Laughter escapes me. "It's okay. I'll make the call."

"Great." She takes a few steps back and begins to turn away but then pauses. "I'm just going to shower. Should I come over afterward?"

"Sure."

She doesn't look as uncomfortable anymore, and I take it as a good sign.

When she begins to walk toward the kitchen, Lick follows her.

I move into the doorway and say, "Dress warm. The news said a cold front is hitting tonight."

"Okay."

Soon, the first snow will fall, and then it will be Thanksgiving. I should ask Kelcie if she's going to spend the holiday with Jordan.

The thought is fleeting as I walk back to my desk, where my phone is lying under a bunch of invoices. I only use the device for my social media accounts and rare calls with my agent.

I google the diner's number and call in an order for three pizzas. I should've asked, but not knowing what Kelcie would prefer, I decide to go with a pepperoni, a Hawaiian, and one called "the Works," which has just about every topping on it. Hopefully, she likes one of them.

While I'm waiting for Kelcie and the delivery, I make sure I've saved my manuscript on my laptop and a portable hard drive. Back when I started writing, I was hit with the blue screen of death when my laptop gave up the ghost and lost forty thousand words. It's one mistake I'll never make again.

Checking my emails, I clear out the spam and reply to an author asking to do a newsletter swap. I won't be sending one to my followers anytime soon, so I decline politely.

Once I'm done, I shut off the laptop and take my phone with me as I head to the kitchen, where I keep my wallet and keys in a bowl filled with stuff I figure I might use at some point.

Kelcie appears in the doorway, and when Lick rushes past her to come inside, she says, "Sorry, she was with me while I showered."

Lucky dog.

I take in the jeans and thin pink sweater Kelcie's wearing and figure I can give her a jacket if she gets cold. Or I can hold her.

Stop it.

A knock at the front door draws our attention, and as I go to open it, I'm conscious of Kelcie behind me.

It feels good having her in my space.

I open the door and barely take in the woman holding the three pizza boxes.

"Hi," she greets me with a friendly smile.

"Hi," I mumble while pulling my black credit card from my wallet.

Kelcie steps closer, and it has the woman saying, "Oh my gosh, I took the order so I could pop over to your place to say hello after the delivery."

"Hi, Waverly," Kelcie says, her tone friendly. "How are you and the family?"

"We're good." Waverly pauses, a sad expression on her face. "We miss seeing you at the diner. How have you been?"

I take the boxes from her and go to set them down on the coffee table, then hang back until they're done catching up so I can pay.

"I'm doing better."

When Waverly reaches out to rub Kelcie's arm, my entire body tenses, and I have to suppress the urge to grab her away from the woman.

I'm caught completely off guard by the unexpected emotion.

". . . or not." I catch the tail end of Kelcie's sentence. "I can pay. I don't mind."

I move forward, and as I come up beside Kelcie, I place my arm around her shoulders and brush my hand up and down her bicep where she was just touched.

Wanting to get rid of Waverly, I quickly tap the card against the little machine in her hand and mutter, "Thanks."

I pull Kelcie back with me as I put some distance between us and Waverly.

"I'll see you around," Waverly says while her eyes dart between Kelcie and me.

"Say hi to your mom for me and give Lucas a hug," Kelcie replies, and as Waverly finally leaves, she shuts the door, then turns to look at me. "Are you okay?"

Realizing I'm still standing with my arm around her shoulders, I quickly let go and glance at the pizza boxes.

Fuck, I'm actually filled with disgust because someone touched Kelcie. It's the exact same reaction I would have if Waverly put her hands on me.

It's the first time something like this has happened, which tells me I'm already in over my head when it comes to Kelcie.

I look at her again. "I'm fine."

"Waverly is one of the good ones," she tells me. "I used to babysit her son."

I nod, then gesture at the coffee table. "Should we eat here in the living room?"

"Sure."

I walk to the kitchen, and opening the fridge, I call out, "Beer, soda, or water?" Since I've been spending more time with Kelcie, I make sure to stock things she likes.

"I'll have a soda, please," she replies as she comes into the kitchen. While she grabs two plates, I work on shoving my strong reaction to Waverly touching her way fucking down.

My gaze follows Kelcie's every movement, drinking in the sight of her beauty, which has placed me under a spell I can't break free from.

A spell I don't want to break free from.

Standing like an idiot with two sodas in my hands and the fridge door open, I realize I've fallen head over heels for Kelcie.

Chapter 10

KELCIE

I can feel Levi's burning eyes on me, and when I dare a glance, I see he's zoned out.

I think he's having a bad day, and I'm trying to come up with an idea of how I can make it better.

Earlier, when he hugged the crap out of me, there was a moment where it felt like he wanted to kiss me, but seconds later, he couldn't get away from me fast enough.

Yeah, I'm not going to lie. Levi is very difficult to read, and I never know what he's thinking.

"Let's eat," I say to get his attention while I leave the kitchen.

My thoughts and emotions are all over the place. Besides not being sure whether he actually wanted to kiss me, there's also the incident of him holding me all possessively and pulling me away from Waverly.

It looked like he was upset because she touched me.

Did it trigger him?

God, I wish I knew what was going on in his mind.

I set the plates down on the coffee table, and when I look at the pizza boxes, it feels like I'm forcefully shoving a dagger through my heart.

Not knowing how I'd react when eating the pizza, I brought a pill in case things spiral and I end up having a panic attack.

"Are you okay?" Levi asks, and it's only then that I notice he's holding a soda out to me.

I quickly take it from him, and deciding to be honest so he'll be prepared, I admit, "The last time I had pizza was the night of the attack."

"Jesus, Kelcie." A harsh breath bursts over his lips. "I can make us something else."

I shake my head and dig the pill out of my pocket. When I place it on the coffee table, Levi says, "Please don't push yourself too hard."

My teeth nervously worry my bottom lip as I nod.

Wanting to be strong for once, I lean down and open the box at the top of the stack. The instant I see pineapple, my breath hitches, and it feels like my heart is being torn in two.

Sage.

Beautiful, clever Sage, who was going to take the legal world by storm.

When she figured out I was giving her all my pineapple pieces to make her happy, she tried to stop me. But I loved seeing her smile and made her take them.

To others, it might seem stupid, or it may not make sense, but it became our thing. I got to give Sage something small that meant the world to her.

In the back of my mind, I'm aware of my breaths bursting over my dry lips, my heart thundering a mile a minute.

"I've got you." Levi's voice sounds weird, as if he's talking underwater.

I feel his fingers by my mouth as he feeds me the pill, and soon after, the soda eases the dryness. I sputter as I struggle to swallow, but finally manage.

As the worst of the panic attack eases a little, I become aware of Levi's arms wrapped around me and the scent of his cologne.

I love the smell.

It feels as if his much bigger body curves around mine, and it gives me a sense of safety I haven't felt since my world was destroyed.

"There you go. Deep breaths," he murmurs, his tone soothing to my frayed nerves.

My fingers are twisted in his sweater, and needing to feel more of him, I flatten my hands over his back.

Finally, the medication kicks in and my breathing returns to normal. Levi presses a kiss to my temple, and his lips pause on my skin for long seconds.

Slowly, I brush my palms up and down the expanse of his back and broad shoulders, and as my emotions get tossed from one extreme to the next, I struggle to think straight.

When I feel a specific part of him hardening against my stomach, my eyes pop open. The next second, Levi yanks back, and picking up the Hawaiian pizza, he stalks to the kitchen.

I lift a trembling hand to my forehead while I suck in a deep breath of air.

I'm pretty sure Levi just got a hard-on. There's no way I imagined it.

But if he's attracted to me, why isn't he acting on it?

Confused and still rattled by the severe panic attack, I sit down on the couch and scrub my palms over my face.

"Are you okay?" Levi asks, his tone gruff and deep.

Is he upset?

My head snaps up, and when I see the uncomfortable expression on his face, I begin to feel rotten. "I'm sorry."

He shakes his head as he comes to sit down beside me. "Don't ever apologize for having a panic attack."

Needing to know why he's upset, I ask, "Did I do something wrong? The touching?"

He shakes his head again and forces a smile to his face. "We're left with pepperoni, and the other has the works on it. How do you feel about those?"

"I'm good with either," I lie, because pepperoni was Dad's favorite.

Levi leans forward and plates two slices of each for himself. When I see a long string of cheese, I swallow hard.

I know I can't avoid everything that reminds me of my parents and Sage.

Enjoy it for them.

The little voice whispering deep in my heart is right. They'd be so upset if they knew how I was spending my time, and I've been getting so much better with Levi's help.

Standing up, I walk to the kitchen, and seeing the Hawaiian pizza on the kitchen table, I pick it up and carry the box back to the living room. I sit down next to Levi again and lift the lid.

You can do this for Sage.

I take hold of a slice and bring it to my mouth. Closing my eyes, I bite into the cheese, ham, and pineapple, the flavors bursting over my tongue.

My chin trembles as I chew, and even though I feel conflicted emotions, I keep eating.

Levi leans back against the couch, and placing his right hand on my back, he uses his left to eat.

His touch is soothing, and slowly the chaotic mess in my chest begins to settle until I'm left with a bittersweet emotion.

God, I miss you, Sage.

My eyes mist up, and I blink quickly.

On the next bite, the image of Mom being dragged by her hair flashes through my mind. It's quickly followed by Dad's groan for me to run.

I ran. I left them and ran.

My stomach churns violently, and shoving the box off my lap, I dart to my feet and run for the hallway. I have no idea where the bathroom is.

"On the left," Levi says behind me.

I make it to the toilet in the nick of time and lose everything I ate, and my body jerks violently.

Levi gathers my hair, and I want to tell him to leave so he doesn't see me like this, but I can't.

When I stop vomiting, I feel drained of all my energy, and a dry sob bursts over my lips.

Levi pulls me back, and he flushes the toilet. He moves his arms beneath me, then I'm lifted from the floor before being set down on a counter.

I watch as he soaks a washcloth, and when he begins to wipe the heated skin of my face and neck, my gaze meets his.

"Pizza is banned," he grumbles.

"We should add chocolate cake to that list," I reply, my voice hoarse from being sick.

Not caring that I'm being selfish, I lean forward and wrap my arms around his neck. I need to hold him for a minute. Or an hour. I need the comfort I can only get from him.

Levi nudges my knees open, and stepping between them, he engulfs me against his chest, his arms solid bands of safety around me.

"I know it's difficult for you, but I need this," I whisper. "It's comforting."

"It's not difficult for me," he murmurs.

One of his hands cups the back of my head, and I feel him dropping kisses on my hair.

Closing my eyes, I focus all my attention on Levi, and it helps a lot. *What is it about this man that makes him have this calming effect on me?*

I have no idea how much time passes before Levi says, "Lick needs to go outside."

I pull back, and when he moves away from me, I slip off the counter. "I'm going to go to my place. I need to brush my teeth a million times."

"Okay."

I begin to feel self-conscious about vomiting in front of Levi and hurry out of his house. I'm hit with a blast of cold air and fold my arms around myself as I dart over the stretch of lawn.

When I pull my back door open, I hear my phone ringing and jog toward the couch where I left it.

Seeing Jordan's name, I answer, "Hi."

"Where were you? I was a second away from calling Sheriff Williams! Christ, Kelcie!"

"I was at Levi's place. Sorry, I didn't mean to make you worry."

"Carry your phone with you. Dammit." I listen as he takes deep breaths. "My fucking heart."

"I'm sorry, Jordan," I apologize again.

"What were you doing at Levi's house?"

I sit down on the couch and rub my palm over my face. "We were having dinner. I've been spending time with him."

"Oh?" I can hear a hundred questions in the single word.

Not wanting to worry Jordan more than I already have, I explain, "I'm doing better. It feels as if I'm making progress when I'm around Levi." I let out a sigh. "It's hard to explain, but he understands me."

There's a pause in conversation before Jordan says, "I'm happy to hear that, Kelcie." Hearing the relief in his voice makes my body relax. "I'm glad you've found someone who can help you."

"He's really nice." I glance at the open door where the cold wind is blowing into the house, and getting up, I go to shut it. I hesitate before I admit, "I like him a lot."

"Oh wow. Really?"

"Yeah." This is a conversation I would've had with Mom or Sage. But Jordan is all I have left, and I need to talk to someone about my emotions. "The attraction is next level, and he is so patient and understanding with me. He even handles my panic attacks like a pro."

Jordan begins to talk, but his voice breaks, and I listen as he takes deep breaths before he's able to say, "You have no idea how happy it makes me to hear that, Kelcie."

The emotion brimming in his voice makes my throat strain and my chin quiver. "I'm sorry for everything the past year," I whisper. "I know it's been hard on you."

"It's okay. I'm just so relieved you're doing better."

"How are Natalie and Brady?"

"They're good. Brady's favorite word is 'but.' Every time I tell him to do something, it's but this and but that."

I let out a chuckle. "He's so cute."

"Are you going to spend Thanksgiving with us?" he asks.

My teeth tug at my bottom lip as I think Levi will be alone if I go to Jordan. "Is it okay if I skip this year?"

"Do you want to spend it with Levi?" my brother asks, a teasing tone to his voice I haven't heard in a really long time.

"Yeah," I grumble playfully.

"In that case, I'll drive through at the end of the month to check on you."

"You don't have to check on me," I argue.

"Fine, but I'm still coming through to visit. I miss you."

The corner of my mouth lifts. "Okay."

We say our goodbyes and hang up. Setting my phone down on the armrest, I get up and go to the bathroom. I spend a few minutes brushing my teeth and gargling with mouthwash. Just as I pat the hand towel over my face, I hear a knock.

When I step out of the bathroom, there's another knock at the back door, and I go to open it.

Without saying anything, Levi holds his hand out to me, and while I place my palm in his, I pull the door shut behind me.

He keeps quiet as we walk back to his house, and when we enter his kitchen, I notice two bowls of soup with slices of bread on the table.

Oh my God. This man is so incredible.

He lets go of my hand and pulls out a chair. "Sit, Kelcie."

As I take the seat, I watch him leave the kitchen, only to return with a warm jacket.

He drapes it over my shoulders and orders, "Put it on."

Having him take care of me makes the first tendrils of love curl around my heart while my stomach does happy cartwheels.

"The chicken soup is store bought, but hopefully it will help settle your stomach," Levi says while he takes a seat across from me.

I wait for him to meet my gaze before I reply, "Thank you. You have no idea how much all of this means to me."

His features soften, and the corner of his mouth lifts in a sexy smirk. "That's what friends are for."

Friends.

The word puts a damper on the happiness I'm feeling, and I hide my reaction by scooping some soup up and swallowing it.

Being friends with him is better than nothing.

Chapter 11

LEVI

When we're done eating, I lean back in the chair and stare at Kelcie. Her face has more color, and it sets me at ease.

Tonight was brutal for her, and all I want to do is hold her. It doesn't help that I love seeing her in my jacket, which she's drowning in.

"Want to move to the couch? We can watch a movie," I say.

She nods, and we get up to clear the table.

God, she fits so perfectly into my space.

When I shut the dishwasher after loading it, Kelcie clears her throat and asks, "What are your plans for Thanksgiving?"

"The same as every other day."

She seems to hesitate before she asks, "Want to spend it with me? I can make us a turkey that will probably feed us for a week."

"You're not going to your brother's?"

She shakes her head, and with a nervous expression, she replies, "I'd rather spend the day with you." Her tongue darts out to wet her lips. "And with Lick, of course."

I know the attraction is mutual, and it makes it all the more difficult to keep my distance.

You can't get romantically involved with her.

Yeah, like only being her friend will hurt less.

When I don't reply quickly enough, she mumbles, "Or not. Don't feel pressured to say yes."

The words rush way too fast from me. "I want to celebrate Thanksgiving with you."

Relief eases the tension on her face. "Oh, good. Then it's settled."

Things still feel a little tense between us as we go to the living room, and I wait for Kelcie to pick a couch before I sit down beside her.

You're looking for trouble.

"What movies do you like?" I ask.

"Let's watch your favorite," she responds. "Then afterward, I can torture you with mine."

"Which is?"

"*Click*," she answers, and when I shake my head, she adds, "With Adam Sandler."

"I don't think I've watched it." While I grab the remote and switch on the TV, I say, "We'll watch yours first."

"Hold on. Which one is your favorite?" she asks.

As I search for Kelcie's movie, I reply, "*Arrival.*"

"What's it about?"

"It's kinda sci-fi, but it's very deep. The first time I watched it, the main plot went right over my head."

Lick jumps onto the couch, trying to squeeze into the small space between Kelcie and the armrest. She scoots closer to me until our sides touch, then Lick flops down and uses her lap for a pillow.

Lifting my arm, I rest it on the back of the couch behind Kelcie. While she pets Lick, I find the movie and press play.

This feels too much like we could be a family. Me, Kelcie, and Lick.

As if my dog is trying to torture me, she turns onto her back, and Kelcie has to duck her head against me to avoid taking a paw to the face.

"Shove her off. She can go lie on the other couch."

"No." Kelcie glances up at me, and then she pouts. "She's just getting comfy."

Holy fuck. Kelcie pouting is too fucking cute for me to handle.

"Fine, but lean against me." Not giving her much of a choice in the matter, I lower my arm to her shoulders and pull her closer.

I have to force myself to focus on the movie, and just as I get into it, Kelcie crosses her legs and turns into me. She lays her head against my chest, and I can't resist trailing my fingers up and down her arm.

I lower my head and almost press a kiss to her hair but stop myself in time.

Watch the damn movie, asshole.

Somehow, I manage to get into it again, and when I realize it's not a comedy but actually fucking sad and deep, I begin to realize why it's Kelcie's favorite. It's about not taking anything for granted.

"I wish I had a remote like that, but instead of skipping forward, I want to go back in time," Kelcie murmurs.

I don't stop myself like I did before and press a kiss to her hair. I take a deep breath of her flowery scent, wishing I could make her mine.

When the credits start rolling, I say, "It was good."

Carefully, Kelcie tries to lift Lick's head off her lap, but my dog wakes up, and when Kelcie climbs to her feet, Lick also jumps off the couch.

"I'll make some coffee and tea while you let her out," Kelcie offers.

We head to the kitchen, and when I open the back door, a freezing wind blows through the room.

"Holy crap," Kelcie gasps, quickly pulling up the zipper of my jacket she's wearing. "Where did you live before moving to Verona? Did you have snowy winters?"

"I have a house in Grand Rapids in Michigan." When a confused expression blossoms on her face, I explain, "I needed a change of scenery. But to answer your question, I'm used to snowy winters."

"What made you pick Verona?" she asks as she turns her attention to preparing our beverages.

Shit.

I don't want to lie to her, but I can't tell her the truth.

"I heard about the inn where Easton stayed," I tell her a believable lie. "I thought I'd check it out. Something about the town called to me, and I decided to stay."

You called to me.

I couldn't stay away, and I watched you like a stalker. I wormed my way into your life, and now I'm making you care about me.

Guilt pours into my chest, and I feel bad about what I'm doing, even though I know I can't stop.

Lick comes back inside, and Kelcie glances my way. She stops stirring the coffee, worry flickering across her features. "What's wrong?"

For someone who hates lying, it comes way too easily to me. "Just a bad memory."

She picks up the mug and brings it to me. When I take it from her, she shuts the still-open back door, then asks, "Want to talk about it?"

My mind races to come up with a memory from my childhood, and when I lock onto one, I say, "Let's go back to the living room, where it's warmer."

She brings her tea, and this time I don't sit on the same couch as her.

I drink some of the coffee before I admit, "I hate birthdays." I suck in a deep breath of air before I let it out slowly. "At first, I thought it was something our family didn't celebrate, but when my half brother was born, our parents would make a big deal about his birthday. Every year, they threw him a party with all the bells and whistles." Hatred and a feeling of worthlessness shudder through me. "For my eighth birthday, I asked for a cake. That's all I wanted. A cake in the shape of a car." A bitter chuckle escapes me. "They said no, and like every other birthday, I was ignored. But then, when my half brother's birthday came around, they gave him the cake I asked for. That's when I realized they hated me."

When I look up, Kelcie is wiping a tear from her cheek. She shakes her head, and as more tears fall, she gets up and comes to sit beside me. She places her arms around me, and when a sob sputters from her, I don't care about the repercussions and pull her onto my lap.

We hold each other as if our lives would end if we didn't, and the tears she's crying for me flow into the cracks in my heart, making the most intense emotion I've ever experienced sprout inside me.

I love her.

Done with another chapter, I save the manuscript before standing up and stretching out.

It's been two weeks since I realized I love Kelcie, and we've spent every night since together. During the day, I write my ass off, too fucking thankful the writer's block is gone.

"Levi?" Kelcie calls.

"In my office." Leaving the room, I walk toward the kitchen.

Kelcie appears, and grabbing hold of my hand, she pulls me out the back door.

"What's going on?" I ask.

"I have a surprise for you." She stops outside of her house, and there's so much excitement on her face, it looks like she's going to burst. "It's something small, and I hope I'm not overstepping."

She opens her door, and I'm pulled inside, then she shouts, "Happy pretend birthday."

My body freezes as my gaze jumps over the blue and white balloons that are floating against the ceiling. When I see the red sports car cake and wrapped presents, the air is knocked from my lungs.

I can't remember when I last cried, but as I stare at everything, my eyes begin to sting.

"Kelcie." I breathe her name like it's a prayer, and the love I feel for her becomes a living force I can't contain.

"Do you like it?" she asks, a cautious smile wavering around her lips.

"I . . ." I shake my head, and when her expression morphs into worry, I hurry to say, "I love it."

I close the distance between us, and lifting my hands, I frame her face. Just as I lean down, it registers what I'm doing, and at the last possible second, I turn my head and press a kiss to her cheek.

I quickly pull away and glance at the decorations, the cake, and the presents. This moment is officially my favorite and more special to me than when I found out about the movie deal.

Kelcie darts to the counter and lights the candles. "You have to make a wish when you blow them out."

I only have one wish.

I step closer and stare at the flickering flames.

I wish that if Kelcie ever learns the truth about why I came to Verona, she'll find a way to forgive me, and we'll be able to love each other without a sword hanging over our heads.

Leaning forward, I blow out the candles, and it has Kelcie excitedly clapping her hands. "Don't tell anyone what you wished for, or it won't come true."

Trust me, I'm not telling a soul.

She picks up a small present that's covered in blue paper with little red cars printed all over it. "Time to open your gifts."

I smile at her, and being careful not to tear the paper, I unwrap it.

"God, you have the patience of a saint. I just rip the paper to shreds."

"I want to keep it," I say. Then I see the little toy version of a Mustang, and my smile widens. "I've always wanted a Mustang."

"Who doesn't?"

"Right?"

I spend the next ten minutes carefully unwrapping all my gifts, and by the time I finish, I have a nice little collection of toy cars.

"I'll even play with you," Kelcie says.

I shake my head quickly. "I'm not taking them out of the boxes. I'm going to put them on the shelf in my living room."

Our eyes meet, and the urge to kiss her hits me again. Instead of giving in, I clear my throat and look at the cake.

"I'll make coffee and tea."

"Thanks," I murmur.

She grins at me as she prepares the beverages. "We can have some of the cake because you can't keep it."

"Wait before you cut it." I hurry out of her house and jog to my place. Grabbing my phone from the office, I head back. When I step into the kitchen, I unlock the device and take a photo of the cake.

"Let me take one of you," Kelcie offers. "Stand by the cake."

I shake my head and pull her in beside me. When I have both us and the cake in the frame, I take the photo. Looking at it, my heart stutters in my chest because Kelcie is unbelievably beautiful, and her smile is filled with happiness.

"Will you please send it to me?"

I nod. "Sure. What's your number?"

She chuckles as she walks to the living room to pick up her phone. "Isn't it weird that we've been friends for . . . holy crap, has it been two months?"

Hell if I know.

"I think so," I reply.

"Anyway, it's funny that we've been friends for so long and haven't even exchanged numbers."

When she gives me her number, I program it into my device before sending her the photo.

"I'm making it my screen saver," she says.

In that case, I'm doing the same. I stare at the photo again, noticing the lines on my face aren't as harsh anymore.

Kelcie is changing me. I don't think she realizes how much joy she's bringing into my life.

Beautiful memories I'll cherish forever.

Chapter 12

KELCIE

Sitting under the tree's bare branches, I look at each of the gravestones.

Hi.

My grief shudders through me, and I close my eyes.

I miss you all so much.

A cold wind blows over the cemetery, and I snuggle into Levi's jacket, which I never gave back to him. I only wear it when I come here because, in a way, it's comforting. It's the second-best thing to having him hold me.

I open my eyes again and read the names engraved into the granite.

Coming to visit you used to be unbearable. But since I've met Levi, it's not so crushing anymore. I wish you could meet him. I think you'd all approve.

He writes books, Mom.

A sad little chuckle escapes me.

And he is soooo damn attractive, Sage.

Dad, you would've probably interrogated him, but once you got to know him, you would've understood why . . . I love him.

God. I love him.

My sight blurs with unshed tears as I realize how I feel about Levi.

But he's made it pretty clear we're only friends.

I look at Mom's grave.

What do I do? Do I keep my emotions a secret from him and appreciate that I have him as a friend?

Sage would've told me to open up to Levi. To take a chance.

That's easier said than done, Sage.

I let out a huff of air.

Levi is so patient and caring. He makes me feel safe. He listens when I talk and understands when I'm quiet.

The corner of my mouth lifts as I think about the man who's stolen my heart.

He hates when anyone else touches him, but he hugs me and even presses kisses to my hair. I gave him a small birthday party, and he kissed me on the cheek.

I roll my eyes.

I can't tell you how many times I thought he was going to kiss me on the lips, but then it didn't happen.

I spend the icy morning talking to my family, and by the time I climb to my feet, I know there's only one thing for me to do.

If I don't tell Levi how I feel, I might miss out on my only chance at happiness.

And, God, have I been happy the past few weeks.

I press a kiss to the tips of my gloved fingers and blow it to my family before I leave.

When I near the street we used to live on, I turn up it and walk down to the cul-de-sac. As I reach the path that leads to my family home, I glance at the front yard and notice how neat it is.

Shoot. The sheriff's department probably sent someone out to clean it again. Pulling my phone from my pocket, I dial the department's number.

Once Libby's done rattling off the usual greeting, I say, "Hi, it's Kelcie. I notice someone cleaned the yard again at my parents' house. Will you please send the invoice to me instead of Jordan?"

"Oh, it wasn't us, dear. The neighbors told us Levi Graye has been taking care of the place, so we've stopped sending someone out."

Levi has been taking care of the upkeep?

"Ahh . . . thanks."

I end the call and stare at the yard. Why didn't he tell me?

I hurry down the street, eager to get home so I can talk to Levi. By the time I reach our houses, I'm out of breath from all the exercise. I make a beeline for Levi's back door, knocking and even trying the handle, but it doesn't open.

Dang, he's probably sleeping.

When I turn away and start walking toward my place, I hear Levi call, "Kelcie."

My head snaps to where he's coming from the direction of the trees. Lick breaks out into a run to get to me and jumps up, her front paws settling against my abdomen.

"Hey, girl. You're always so excited to see me." I scratch behind her ear. Looking up, I take in the sweatpants and hoodie Levi's wearing. "Did you go for a walk?"

He shakes his head. "I run along the trail to the creek every morning. Lick needs the exercise."

That's quite the distance. No wonder the man has abs for days.

He uses his sleeve to wipe the sweat from his forehead. "Were you looking for me?"

"Oh, right. I passed by my parents' place and noticed the yard was neat. The sheriff's department told me you've been taking care of the upkeep."

Levi instantly looks uncomfortable and glances down at Lick. "I'm sorry if I overstepped."

"No!" I dart forward and grip the front of his hoodie. "You didn't have to." My eyebrows pull together, and my heart expands to twice its size with love for this man. "But it means so much to me. Thank you."

His expression relaxes. "I just want to make things easier for you."

"You do." I lift myself onto my tiptoes and press a very quick kiss to his mouth, which has my heartbeat setting off at a crazy pace. Pulling away, I walk to my back door. "Anyway, I'll let you get some sleep. See you later."

I don't dare look at his face as I go inside, afraid I'll see that he disapproves of the kiss.

So much for telling him how you feel about him. One thank-you kiss, and you run for the hills.

I shut the door behind me and lean my forehead against the wood. A few seconds later, I carefully peek out of the window, and not seeing Levi, I sit down right on the spot while a nervous chuckle bursts over my lips.

Well, I kinda did try. Now the ball's in his court.

The doorbell rings, and I climb to my feet. When I peek through the peephole and see Colby, my shoulders slump.

Unlocking the door, I open it and say, "Hi."

"I was visiting with my parents and saw you come home. It's been a while. How are you?"

"I'm great, and you?"

"I'm doing okay. Things would be better if the prettiest girl in town finally stopped playing hard to get and agreed to go on a date with me."

Not this again.

Desperate to make him understand it will never happen, I totally take advantage of my friendship with Levi and lie, "I'm actually dating Levi."

Shock flashes over Colby's face, then he frowns darkly at me. "What the fuck, Kelcie? I was there for you when your family was killed. I helped you get this place." His voice keeps rising until he shouts, "The fucker moves in, and you jump into his arms?"

My lips part with shock, and I take a step backward from Colby's aggressive reaction. "Don't take that tone with me!"

He shakes his head, and just as he moves toward me, Levi's voice snaps, "Back the fuck away from her."

Colby's head turns to the side, and when he moves backward, I'm able to peek out the doorway. Levi cuts across the dead grass between our houses, his expression downright pissed off.

"You better go, Colby," I say, not wanting a fight between the two men.

"Oh, look," Colby sneers. "If it isn't the great Levi fucking Graye. You think you can tell me what to do just because you're some big-shot author?"

"I'm going to call the sheriff," I warn him.

His eyes flick back to me, the anger in his gaze scaring me, as he hisses, "I see how it is." Levi steps between Colby and me, but it doesn't stop Colby from continuing, "Don't come running to me when he drops you like a sack of potatoes. People like him never stay in one place for long."

"Leave," Levi growls, the sound of his threatening tone making goose bumps erupt over my skin.

"Fuck both of you," Colby angrily mutters as he walks away, crossing the street to where his car is parked in his parents' driveway.

"I'm so sorry," I say while letting out a heavy breath. When Levi turns around, I step out of the way so he can come inside the house. "Where's Lick?"

"At my place. I didn't want her attacking Colby."

"Yeah, we don't want that to happen," I agree. My shoulders sag as I wrap my arms around myself. "Colby is probably going to tell the whole town who you are."

"Let him. I don't care." Levi shuts the door behind him and locks it. When he turns to face me, he lifts his hand and rubs it up and down my arm. "Are you okay?"

I shrug, feeling rattled by the unpleasantness. "I hate that it happened, but Colby needed to understand I'll never date him. I just don't get why he has to be so difficult." I give Levi a weak smile. "I mean, I'd give up after the first time I'm rejected."

Levi's eyes drift over my face. "How many times did you reject him?"

"I've lost count." Turning around, I walk to the kitchen. "Would you like something to drink?"

"Hold up." Levi grabs my shoulder and stops me from walking. Coming to stand in front of me, he asks, "Countless? Has he spoken to you like that before?"

"No, usually he just flirts and tries his luck. But it's been going on for six years. It's exhausting."

Levi's expression turns angry again. "Have you told the sheriff?"

I shake my head, and not wanting Levi to worry, I explain, "Colby is harmless. He is all bark and no bite. I'm sure he got the message this time." Knowing word might spread through town, I glance down at my feet as I admit, "I kinda threw you under the bus and told him we're dating, so if you hear the rumor, you know where it started."

"You can throw me under the bus any day."

Surprised, I look up again, and seeing Levi isn't angry with me, I let out a breath of relief.

"I'm going home," he says. "I need to jump in the shower."

"Okay." When he walks to the back door, I ask, "Will I see you later?"

"Yes. Dinner and movies at my place," he replies before pulling the door shut behind him.

A deflating sound ripples over my lips while I go to the couch and sink down on it.

Well, that sucked.

I meant it when I said I wish it hadn't happened. We could've been friends, and I hate that things had to escalate like that.

I kick off my sneakers, and lying down, I pull the blanket over me. I snuggle into my pillow and stare at the black screen of the TV.

Levi didn't say anything about the kiss. Maybe he's going to pretend it didn't happen.

For a day that started so well, it sure turned to crap at the speed of light.

If friendship is all I'll ever have with Levi, at least I got to kiss him today. Even if it was just a peck on the lips.

My head pops up as I remember the security cameras. I sit up, and grabbing my phone, I go into the security app. I find the camera that's focused on the back of the house and rewind to where I'm talking with Levi.

I drink in the sight of his face, the week-old beard I'm really growing fond of, and as I go in to kiss him, I see his eyes closing. When I pull away, there's a flash of shock tightening his features, and he stares after me.

Then he lifts his hand and brushes the pads of his fingers over his lips. When he begins to walk back to his house, the corner of his mouth lifts.

I rewind the footage, needing to make sure I didn't imagine his reaction.

Watching it again, a smile forms on my face, and hope blossoms in my chest.

Okay. Chill, Kelcie. You've made it pretty clear how you feel by kissing him. Let him make the next move.

I rewind the footage again and pause on the time stamp where Levi's smiling as he walks away. Staring at the screen, I memorize it until my eyes drift closed.

The ringing of the doorbell rips me out of a deep sleep, and when it's followed by someone banging on the door, I dart up off the couch. My eyes feel as if there's sand in them, and I rub them before I look through the peephole. Seeing Mrs. Adams, Colby's mother, I let out a groan.

There's a strand of hair sticking up at the back of her head, and her cheeks are red with anger. Where Colby has an athletic build like his father, his mother is short like me.

I pat over my messy hair before I unlock the door and open it for her. "Hi, Mrs. Adams."

"Don't 'Hi, Mrs. Adams' me," she snaps angrily. "How could you be so cruel, Kelcie? Colby has been nothing but kind to you, and you broke his heart. All for some stranger?"

My eyes grow wide from the sudden attack, but needing to make her understand, I reply, "Even if Levi weren't in the picture, I still wouldn't date Colby. I told him so many times that I only feel friendship for him, but he wouldn't listen."

"Many marriages built on friendship have been successful."

I give her a what-the-heck look. "I'm not talking about this with you. I'm sorry Colby is hurting, but that's not on me. Excuse me."

When I begin to push the door shut, she darts forward, and her palm connects hard with my cheek.

"Your parents must be turning in their graves," she spits at me while I lift my hand to my stinging face, too shocked to react. "Shame on you, Kelcie. They raised you better than this."

Still stunned out of my mind, I watch as she stalks back to her house.

Slowly, I shut the door and lock it, then turning around, I walk right through the house and out the back, going straight to the only place I feel safe.

Chapter 13

LEVI

Done showering and on my way to my bedroom, I hear a soft knock at my back door. Knowing it can only be Kelcie, I turn around and head to the kitchen.

Lick starts wagging her tail, confirming my thoughts.

I open the door, but when I see Kelcie cupping her cheek, tears swimming in her eyes, worry pours into my chest.

"What happened? Did Colby come back?" I ask while taking hold of her arm and pulling her inside. I slam the door shut behind us before giving Kelcie all my attention.

"No," she whispers, her face pale. "His mother came over." Her eyebrows pull together, and she gasps before she continues, "She laid into me for breaking Colby's heart, and when I told her I'm not taking the blame, she slapped me."

Anger explodes in my chest because someone dared to raise a hand against the woman I love.

Knowing I'll land my ass in jail if I go over to the Adamses' house and that won't help Kelcie at all, I do the only thing I can. I pull her against my chest and rub my hand up and down her back.

"I'm so tired," she admits in a small voice. "I'm sorry I came here, but it's the only place I feel safe."

"You did the right thing," I grumble. "If anyone comes knocking on my door, I'm putting them on their asses."

Keeping my arm around her shoulders, I guide her out of the kitchen and down the hallway with Lick right behind us. When we enter my bedroom, I say, "Sleep here for today. I'll take the couch."

When I let go of Kelcie, her hand darts out and she grabs hold of my sweater. "No. I mean, I feel safe with you." She glances at the king-size bed. "It's a huge bed. There's enough space for both of us."

I should do the right thing and leave Kelcie alone. Nothing good will come of this.

Colby already knows who I am. He's a reporter. He can make things bad for me.

The thoughts are fleeting and don't manage to take root.

Fuck Colby. I don't care what he prints about me. Only Kelcie matters.

"Okay. I'll take the side closest to the door."

When she climbs onto the bed, and I notice she's barefoot, my anger spikes again, and I let out a growl. She must be fucking freezing.

"What?" Kelcie asks.

"I'm just pissed off because people won't leave you alone," I mutter while I get into bed beside her. I pull her into my arms, and leaning over her, I tuck the covers tightly in behind her before I settle into a comfortable position.

Rubbing my hand up and down the length of her back, I'm hoping my body will heat hers quickly.

"Thank you," she whispers.

I dip my head down and press a kiss to the red mark on her cheek. "Get some sleep, my muse."

She tilts her head back, and I feel her warm breath fan over my neck and jaw. "Your muse?"

"Since I've been spending time with you, the writer's block is gone, so you're my muse."

"Oh my gosh. Really?" Her face lights up with happiness. "That's such good news."

"I've already written forty-five thousand words. I'm halfway done with the book. At this rate, I'll be able to send it in before Christmas."

She pushes herself up into a sitting position. "Levi, that's amazing!"

"It is, so we'd better sleep or I won't get any writing done this afternoon." I pull her back down, and when she rests her head on my chest, I feel content.

"Sweet dreams," she murmurs as she places her hand over my heart. "You too."

I lie awake, soaking in how perfect it feels to hold Kelcie. Eventually, her breathing evens out, and I wait another ten minutes to make sure she's asleep before I whisper, "I love you."

It might be the only chance I get to say the words to her, and I'm not letting it slip through my fingers.

Finally, I drift off, and when I wake again, it's to Kelcie's face pressed into the crook of my neck, her arm and leg thrown over me. She's half on top of me, the V between her thighs dangerously close to my cock.

The room has already started to grow dark as the sun sets, and Lick jumps off the foot of the bed, coming around the side to boop me with her nose.

As gently as possible, I extract myself from beneath Kelcie, and once I'm out of the bed, I adjust the covers over her. With her hair all over my pillow and her lips slightly parted, she looks absolutely breathtaking.

I indicate for Lick to go and follow her out of the bedroom, pausing to shut the door softly behind me.

When I get to the kitchen, I mutter, "You couldn't wait a little longer, could you?"

She lets out a bark, and I quickly sign for her to stop so she won't wake Kelcie.

I open the back door and shiver when the cold hits me in the face. I should've grabbed a jacket before I left the room.

I get busy preparing Lick's food while thinking about what Kelcie and I can have for dinner.

I've been eating much healthier since she came along. Before I started spending time with her, I used to live off sandwiches.

While Lick's food is warming in the microwave, I make myself coffee, then lean back against the counter, sipping on it.

It's Thanksgiving tomorrow. It will be the first time since my divorce that I'll spend the day with someone.

My thoughts are filled with the past few months and how much my life has changed because of Kelcie.

I want her in my life forever.

When the microwave dings, I quickly mix everything together and place the bowl on the floor. While Lick goes to town on her meal, I open the freezer and look at the contents.

Pulling out a steak, I let it thaw in the sink, adding hot water to help it along. The second Lick is done eating and doing her business outside, I shut the door and lock it.

"Let's go to the office, girl."

I bring my coffee with me, and sitting down, I open my laptop and get to work.

Knowing Lick will notify me when she hears Kelcie moving in the house, I get lost in the story, writing page after page.

By the time Lick's tail starts wagging, I've written three chapters.

"God, what's the time?" Kelcie grumbles in the living room.

I check on my laptop, then call out, "Eight fifteen."

"Holy crap!"

She appears in the doorway, not a hair out of place, and I assume she used my brush. The thought makes me grin at her.

"I can't believe I slept for so long."

"Do you feel rested?" I ask as I get up.

"Yes. Thank you."

"I'm going to make pasta with cream and strips of steak. Are you good with that?"

"It sounds delicious. Can I help?"

"Of course. I'll cut the meat, and you can take care of the pasta."

Going to the kitchen, we get to work, and while I'm frying the slices of steak, I can sense Kelcie's eyes are on me.

"Do you feel better after the rough day?" I ask.

"Yeah," she sighs. "But I'm going to have to move. I can't keep living across the road from Colby's family. It will be awkward."

"Have you ever thought about leaving Verona?"

It takes a few seconds before the answer bursts from Kelcie. "I can't."

I glance over my shoulder and see the panic tightening her features. "Is your medication at your place?"

She nods as she focuses on taking deep breaths.

I turn off the gas, and not caring that I'm barefoot, I hurry over to her house. Finding the back door open, I make a mental note to talk to Kelcie about locking it behind her whenever she comes over.

I find the box in one of the cupboards and rush back to her. By the time I burst into the kitchen, Kelcie is calmer and giving me a sheepish look.

"We should keep some here," I say as I set the box down on the table.

"You're right," she agrees.

I turn on the stove again and get back to work.

"Jordan's asked me a hundred times to move to Naperville so I'm closer to him, but I just can't bring myself to leave my family behind."

When the steak is done, I set the pan aside and get to work on making the cream sauce.

"You can move to one of the other towns in the Sugar River Valley area and still be close enough to visit them daily," I mention.

"I never thought of that," she murmurs. "Maybe I should get a farm. I can milk cows for a living."

"Yeah? You think you'll like living on a farm?"

She lets out a chuckle. "Hmm . . . all the space. No neighbors right across the road." She's quiet for a moment. "I think it would be awesome."

I glance over my shoulder at her. "Then why don't you?"

Kelcie shrugs. "I like living next door to you."

"I'm not attached to this house. I can sell and move as well."

The idea of living on a farm with Kelcie sounds heavenly.

"All jokes aside," she mutters. "I hope this nasty business with Colby and his family is over."

I wasn't joking. I would follow Kelcie to the ends of the earth if she let me.

When the pasta is ready, I drain it and mix all the ingredients together. Letting it rest in the pot, I lean back against the counter and cross my arms over my chest.

"If they come looking for trouble, let me know and I'll handle it."

She shakes her head. "I can't expect that of you. You hate talking to people, and I'll never forgive myself if you get in a fight because of me."

"Kelcie." I wait for her to look at me. "I'm not going to sit back and let people walk all over you." Needing her to understand what she means to me without saying the actual words, I admit, "You're important to me."

Emotion washes over her face, and her voice is soft when she replies, "You're important to me too."

"You would stand up for me, so let me do the same for you."

She nods and climbs to her feet from where she's sitting by the table. When she comes toward me, I uncross my arms and open them. We hug, and she rests her cheek against my chest, letting out a sigh.

"I'm so thankful for you, Levi. I was drowning until you came along."

"Ditto."

Her voice is vulnerable as she whispers, "Promise you won't just up and leave me."

"Not unless you ask me to."

"Promise," she insists.

"I promise."

She tilts her head back and looks up at me with so much hope that it makes my heartbeat speed up. My eyes lower to her mouth before flicking back to her gaze, where I can see my entire future in her soft brown irises.

God only knows where I get the strength to let go of her. I extract my body from between hers and the counter and grab two plates out of the cupboard.

"Why do you do that, Levi?"

With my back turned to her, I set the plates down and close my eyes.

"Is it my imagination?" she asks. "Am I seeing something that's not there?"

Unable to lie, I shake my head. "No."

"Then why do you keep pulling away?" When I don't answer her, she says, "Look at me and tell me why you keep breaking the moments instead of kissing me."

I grind my molars, trying to come up with a way out of this mess.

"I already failed at one marriage," I spit out the first thing that comes to mind.

"So you think we would fail?"

I hear her move closer to me, and I quickly dart to the side and out of her reach. "Can we not do this?"

Pain ripples over her face, and she wraps her arms around her middle. "Okay." She looks at the back door. "I think it will be best if I go home. I'm sorry I brought it up."

The look of rejection in her eyes tells me I'm about to lose her, and it's the one thing I can't deal with.

She never promised not to leave me.

As Kelcie walks toward the door, I dart forward and grab her wrist. When she spins around, I bring my other hand to the back of her neck and slam my mouth to hers.

Unlike the times I kissed my ex and hated swapping spit, the pleasure I feel when my tongue pushes past Kelcie's lips draws a groan from me.

Holy fuck.

Kelcie is pure heaven.

Chapter 14

KELCIE

I had my first kiss a year after graduating from school, and I lost my virginity to a carnival worker who upped and left town before I even woke up. I didn't even know the guy's last name.

To say my romantic history is sad would be the understatement of the year. It was never something I gave any thought to until Levi.

So when Levi grabs me by the back of my neck and yanks me toward him, shock ripples through me. His mouth crashes against mine, and I struggle to play catch-up as he practically devours me.

His lips knead mine roughly, and his tongue sweeps into my mouth with such dominance, I don't know if I'm coming or going.

Letting go of my wrist, Levi moves closer and presses his body against mine while his arm wraps around me, locking me firmly in place.

I'm standing still like a dumbfounded idiot, unable to think a single coherent thought while Levi claims every inch of my mouth.

Good. God. This is . . . This is . . .

When his teeth tug at my bottom lip and his tongue strokes roughly over mine, an embarrassingly loud moan escapes me.

Heat flushes my face, my abdomen clenches hard, and tingles spread over every inch of my body.

Finally, I think of lifting my arms and wrapping them around his neck. I push up on my tiptoes, and tilting my head, I begin to taste and worship Levi as if he's my beginning and end.

I don't know if this will be my only chance to experience him like this, so I'm taking full advantage of it.

We hold onto each other as if we'd stop existing if we were to separate, and we kiss like people who've been starved of love.

Every good emotion known to mankind floods me until it feels like I'm floating in Levi's arms.

He slows the kiss down until he's lapping at my mouth, the kiss feeling so deep and intimate that it brings tears to my eyes.

Moving my hands to his face, my fingertips brush over his light stubble. I love the scratchy feel and how his jaw moves.

I'm surrounded by his cedarwood scent, and his much stronger body pressed against mine makes me feel delirious with desire.

I want all of him.

I have no idea how much time passes before he nips at my mouth one last time. Lifting his head an inch, I feel his breath on my swollen lips.

"Open your eyes," he says, his voice hoarse and cracking over the words.

Slowly, I lift my lashes until Levi comes into view. Seeing the emotion that can only be described as love all over his face has my heart bursting into a wild gallop of happiness.

"I'll never reject you, Kelcie. Don't ever think that."

Nodding, I clear my throat. "Okay."

Levi lets go of me and takes a step backward. "We should eat."

I shake my head. "Uh . . . no. I think we need to talk about what just happened."

I watch as he swallows, and picking up the plates from where he left them on the counter, he moves them to the table. He begins to scoop pasta into them, and only when he sets the pot back on the stove does he look at me again.

"I'm not ready to talk about it."

Seeing the worry in his eyes dims my happiness, and confusion spills into my chest.

Levi just gave me the best kiss of my life, and he doesn't want to talk about it? Why?

I move to the table and take a seat. Staring at the pasta, I think for a moment before I ask, "Did your previous marriage end badly?"

He sits down, and picking up his fork, he shakes his head. "I couldn't give her what she needed. The divorce went pretty smoothly."

"What did she need?"

He lifts his eyes to mine. "For me to show her affection." He lets out a sigh. "She didn't repulse me, but I felt uncomfortable touching her. Kissing her was . . ." There's a flash of disgust on his face. "I did it as little as possible."

Fear trickles through me as I ask, "And kissing me?"

"You're . . ." He shakes his head again, and my stomach drops. "You're unlike any person I've ever met. I love touching you, and kissing you was one of the best things I've ever experienced in my life."

Oh, thank you, sweet baby Jesus.

His words register, and happiness pours back into my heart.

Needing to know the answer, I ask, "Why did you marry her?"

"I didn't want to be alone. I thought I could make it work, but I quickly realized I'm too fucked up to be with someone."

"You're not fucked up."

Levi puts down his fork, and his eyes lock with mine. For the longest moment, he just looks at me, then he says, "I am, Kelcie. I'm still a grumpy asshole when I'm not with you. I still avoid talking to other people. I still crawl out of my fucking skin when someone touches me. None of that has changed."

"You're not fucked up," I repeat myself. Getting up, I move around the table, and I frame his face with my hands. As Levi looks up at me, I say, "You're the most incredible man I've ever met. You're the only one who got through to me. I wish you could see yourself the way I see you."

He sucks in a deep breath as if he's trying to inhale my words.

Leaning down, I softly press my mouth to his. I keep the kiss tender, and when I pull back, I whisper, "I've never been in love until you. My parents raised me to have super-high standards, and you've met them all." I give him a pleading look. "We won't fail if we give this a go, because I feel we're perfect for each other."

Levi grips hold of my hips and tugs me down onto his lap.

A myriad of expressions flashes over his attractive features. After what feels like long minutes, a determined expression settles in his hazel eyes.

"The last thing I want to do is hurt you," he whispers.

"I know."

Please, Levi. We're meant to be.

"I only want to make life easier for you. I want you to be happy, Kelcie."

My eyes mist up, and my chin begins to tremble from all the intense emotions I'm experiencing. "I've been happy every moment I've gotten to spend with you." I suck in a quivering breath. "I was dead until you came along."

I wish he would see that he is the only reason I've started living again.

Levi lifts his hand and brushes some hair away from my face while looking at me with something that can only be described as wonder.

His fingers trail over my temple and cheek until his thumb tugs at my bottom lip. My breathing instantly speeds up, and my heart skips a beat.

His gaze turns downright predatory, and I'm glad I'm sitting on his lap because I swear, I go weak in the knees.

I feel how Levi tenses. "Once we cross the line, there's no going back."

I cup the sharp line of his jaw and shake my head. "We've already crossed the line, Levi." Thinking he might need to hear it, I say, "I want all of you. Every single broken piece. The good. The bad. There's nothing you could do to make me feel any different."

His eyes flick away from me, worry flashing over his face.

"Hey," I whisper. He brings his gaze back to me, and I smile. "Stop overthinking things."

When Levi remains silent, I give him the time he needs, and it pays off because the determined expression that's super hot returns to his face.

I lean in a little closer until I'm able to press a soft kiss to his lips. His week-old beard is scratchy on my skin, causing tingles to spread out over my body.

I pull back an inch or so, and when Levi follows, his mouth nipping at mine, once . . . twice, I let out a needy moan, desperate for more.

A sexy grin forms on his face, and I realize he's teasing me. I playfully slap his shoulder and move to get off his lap, but his hand shoots up, and he grips me by my throat.

My brain completely misfires at how dang hot the move is, then his mouth takes mine in an urgent kiss that has me seeing fireworks.

The level of heat between us becomes damn near combustible, and I feel his manhood harden beneath me.

I'm overcome with satisfaction that I'm the only one who brings out this side in him.

Somehow, the kiss is both gentle and demanding, his tongue and lips alternating between different pressures that have me melting into his embrace. I move one hand to the back of his head, my fingers finding the short strands, while my other palm greedily explores the hard planes of his chest.

His stubble keeps scraping against my sensitive skin in the most delicious way, and I'm a second away from begging him to strip me naked when he wisely slows the kiss down until we're both keeping still, our rushed breaths warming the air between us.

"Holy crap," I whisper. "For a man who hates touching and kissing, you sure are good at it."

A deep chuckle rumbles from his chest as he pulls me into a hug. I press my face into the crook of his neck and hold him as if he might up and vanish at any time.

I've learned the hard lesson to appreciate every single moment you have with a person because you never know when it will be your last.

Please, God. Don't ever take this man from me. I won't survive it.

By the time I lift my head and slip off Levi's lap, our food is cold, and Lick needs a toilet break.

"I'll warm our plates while you let Lick out," I say, getting to work.

My steps feel light, and there's an excited buzz all over my body. My stomach keeps fluttering as if a kaleidoscope of butterflies has taken up permanent residence inside me.

Mom pats my cheek. "One day you'll meet someone who'll make you feel differently."

I shake my head. "Nope. I have zero desire to date."

"You might change your mind a few years from now."

The memory flashes through my mind, and I stop what I'm doing, suddenly realizing Mom was right.

I wish you were here, Mom. I wish I could tell you I've fallen in love with the most perfect man.

Grief ripples through me like a wave spilling onto the shore before it withdraws back into the darkness, where all my trauma is locked in the deepest corner of my heart.

"Kelcie?" Levi's hand brushes up my back in a comforting way and settles against the side of my neck as he leans down a little to catch my eyes. "Are you okay?"

"I just remembered something my mom said."

"Want to share it with me?"

Lifting my arm, I take hold of his wrist. "Before that night, I had no interest in dating because I was so happy with my life. My mom said one day I'd meet someone who would make me feel differently." An emotional smile wavers around my mouth. "She was right."

Levi's eyes narrow slightly, and he tilts his head. "Have you dated before?"

Glancing to the side, I shake my head. "Not really. After I was done with school, I had my first kiss. It was with one of Jordan's friends, but nothing ever came of it, because my brother would've lost his shit if he found out."

Levi's expression remains serious as he asks, "And sex?"

I pull a disgruntled face and roll my eyes. "Promise you won't laugh."

"Promise." The word bursts from him, his focus solely on me.

"I lost my virginity in a field to a guy who was working at a carnival passing through town. It's the most irresponsible thing I've ever done. When I woke up alone and saw they packed up and left during the night, I felt disgusted with myself." My shoulders lift as I shrug. "And that sums up my entire experience with dating."

Levi shakes his head. "I hate that for you."

Curious as heck, I ask, "What was your first kiss and losing your virginity like?"

I place each plate in the microwave for a couple of minutes, and Levi waits until we're seated at the table before he answers, "Margo, my ex-wife, was my first everything. I was drawn to her gentle nature. She tried to be patient with me, but in the end, she had to think of herself. Honestly, I was relieved when she divorced me." Levi pauses to take a sip of water. "The first time I kissed her, there was no tongue, and it wasn't too bad. No fireworks, but bearable, you know?"

He scoops some pasta onto his fork and brings it to his mouth. While he eats, I wait patiently for him to continue.

Resting his left forearm on the table, his pointer finger brushes along the rim of his plate.

"She initiated the first time we had sex." He lets out an embarrassed chuckle. "Fuck knows why she married me. I just laid still and let her do all the work."

"Me too," I admit. "I had no idea what to do, so I kept my arms crossed over my chest and kinda prayed for it to be over as quickly as possible."

His gaze softens on me. "Two peas in a pod."

As I spear a strip of steak, I say, "I'm sure that won't be the case if we . . . do the deed."

"Yeah?" Levi's lashes lower, and his features tighten with hunger, his eyes dilating. Then the man's teeth tug at his bottom lip.

Heat flushes my core, and my abdomen clenches hard. The fork clatters against my plate as it slips from my fingers.

"Yep." My voice is hoarse, and I clear my throat before continuing, "I'm willing to bet everything I have that things will be pretty explosive."

Levi keeps looking at me as if he prefers to have me for a meal instead of the plate of pasta. "I think you're right."

Chapter 15

After showering, I pull my brush through my damp hair before I walk to my study. It's Thanksgiving, but I'll only see Kelcie later this afternoon.

Sitting down behind my desk, I turn on my laptop. While I wait, I check my emails on my phone and see one from my agent, checking in with me.

I type out a quick reply, telling him to relax and that I'm halfway done with the book. Just as I set the device down, another email pops up. The subject heading has my eyes narrowing.

One and only warning.

I open the email and stare at the two words.

Leave Verona.

My author email is on my website, and this message can be from anybody, but my initial thought is that it's from Colby or someone in his family.

Kelcie said Colby is more bark than fight, and this is probably him barking.

Anger simmers in my chest as I read the words again before blocking the sender's email.

Letting out a sigh, I roll my shoulders, then opening my manuscript, I read the last piece I wrote and get to work.

The words struggle to come, and after trying for an hour, I lean back in my chair and glare at my laptop.

Lick lifts her head and wags her tail.

I quickly save the little work I've managed to get done and shut my laptop. When I climb to my feet, Lick darts up and pads to the kitchen, impatiently waiting by the door for me to open it.

I let her out, and noticing the snowflakes floating to the ground, I take the steps down to the backyard. Holding out my hand, I catch one in my palm and watch as it melts.

It feels like a forewarning. Kelcie is fragile like this snowflake, and being with me might lead to her getting hurt in such a way that she can't come back from it.

What if she somehow finds out I watched her like a creep for a year?

What if she learns I bought this house because it was next door to her?

What if . . . What if . . . What if . . .

So much can go wrong, and if the worst happens and she realizes who I am and what I've done, I know it will kill whatever love she feels for me.

She'll hate me.

I hear Kelcie's back door squeak as it opens, and turning my head, I see her dart out into the yard and twirl in a circle with her hands in the air. Laughter bubbles from her, the sound making a sad smile tug at my mouth.

Just thinking about losing her has unbearable pain ripping through my heart.

I want to steal her away from the world. Carry her off to our little farm, where she can milk cows and do whatever she desires.

I want to give her the whole goddamn world.

Kelcie quickly jogs back to lock the door, then her laughter fills the air again as she runs toward me. Her happiness is so bright that it shines from her, making the shadows around me retreat.

I open my arms as Kelcie launches herself at me, and when I catch her, I hug her as tight as I can while she hooks her legs around me.

I walk into my house and wait for Lick to follow before I shut the door behind us. Heading to the living room, I sit down on one of the couches, and Kelcie adjusts her legs as she straddles me.

"First snow," she whispers. "Make a wish."

I wish Kelcie will never leave me and we'll be happy together forever.

Lifting my arm, I brush the tips of my fingers over her temple and cheek. I revel in how soft her skin is while I memorize every inch of her face.

I notice a scar beneath her left eye, and when she realizes what I'm looking at, her smile fades.

"I got it during the . . ." She swallows hard but finds the strength to push through. "During the attack."

Keeping quiet, I wait to see if she wants to tell me more.

She finds a spot on my chest that she stares at, then she asks, "Memory for a memory?" When I nod, she says, "You go first."

My teeth tug at my bottom lip while I think of something to share. Wanting Kelcie to open up to me about the attack, I decide to share one of my worst memories.

I clear my throat, and taking hold of her hand, I link our fingers. "There's a reason I'm antisocial." I suck in a fortifying breath before continuing, "My parents, if you can call them that, would take my half brother out for fun days. They'd spend all week talking about their plans. Going to the zoo. Camping. A day at a water park. They would get all excited while I was consumed with dread." I shake my head and glance down at our joined hands. "I never got to go with them. Instead, they would lock me in the guest restroom while they were out having fun. I suppose I should be thankful I at least had access to water." A bitter chuckle escapes, then I have to shut my eyes as the memories flash through my mind.

Slamming my fist against the door until my skin turned purple and blue.

Crying until I passed out from exhaustion.

The loneliness.

Fuck, the horrible feeling of being abandoned.

Kelcie rubs her free hand up and down my chest, drawing me out of my thoughts. I look at her again, and seeing the tears shimmering in her eyes, I shake my head. "Hearing my memories isn't doing you any good."

"This isn't about me." Her hand moves up to cup my jaw. "It's about you, Levi. Maybe if you share your trauma, I can help you bear the weight."

Our gazes lock as I realize the memory-for-a-memory deal isn't for Kelcie's benefit. All this time, she's been doing it for me.

For once, someone is putting me first, and I can't describe how it makes me feel.

"Tell me more," she encourages me to continue.

My eyebrows pull together. "One Christmas Eve, they left me locked in the restroom for four days. I think they went skiing. There was a blizzard on the third night. It sounded like the house was going to cave in on top of me from the strong winds. Then the power and heat went out. I was wearing a pair of shorts and a T-shirt, so they didn't do much to keep me warm."

"Oh my God, Levi," she whispers, horrified.

I remember how helpless and cold I felt.

When my chest begins to rise faster and my breaths become shallow, Kelcie frames my jaw and locks eyes with me.

"Focus on your breaths and count backward with me. Ten . . . nine . . . eight . . . seven . . . six . . . inhale . . . five . . . four . . . three . . . two . . . one . . . exhale . . ." Kelcie keeps going through the exercise with me, and when the claustrophobic sensation subsides, she yanks me into a hug, her palm cradling the back of my head.

She holds me as if I'm the most precious thing to her while cooing, "You're not in that restroom anymore. You're here with me, where you're safe and loved." She drops kisses on the side of my face. "I want you. You're important to me. I love you."

I tilt my head back so I can see her face, and desperately needing to hear the words again, I beg, "Please say that again."

"I want all of you." Her features tighten with so much love for me, it bathes me in comforting warmth. "You are the most important person in my life." My heart squeezes in my chest. "I love you with all of my heart, Levi Graye."

My chest expands with one emotion after another, filling the space until it feels like it might explode. I feel everything from love to damn near obsession when it comes to Kelcie.

Then there's a moment when I wonder if this is even real. Am I dreaming? How is it possible that this beautiful creature is here with me?

To make sure this is not a dream, I press my palm to Kelcie's cheek, then to the side of her neck, before settling it over her heart. I feel every beat, and shaking my head, my tone sounds incredulous as I ask, "How can someone as amazing as you love someone like me?"

The corners of her mouth tip up in a tender smile. "Loving you is as easy as breathing."

Her words patch the cracks in my soul, and I know this is one of those moments I'll think back on when I'm lying on my deathbed.

This moment is what makes life worth living.

With my eyes imprisoned by hers, my voice is hoarse as I say, "I always believed I wasn't capable of loving another person." I move my hand up to the side of her neck and brush my thumb over her jaw. "But you showed me how wrong I was." I pull her closer until I can press my forehead to hers. "I love you, Kelcie." My eyes drift closed as the intensity of my emotions for her overwhelms me. "You own every inch of my heart." I press a kiss to her mouth. "Only you." My lips nip at hers again. "You're everything to me."

I take her in a crushing kiss filled with desperation to show her just how much she means to me.

Kelcie's hands move into my hair, then down to my chest, before going back up to find my hair again. It's like she can't get enough of touching me.

Breaking the kiss, I grab the back of my collar and rip the shirt over my head.

My woman's eyes zero in on my chest like a heat-seeking missile, her pupils dilating with desire, and not even a second later, her palms and fingers explore every inch of my tattoo.

"So beautiful," she whispers, looking at me as if I'm a work of art.

The tip of her pointer finger traces the scars she can feel beneath the ink, and her eyes dart up to mine, asking the silent question.

"My mother was ironing clothes when my half brother tugged at the cord. It fell and missed him by mere inches. My stepfather grabbed the iron and pressed it to my chest to show me how badly his son could've been hurt."

"Jesus," Kelcie whimpers. "And your mother did nothing?"

"She never tried to stop him. My stepfather gave her everything she wanted, and letting him abuse me was the price she was willing to pay for her comfortable life."

Kelcie's face crumples with heartbreak. "I'm so sorry, Levi."

Shaking my head, I say, "It wasn't your fault or doing."

"I know, but someone has to say the words to you." She closes the distance between us and gives me a soft kiss before she begins dropping them all over my neck and chest.

Her kisses and touches turn sensual, and it has me hardening beneath her. The instant she feels me, she presses down on me, and her hips swivel.

Jesus.

Pushing my hands through her hair, I grip fistfuls of the silky strands and pull her head back. Her lips are parted and her eyes hooded from desire, making her look fucking sexy.

With our gazes locked on each other, I thrust up, and we both groan at how good it feels. I do it again, and our breaths burst over our lips.

"Levi."

Kelcie makes my name sound like a desperate prayer, and it has me yanking her against me while I crush my mouth to hers. I kiss her with every ounce of need I've ever had to be loved. I greedily take whatever she's willing to give me.

Her hips begin to move at a steady pace, and as she presses down on me, I keep thrusting up.

Her palms frantically brush all over my chest, and when she begins to rub herself faster against my cock, she grabs hold of my neck and lets out a needy sound.

Pulling one hand away from her hair, I find the swell of her breast. Getting to touch her so intimately while we grind against each other has me losing my mind.

Breaking the kiss, I yank at her shirt and roughly rip it over her head before tossing it God knows where. I shove the lace of her bra down, and getting my first look at her breasts, I almost come right then and there.

I stop thrusting, but Kelcie keeps moving, pushing me dangerously close to the edge.

My palm covers her breast while I bring my other hand down to feast on all her silky skin that's on display for me.

"Fuck," I hiss, sweat breaking out all over my body.

I thrust harder, and Kelcie rides me as if her life depends on it, our movements turning choppy.

Even though I know the pleasure has been building, I'm totally caught off guard when ecstasy rips through me. It's unlike anything I've ever felt.

My arms shoot around Kelcie, and I squash her to me while I bury my face against her neck. I come so fucking hard, my vision goes spotty, and it rips a growl from my chest.

My body jerks as I empty myself in my goddamn jeans, and I lose all sense of time.

As the pleasure begins to ebb away, my senses return one after the other.

Finally, I'm able to lift my head, and I'm met with a proud grin on Kelcie's face. "It looked like you *really* enjoyed that."

"You have no fucking idea," I say while trying to catch my breath.

Then I realize, I held her so tight she couldn't reach her own release because I stopped her from moving.

In a single move, I get up, turn us, and lay Kelcie down on the couch. It's only then I see the long surgical scar down the middle of her chest.

As I bring my fingers to the swollen skin, I notice I'm slightly trembling.

"It's an eyesore," Kelcie whispers.

I shake my head hard. "Don't ever say that again." I lean down and caress her scar with my lips. "There's not an inch of you that's not beautiful."

My mouth finds her nipples, taking turns to lavish each one with attention while I undo the button on her jeans and pull down her zipper.

I press kisses over her stomach before I tug the fabric off her legs. Pushing her knees apart, I look down at where she's wet for me, and for the first time ever, I'm filled with hunger to taste a woman down there.

Grabbing hold of Kelcie's right thigh, I pull her leg over my shoulder as I duck down to swipe my tongue over her.

One taste is all it takes. I'm instantly addicted.

Unable to get enough of her, I lick and suck, drinking every drop of arousal she gives me.

So fucking incredible.

"Levi," Kelcie cries, her fingers gripping my hair as she holds on for dear life. "Oh God. Please. Please. Please."

Moving one of my hands to between her thighs, I push my middle finger inside her tight warmth and groan against her clit.

Kelcie arches and tilts her head back, and a second later, I feel her inner walls grip the fuck out of my finger as she comes.

My woman unravels fast, her body shaking from the pleasure I'm giving her, and it fills my chest with pride and satisfaction.

I lap up all of her arousal until she comes down from her high, then I crawl up her body, kissing every inch of skin I can until I reach her mouth.

Lying down on top of Kelcie, I rest my forearms on either side of her face and take my sweet time kissing her.

When I eventually lift my head, there's a dreamy look in her eyes.

"Happy Thanksgiving," I say.

She nods while chuckling, a beautiful smile splitting over her face. "I have a lot I'm thankful for right now. Best orgasm of my life. Watching you come. You on top of me. The list is endless."

Lowering my head, I kiss her again, and we lose track of time until Lick nudges her snout against our shoulders to get us to let her out.

Chapter 16

KELCIE

With the snow covering the ground, it's way too cold to sit down beneath the tree, and I remain standing in front of my family's graves.

My cheeks are flushed, and my breaths turn white as they leave me.

Winter is officially here. It's freezing, so I can't visit for long.

A sad smile tugs at my mouth.

I feel guilty for finding happiness with Levi. I know it's stupid and that you would want me to go on with my life.

Letting out a sigh, I glance over the cemetery.

He loves me.

A breath shudders from me as my eyes begin to sting.

And I love him.

I look at the three headstones again and lift my gloved hand to rest over my heart.

You'll always be in here, but I think I have to put some distance between us. I'll always love you. I'll visit once a week, okay?

I can picture my parents and Sage jumping up to hug me while saying they understand. They would tell me to grab on to Levi and hold on as tight as I can.

That's what I'm going to do. I'm going to start living again and build a future with the man I love.

I lift my hand to my mouth and press a kiss to my fingertips before blowing it at the three graves.

Turning around, I walk as quickly as I can, my throat closing up. A tear escapes, and I wipe it away. When another rolls down my cheek and they start falling faster, I keep brushing them away.

Exiting the cemetery, I suck in a deep breath and head for the main street that runs through the middle of town.

Yesterday, Levi showed me how much he loves me, and it felt like an unbreakable bond was formed between us.

So this morning, when I left his house to visit my family, I made the decision to start letting go of the past. I know it's going to be difficult, but it's something I have to do if I want a future with Levi.

When I pass the general store and I see the sign for Dixie's Coffee, I lift my chin and go inside.

Mrs. Dixon glances at the door, and when she sees me, shock flutters over her face. "Kelcie! Oh my gosh, aren't you a sight for sore eyes." She hurries around the counter, and I brace for impact as she comes to hug me. "This makes my old heart so happy." Pulling back, she holds me by my shoulders and looks me up and down. "You look so good. How are you doing?"

Smiling, I answer, "I'm doing very well, Mrs. Dixon. How have you been?"

"You know me, dear. I don't complain." She walks back behind the counter while asking, "What can I get you?"

I glance over the menu, then say, "A pumpkin spice latte, please."

"It's the perfect thing for such a cold day," she agrees. She gets busy preparing the beverage. "I hear you're dating the new guy in town."

"He's lived here four months, but yes, I'm dating Levi."

She gives me a curious look. "Is it safe to assume the rumors about him aren't true?"

I lean against the counter and rest my forearms on the black slab of marble. "Which rumors would those be?"

"Folks say he's rude and to steer clear of him."

"Levi is an introvert and the kindest person I know," I defend my man. Frowning, I ask, "Are those rumors still making the rounds?"

Mrs. Dixon nods. "You know how it is. It will take months before the gossip mill finds something new to talk about."

"True," I sigh.

She places the steaming cup down in front of me. "It's on the house, dear. I hope you won't be a stranger and I'll get to see more of your pretty face."

"Thank you." I pick up the cup and take a sip. "Mmmh. I'll definitely pop in soon again." Walking to the door, I give her a smile. "Have a good day, Mrs. Dixon."

"You too, dear."

Walking up the street, I enjoy my beverage until Mom's old store comes into view. I notice it's now a gadget repair shop, and there's a stabbing sensation in my heart.

When I peek through the window, I'm sad to see everything has changed.

I quickly walk away, and as I near the corner, I hear Waverly shout, "Kelcie!" My head snaps in her direction, and I watch as she crosses the road. "When I saw you walking by the diner, I thought there's no way you wouldn't pop in to say hello."

I give her a sheepish look. "I'm sorry." I gesture at the repair store. "I got rattled by that."

"Ugh. It's such an eyesore. Come sit with me for a little bit." I hold up my cup, and she rolls her eyes. "I'm the owner, silly. I don't care what you're drinking in the diner as long as I get to spend a few minutes with you."

"Okay," I agree. We wait for a car to drive past before walking across the road.

Stepping inside the diner, I relish the warm air and take a seat on one of the stools by the counter.

"If it isn't my favorite neighbor I hardly get to see anymore," Jill says as she comes up behind me.

I glance over my shoulder and smile. "Oh, hey."

She sits down beside me, a mischievous expression on her face. "Soooo, how are things with you and Levi?"

Waverly's eyebrows fly up. "Are we talking about Mr. Hottie that lives next door to you?"

Jill winks at Waverly. "That's the one. I've noticed Kelcie is at his place every night." My neighbor looks at me again. "Girl, for someone who's seldom seen out and about, you sure are the talk of town."

"Is it true you finally told Colby to hit the road?" Waverly asks.

My cheeks flush from all the attention, and I grumble, "Hush. Both of you."

"No, no, no. You don't get to live this exciting life and not share the juicy details with us," Jill says.

I drink the rest of my latte, making them suffer, then I grin. "Yes, I made it clear to Colby that I will never date him. After he left, his mother came over to tell me what an awful person I am for breaking his heart. She even slapped me."

My friends gasp, then Waverly mutters, "That's it. Next time she comes in, I'm spitting on her food."

Laughter tumbles past my lips. "Oh God. Please don't do that on my account."

"Okay, enough about the dipshit and his family. I want to know about you and Levi. What goes on in that house all night long?" Jill asks, wagging her eyebrows suggestively.

Just thinking about Levi, my smile widens.

Jill slaps her hand on the counter, surprise flickering over her face. "Holy crap. You're in love with him."

Waverly grabs hold of my forearms. "Really?"

When I nod, they both shriek, looking so happy for me that it warms my heart.

"And? Does he feel the same about you?" Waverly asks.

I nod again.

Jill yanks me into a sideways hug while Waverly says, "We need to celebrate with hot chocolate."

I wait for Waverly to prepare the three drinks, and when we each have a steaming mug in our hands, I tell them, "Levi is the most incredible man ever. He makes me so happy."

Jill impatiently gestures for me to keep talking.

A shy smile tugs at my mouth. "And he's a damn good kisser. I go weak in the knees for the man." When she gestures again for me to say more, I shake my head. "No. The rest is private."

"Ooooh," both women tease me, then Jill says, "Private means sex."

"Hush," I chastise her. "I don't want the whole diner to hear."

We all burst out laughing, and to get the spotlight off me, I ask Jill, "Did you let Holly go on that date we talked about?"

"Yes." She looks downright disgruntled. "The little bastard kissed her right in front of me. I pulled them apart by their ears, and now my daughter hates me." My mouth drops open, but before I can say something, Jill continues, "But get this. She didn't want to kiss him anyway. And I'm the bad guy?"

"Mothers are always the bad guys," Waverly mutters. "I wouldn't let Lucas go to a sleepover, and he dumped all his LEGOs in my bedroom as revenge."

"That's just diabolical," Jill says before she starts to laugh. "Did you step on any?"

"What do you mean, *did I step on any*?" Waverly scowls at her. "I freaking tap-danced all the way to the bathroom."

Our laughter fills the air, and it feels so good to hang out with them, I don't even keep an eye on the time.

Jill glances at her phone, then shoots up off the stool. "Oh crap. My lunch hour ended thirty minutes ago. The boys are going to fire my ass."

Jill's been working for the Woods brothers as a receptionist at their auto repair shop.

Just as she turns around, she slams into Deputy Stone's chest.

"God, Jonas. Are you made of steel?" She scowls at him before moving to dart around him, but he leans back and grabs hold of her wrist.

My eyes widen when I hear her call him by his first name, and I'm completely entranced by what's happening right in front of me.

"Hold up. It's bad out," he tells her. "I'll give you a ride."

"Oh. Thanks." Jill practically bats her eyelashes at him.

Waverly gets so excited that she starts patting relentlessly at my shoulder.

"I'm looking," I whisper at her. "Stop hitting me."

"Shoot. Sorry."

When we turn our attention to Jill and Deputy Stone again, they're staring at us.

"So . . ." Waverly wiggles a finger between them. "Anything the two of you care to share with us?"

"There's nothing to share," Jill replies.

Deputy Stone, on the other hand, places his arm around her shoulders. "I beg to differ."

Not wanting to miss a single second, Waverly and I lean forward.

"You can beg all you want," Jill snaps at him.

His expression fills with a look of warning. "Is that so?"

"Yep."

Before the word is even cold on her lips, he tips her backward and plants a searingly hot kiss on her mouth.

"Ooooh!" Waverly starts hitting my shoulder again until I grab hold of her hand, then we cling to each other as we watch the deputy kiss the living daylights out of Jill.

When he ends the kiss and rights her on her feet, Waverly gives him two thumbs up. "Five stars, Deputy Stone. Your next coffee is free."

"All my coffees are free anyway," he says, a smirk on his face.

He steers a stunned Jill out of the diner and takes her to his cruiser. Suddenly, she slaps him on the chest, and I can't hear what she's saying, but it's clear she's laying into him until he silences her with another kiss.

"Jill's lunchtime is at eleven thirty every day. Be here tomorrow so we can get all the juicy tidbits about what's going on between her and one of Verona's most eligible bachelors."

"The things you must see in this diner," I say as I turn to face the counter again.

"Every other day, a new drama unfolds right before me. Just last week, Patrick and Ellie were in here. She caught him chatting up some woman who lives two towns over." She points at the corner. "Right in that booth, Ellie let him have it, and he ended up shouting, for everyone to hear, that he has been sleeping with the woman and wants a divorce before storming out of here. Poor Ellie was devastated."

"Oh no," I gasp. "That's awful."

How's that piece of news not the talk of the town? Instead, people are still harping on Levi.

"Yep. It's splitsville for those two."

Pushing my empty mug across the counter, I ask, "How much do I owe you?"

"Nothing. I asked you to come in." Her features soften. "This was fun, Kelcie. I hope we'll get to spend more time together."

Smiling at her as I slip off the stool, I say, "I'll be here tomorrow at eleven thirty sharp to get Jill's juicy news."

"Oh, right! See ya."

When I leave the diner, I pull my coat tighter around myself and cross my arms to keep the wind from getting inside.

Chapter 17

Kelcie

As I turn up my street, my phone rings, and I pull off my glove before digging it out of my pocket.

I swipe over the screen to accept the call, then pinning the device between my ear and shoulder, I put the glove back on. "Hi, Jordan."

"Hey. I know we spoke yesterday, but Natalie wants to know whether you're coming to us for Christmas."

When he called, we didn't get to talk for long because Natalie's parents arrived and Jordan had to go.

"Natalie or you?" I tease him.

"Fine," he grumbles. "Me." I chuckle while he continues to say, "I want you here for the holidays. I need my sister because I'm always outnumbered by Natalie's family."

"I'll come, and I'll bring Levi as well, so you'll have two people on your team."

"I didn't get to ask. How are things between the two of you?"

"Very good." I probably have a ridiculously happy grin plastered to my face. "I'm really happy, Jordan."

"Then I'm happy," my big brother replies. "That's all I want for you."

"I know."

"If you're going to drive here for Christmas, you need to have your car checked. And put on snow tires."

"Don't worry about my car. We'll probably take Levi's."

I still haven't replaced the battery, but I should get it done before the snow gets worse. I won't be able to walk around town for much longer.

"Thank God," Jordan sighs with relief. "Then it's settled. We'll see you and Levi on the twenty-third of December."

"That's two whole days before Christmas."

"I know. Pack a bag and visit for a week. It will be nice."

"I'll talk to Levi and ask what he wants to do."

"Tell him he'll score brownie points with your older brother, whose blessing he'll need if he ever wants to marry you."

I laugh at Jordan while shaking my head. "Oh, you're resorting to blackmail now?"

"Of course. Anyway, let me get back to work."

"Have a great day."

"You too," Jordan replies before we end the call.

When I walk past Levi's house, I glance at it and wonder if he's sleeping or writing.

"Kelcie."

Hearing Colby's voice, my head snaps toward his parents' place, and seeing him jog across the road, I shake my head and quickly rush up Levi's driveway.

"Go away, Colby. I'm done talking to you and your family."

"Wait up. I'm sorry my mom slapped you. She shouldn't have done that."

I quickly ring Levi's doorbell repeatedly, praying he isn't sleeping.

Glancing over my shoulder, I groan when Colby comes up behind me, and abandoning the doorbell, I pound against the wood. "Levi!"

I hear Lick barking like crazy.

"Come on. Don't be like that," Colby snaps.

He grabs hold of my shoulder and spins me around. I'm so startled, I stagger backward, but there's no door, and strong arms wrap around me.

Oh, thank God.

Levi lifts me off my feet and sets me down inside before he turns to face Colby while he indicates for Lick to stay.

"Get off my fucking property." There's so much anger brimming in his voice. I've never heard it so deep before. "And stay the fuck away from Kelcie. She's mine."

Colby steps right up to Levi, and just before their chests can touch, I grab hold of Levi's arm and pull him backward while Lick snarls, the fur on the back of her neck rising.

"We'll see how long you can hold on to her," Colby sneers, a vindictive expression on his face. "Just know, when Kelcie needs a shoulder to cry on, it will be mine."

Levi takes a step forward again, but I tighten my hold on his arm.

"Dammit, Colby!" I snap, my heart beating fast because of the volatile situation. "Just go away and leave us alone!" I reach for the door and slam it shut. Moving to the window, I watch as Colby finally leaves and let out a sigh of relief. "We're really going to have to consider moving."

"Just say when, and I'll buy you your farm," Levi grumbles, still wound tight. He pets Lick's head. "Good girl."

Not wanting the incident with Colby to spoil my good day, I smile at Levi. "Aww. You'll buy me a farm?" I close the distance between us and wrap my arms around his neck. "Can I have cows?"

"Yes."

"And chickens?"

He nods, the tension draining from his face.

"And baby goats?"

He nods again, then leans down and presses a kiss to my mouth. "You can have anything you want, my muse."

"Talking about muse. Did I interrupt your writing?"

He instantly looks upset again. "You didn't. That asshole did."

I place my hand on Levi's jaw and give him the sweetest smile I can conjure on my face. "Thank you for coming to my rescue."

"I'll always come to your rescue."

"How can I thank you?" I ask, rubbing my hands over his shoulders and down his chest.

God, I'll never get enough of touching him.

"You can cuddle with me and sleep here."

"Oooh, I like the sound of that."

Levi chuckles as he pulls away and walks to the kitchen, where he lets Lick go out quickly.

I come up behind Levi, and wrapping my arms around his waist, I rest my cheek against his back. He covers my hands with one of his.

She's mine.

Remembering his words, I grin like an idiot.

LEVI

After Lick comes back inside, I shut the door and lock it.

Kelcie lets go of me, and I take her hand, leading her to my bedroom.

While I kick off my shoes, she shrugs out of her coat and removes her gloves and beanie.

"Jordan called and invited us to spend the holidays with him. Are you okay with that?"

It will probably be overwhelming for me, but I can't refuse Kelcie a single damn thing. "Sure."

"He also wants us to visit for a week. He said you would score some serious brownie points with him."

Shit. A whole week.

"What about Lick?" I ask, not willing to put her in a shelter.

"She comes with us," Kelcie replies while we climb into bed.

Lick jumps up to find a comfortable spot by Kelcie's feet while I pull my woman into my arms.

"I guess we're spending a week at your brother's, then."

"Thank you," she murmurs while snuggling into my side.

When she's quiet, my thoughts turn to Colby, and I worry that he's not going to back down.

"This morning I decided to scale down my visits to the cemetery to once a week."

Surprised at the news, I glance at Kelcie. "Yeah? And you're okay with that?"

"I can't live in the past while trying to build a future with you."

The corner of my mouth lifts. "I know it must've been difficult for you to do. I'm proud of you."

Kelcie falls silent again, and just as I think she's asleep, she asks, "Memory for a memory?"

"Sure."

She begins to draw random patterns on my chest.

"Sage came home for a long weekend. We were so happy because she'd been busy with a trial and wasn't able to visit for months. I'd just finished the biggest order I've ever received, and we had pizza for dinner to celebrate."

Realizing that she's sharing a memory from the night of the attack, I hold her tighter and brush my hand up and down her back.

"Sage and I were going to watch a movie, but I had to dry my hair, or it would be all poofy and unmanageable." She pauses for a long while, and when she continues, her voice is hoarse. "I was blow-drying my hair when I heard a scream. It all happened so fast, but at the same time, it feels like the longest night of my life."

I press a kiss to her temple and keep caressing her back.

"When I ran out of my room, one of the men was dragging Mom by her hair." She clears her throat. "Wesley Porter. Such a plain name for such an evil person."

Every muscle in my body tenses, and I clench my jaw.

"I tried to stop him, but he was so much stronger than me. He hit me before shoving me down the stairs. In the living room . . . one of the men was kicking Sage. I think he'd already killed her, because she was so pale and had a big gash on the side of her head."

Her voice breaks, and I almost tell her to stop. To not put herself through the horror again, but by some miracle, I keep quiet.

"The third bastard was stabbing Dad." Her voice cracks. "God, Levi." A sob bursts from her, and I turn onto my side, trying to engulf her smaller frame with my body.

Her voice is muffled against my chest as she somehow finds the courage to go on. "I was stuck in a horrified trance while that evil monster kept plunging a knife into Dad's stomach and chest. He was so aggressive. So deranged." Kelcie begins to cry heartbreakingly, and her words are strained. "I heard a sound as if someone was choking, and when I looked at the top of the stairs, Mom . . . my mom . . ."

Kelcie loses control of her emotions and weeps in my arms, and I feel so fucking helpless, not being able to take the gruesome memories from her.

I'm well acquainted with hatred, but after hearing what those bastards did to her family, I wish I could reach into their jail cells and tear them apart.

Kelcie sounds broken when she manages to continue. "He slit my mom's throat, and I watched as she bled out. Dad told me to run."

Her breaths speed up until they're coming too fast, and I pull back so I can see her face. "Take a break and focus on your breathing, baby. Ten . . . nine . . . eight . . ."

I go through the same exercise she did with me last night, and when she calms down, I wipe the tears from her cheeks.

"I ran," she whispers.

I see the guilt in her eyes and quickly shake my head. "You had to run."

"I ran and left my parents and sister behind. I didn't even make it to the front door when one of them shot me in the back. That's the last thing I remember. The sheriff told me I stumbled out onto the porch just as he got to the house. Our neighbors heard our screams and called for help."

The guilt doesn't ease from her face, and it has me gripping hold of her chin and forcing her to look at me. "There is nothing you could've done to save your family. Don't for one second feel guilty."

Because that's on me. If I had done things differently in the past, I could've changed the trajectory of our lives and maybe prevented that night from happening altogether.

Her face crumples under the weight of her grief and trauma. "Those monsters killed my family because my dad was the mayor, and he was clamping down on crime and drugs. They didn't like it one bit and thought if they could get rid of Dad, they could go on doing whatever they wanted." She shakes her head. "They were so high on drugs, two of them barely remembered what they did. Trent Crawford and Dustin Baker. But Wesley Porter . . . he remembered every detail and sat in that courtroom looking proud of what he did." Her eyes meet mine again. "His parents were even there to support their murderous son. His father had the same evil look on his face. It terrified me."

Jesus Christ.

I close my eyes, and squashing Kelcie to me, I breathe through the destructive mess I feel.

We lie for the longest time, clinging to each other as the horrors of that night hang like a dark cloud over us.

Chapter 18

KELCIE

I quickly came home to shower before I go back to Levi's place.

At this rate, I might as well move in with him.

While I hurry through my routine, I think about earlier. It was so difficult to tell Levi what happened to my family, but I managed. Even though I started having a panic attack, it wasn't too severe.

Now that I've finally spoken about it, I have to admit, I feel a little better. By taking one step at a time, I'm moving forward.

Levi once told me I had to create a new version of myself, and that's what I'm trying to do. A version who can be happy with him, and even though the grief might never fade, I hope to learn to live with it.

I've taken two giant steps today, and I need to process them before I can even think of what to deal with next.

Once I'm done at my place, I rush out the back door and quickly walk across the stretch of lawn before letting myself into Levi's house. When I see the lit candles on the table, I shut the door so the wind doesn't blow them out.

Levi comes in from the other doorway, and seeing me, he says, "That was fast."

"Candles?" I ask.

"I wanted to do something special for you, and it's the best I could come up with on such short notice." He walks to a cupboard and takes two plates out, setting them down on the table. "I'm making us turkey sandwiches. I hope you're okay with that?"

"Of course."

When I move in the direction of the fridge so I can help, Levi shakes his head and points at the chair nearest to me.

"Sit down. I'll take care of everything."

I take a seat and track his every movement as he prepares our sandwiches.

I notice Lick watching Levi anxiously, and getting up, I steal a piece of white meat and break it in two before feeding her. She takes it gently from me, bringing a smile to my face, and I say, "We should get another puppy so Lick isn't alone."

"Yeah?"

I crouch down and scratch behind her ears, giving her attention, until Levi murmurs, "Come eat, my muse."

Climbing to my feet, I go to the sink and wash my hands before I sit down at the table. "Thank you for making dinner for us."

"You did most of the work yesterday. I just had to slap sandwiches together."

"Levi." When his eyes flick to mine, I repeat myself. "Thank you."

A slight smile tugs at his mouth. "You're welcome."

I pick up one half of my sandwich, sinking my teeth into it. Once I've swallowed, I say, "You owe me a memory."

Levi glances at me and swallows before he says, "I'll have to make it a happy one."

Nodding, I grin.

"Lick was in the backyard doing her thing when my beautiful neighbor came outside."

I let out a burst of laughter. "It sounds vaguely familiar, but go on."

"You sat down at the table, and Lick did me a favor by going over to you and getting your attention. It opened a door for me to talk to you, even though I was awkward as fuck."

"We were both awkward," I mention.

Levi tilts his head. "You blushed that day. Why?"

"It was the first time I got to see you up close." When Levi frowns, I say, "You have to know how attractive you are." He begins to look uncomfortable. "Is it hard for you to accept compliments?"

He nods. "It's not something I got growing up, so I'm not used to it."

"Well, brace yourself, because I like giving compliments. You're easily the most attractive man I've ever seen. That's why I blushed. The attraction hit me so hard, and when I looked into your eyes, I think I knew right then it would only be a matter of time before I fell in love with you."

"It was the same for me," Levi murmurs.

Once we're done with our meal, we clear the table before moving to the living room. We get comfortable on a couch while Lick jumps up on the other one.

"It's your turn to pick a movie," I remind him.

"Would you think it's weird if we watched *The Elimination Project*? I haven't seen it."

My eyes widen. "Why?"

Levi shrugs. "I was too overwhelmed by everything that happened, and I was scared it would suck."

"It's sooooo good." I grab the remote, and switching on the TV, I quickly find the movie and press play. "By the way, it's one of my favorites."

"Yeah?"

"I might sob my little heart out at the scene where Easton cries," I warn Levi.

I snuggle into his side, and when he places his arm around my shoulders, I let out a happy sigh.

While the movie plays, I keep stealing glances at Levi. Emotions flash over his face as he watches his hard work come to life.

When we get to the sad part and Easton lets out a heartbroken cry before breaking down, my throat strains. I wait until the credits run before I say, "I read Easton was really crying. He lost his sister to cancer a few weeks before they shot that scene."

"Yeah. I was told they might postpone filming, but somehow they still got the movie done on time." Levi lets out a sigh, then looks at me. "That was . . ."

"Incredible?" He nods, and I add, "The best thing ever?"

A proud smile spreads over his face, and he even looks a little emotional.

"You wrote a damn good book, Levi. You should be very proud of yourself."

"Thank you."

I switch off the TV, and turning my body toward his, I ask, "What are you thinking?"

"I'm thinking how lucky I am to have you in my life, and I don't want to waste a single second I get to spend with you."

I grin at him. "Hopefully, we'll live long and happy lives together."

"Hopefully."

There's something in his voice that tells me he doesn't believe we'll make it, and it has worry creeping into my heart.

"You don't sound so sure," I mention.

He turns his head toward me. "Oh, I'm sure."

"But?"

"You might change your mind about us at some point."

I climb onto his lap and rest my hands on his shoulders. "Once I make up my mind about something, I see it through." I lean forward and press a soft kiss to his lips. "And I've made up my mind about you, Levi. I want a future with you."

Gripping me by the back of my neck, he pulls me closer and seals his mouth to mine.

This time, the kiss feels different. It's as if Levi is savoring every swipe of our tongues. I can feel his love for me as his lips massage mine.

By the time he pulls back, I'm a little emotional, and I can see by the expression tightening his features, he feels the same.

"The things you make me feel. The emotions you bring out in me," Levi murmurs, staring at me with so much wonder in his gaze, there's no doubt in my mind that he loves me. "I want to build a future with you, Kelcie."

Not wanting to disrupt our intimate bubble, I whisper, "I want that too."

When I hear Jordan's car pull up, I shoot to my feet and hurry to open the front door.

There's a happy smile on my face, and as my brother climbs out of his car, his eyes lock on me. He stops moving and just stares at me, an emotional expression tightening his features.

"Why are you standing out there? It's freezing," I say. "Come inside!"

Jordan begins to move again, and I quickly step aside. The instant I shut the door behind us, blocking out the icy wind, he grabs me into a tight hug.

"God, Kelcie. You look so much better," he murmurs near my ear. "I'm so relieved."

Even though I know the answer, I jokingly ask, "Was I such a big mess?"

Jordan pulls back so he can look me over from head to toe. "I was worried. I didn't think you'd be able to pull yourself out of your grief."

My smile fades a little because it's still difficult to talk about our grief and family.

"I didn't. It's all Levi."

My brother glances at the sparsely decorated living room and kitchen. "Where is he?"

"Next door. I wanted ten minutes alone with you." I gesture at the couch. "Have a seat while I make us some hot chocolate."

Jordan sits down and asks, "Did you talk to Levi about spending the holidays with me?"

"Yes, and he agreed, but we're bringing his dog. She's really well trained."

My brother lets out a sigh of relief. "I'm just glad you're coming."

I carry our steaming mugs of chocolaty goodness to the living room and hand one to Jordan. Sitting down, I turn slightly to face him before I say, "Levi isn't very social, but it doesn't mean he's rude, so please don't be offended if his replies are short." I give my brother a pleading look. "It's very important to me that the two of you get along."

Jordan tilts his head, and his gaze searches mine before he asks, "Do you love him, Kelcie?"

I'm overcome with everything I feel for Levi as I nod. "With all my heart."

"Is he good to you?"

"Yes. He's so patient and understanding. God, Jordan, Levi is the most incredible man I've ever met." My brother scowls at me, and I quickly add, "Obviously, that doesn't include you."

His scowl morphs into a playful expression. "Just kidding. I know what you mean."

I drink some of my hot chocolate, then say, "There's one more thing."

Jordan's right eyebrow lifts. "What?"

"I want you to know so you don't find out and make Levi uncomfortable. Remember *The Elimination Project* that Easton Rowe starred in?"

"Oh yeah. One of my fav . . ." Jordan's voice trails away, and his eyes go wide as saucers. "Holy shit!" he gasps. "Is he the same Levi Graye who wrote the book?"

When I nod, Jordan stands up, too excited to remain seated. "I thought he just had the same name as the author. I've read the book. Wow. Do you think he'll sign a copy for me?"

"Jordan." I pat the couch. "This is why I'm telling you now, so you don't get excited in front of Levi. It will have him running for the hills."

My brother reins in his excitement and sits down again. "Okay. I can act calm around him."

Reaching out, I rub his shoulder. "Thank you. And don't worry, I'll ask him to sign a book for you."

While we finish our hot chocolate, I ask, "How are Natalie and Brady?"

"They're good. Natalie found a new job, so she's currently working her notice period. She'll be closer to home, and it pays more."

"Oh my gosh! That's such good news. I'll send her a text to congratulate her."

An apprehensive expression ghosts over my brother's face, and I already know what he's going to ask.

"Just give me a little more time," I answer his unspoken question. "Levi's been taking care of the garden, so you don't have to worry about it."

"I'm not worried about the garden. It's been over a year, and you seem to be doing so much better. We need to talk about selling the house."

My heartbeat speeds up, and my palms grow sweaty. Even though my anxiety spikes, it doesn't spiral out of control and into a full-blown panic attack.

Surprise ripples over Jordan's face. "You're actually okay to talk about it."

I shrug while I breathe through the anxiety. "Yes, but I'm not ready to sell. Can you give me six months? I want to prepare myself emotionally before I go to the house."

Jordan nods as he leans in to hug me. "I can wait six months."

Pulling away, I climb to my feet. "Let's go next door."

He darts up and hurries to the kitchen to place his mug in the sink. "You don't have to tell me twice."

A chuckle escapes me, and as we step out into the cold, Jordan places his arm around my shoulders. "I'm happy for you, Kelcie."

"Thank you for being patient with me over the past fifteen months."

"It feels like I should've done more for you, but I didn't know how to help."

"I know. Don't forget that you were dealing with your own grief as well. We both did the best we could."

He presses a quick kiss to the side of my head as we reach Levi's back door. I knock once before opening it, and I gesture for Jordan to follow me inside.

Suddenly, Lick starts barking, and the sound of nails slipping on the floor sounds up. The instant she barrels into the kitchen, I hold up my hand to show her to stay.

She stops running, her eyes on Jordan.

"Just hold your palm out so she can sniff you," I tell my brother.

He leans down and does as I say. Lick takes one sniff, then her tongue darts out and she slobbers all over Jordan's hand.

"And that's the reason her name is Lick," I mention, laughter tumbling past my lips.

"Hi, Jordan." Levi's tone is much quieter than it usually is when he talks to me.

My head snaps to where he's standing in the doorway, and noticing his discomfort at having Jordan in his personal space, I walk to him and link my arm through his.

"Hi," Jordan chuckles while glancing between his spit-covered hand and Levi. "I'd shake your hand, but your dog just went to town on mine."

I point at the sink. "You can wash your hands there, and Levi doesn't touch people."

"Oh, right. I forgot."

While Jordan washes his hands, I go to the paper towel roll and rip two off for him.

Smiling, he takes them from me, then turns his attention to Levi and says, "Kelcie tells me the two of you are dating."

Levi nods. "We are." He gestures at the coffee machine. "Would you like something to drink?"

"I'm good. We just had hot chocolate," my brother replies.

Before things can get too awkward, I suggest, "Let's sit in the living room."

We move to the other room, and once we're sitting on the couches, Jordan's gaze lands on the shelf. He gets up again and moves closer, looking at the books and awards with admiration.

He gestures at one of the toy cars I got Levi for his pretend birthday. "I loved playing with these as a kid." My brother takes a deep breath, then glances at Levi. "Kelcie told me not to make a big deal of it, but I have to say I love your books. I own every single one."

I look at Levi, seeing the discomfort ghosting over his face, but the corner of his mouth lifts. "Thanks."

"Are you still writing?" Jordan asks as he goes to sit on the other couch again.

"Yeah. I struggled with writer's block until Kelcie came into my life. That's why there's been such a long break between books."

Jordan grins at me. "So all his fans should be thanking you."

I shrug, a wide smile on my face as I joke, "Oh, definitely."

I begin to relax because it's going much better than I thought it would.

Jordan changes the subject, asking, "Have you replaced the battery in your car yet?"

I shake my head while letting out a sigh. "I'll call Malakai and Asher this week and have one of them come out."

My brother glances at Levi. "You need to keep an eye on her car, or she'll let it fall apart in the garage. It needs a service."

"I'll take care of it," Levi assures him, lifting his arm to wrap it around my shoulders.

The conversation flows, and we talk about what we did for Thanksgiving and even discuss things we could do while we're visiting Jordan over the holidays.

I take in how relaxed my brother is and that there are no worry lines on his face. It's the first time we've been able to get together without my grief dragging him down, and it's all because of the change Levi has made in my life.

Chapter 19

KELCIE

This morning, Levi took me to the auto repair shop to get a new battery. I told him he didn't have to, but he insisted.

When he starts the car and the engine purrs to life, I clap my hands and lean down to press a kiss to his cheek. "Thank you! Now Jordan can get off my back."

"You're welcome, my muse," Levi replies. "I'll go get snow tires put on later today."

I step back so he can get out of the car and shut the door.

"Levi."

Hearing a woman's voice, we both glance toward the end of the driveway where Colby is standing with a microphone in his hand, a cameraman, and some lady who looks awfully familiar. For a few seconds, I can't place where I know her from, but then recognition shudders through me like an earthquake.

Wesley Porter's mother.

"Why would you bring her here, Colby?" I exclaim in complete shock. Does he hate me so much?

"Fuck," Levi mutters under his breath.

Feeling completely rattled, I glance at Levi, who's staring at the three people with a grim expression, the blood draining from his face, and his jaw clenching hard.

Suddenly, he grabs me by my wrist and begins to drag me toward the front door, but Colby calls out, "Levi, your mother came all this way to see you. Don't you have anything to say to her?"

Mother?

A weird pins and needles sensation spreads from the top of my head to my toes as I'm hit with a wave of shock that threatens to wash my feet from right under me.

"Levi," the woman says, her tone urgent as she walks closer to us, "I just want to talk to you."

Levi shoves my front door open, and I'm hauled inside.

"What's going on?" I ask, air bursting over my lips and drying them quickly. "Why . . . ?"

My heart clenches into a tiny ball as the grief I've worked so hard to deal with consumes me.

"Kelcie, did you know your boyfriend is related to the man who killed your mother?" Colby shouts for half the neighborhood to hear. "Wesley Porter is Levi Graye's brother."

No. No. No.

I shake my head, unable to process what Colby is telling me. There's no way it's the truth.

Lifting my eyes to Levi's, I don't even have to ask whether what Colby is saying is the truth. The guilt is written all over his face.

No!

Somewhere deep inside my soul, something breaks.

It's only then that I begin to make sense of everything, and I rip my wrist free from Levi's tight hold. I slowly shake my head, the initial blow of heartache so intense it forces me three steps backward.

"Levi," his mother says, trying to get his attention.

He turns his head, hatred and disgust darkening his features as he snaps, "Fuck off, Rene!" He slams the door shut in her face. After locking it, he keeps his head turned away from me. "I can explain."

Oh God.

A sob threatens to escape from me. I take another step backward, shaking my head faster as my breaths turn to short puffs. "No, Levi," I whisper, my tone filled with unspeakable fear. "Tell me Colby is lying. Tell me this isn't true."

It feels like I'm being sucked into a world where everything is turned upside down and nothing makes sense. I lift my hands to cover my mouth as another wave of shock shoots through me.

Finally, Levi looks at me, his eyes filled with guilt and pain.

"I wanted to tell you," he replies, his tone desperate. "But I didn't know how, and then I fell in love with you, and I just couldn't."

"No!" I cry, my chest heaving as sobs begin to build in me. The pieces of my heart he carefully glued back together over the past few months shatter into an unrecognizable mess around me, and I whimper, "No, Levi."

"I saw the article and recognized Wesley's name," he says while giving me a pleading expression. "Even though I knew it had nothing to do with me, I felt guilty because he's my half brother. I followed the trial, and it broke my heart to see how you and Jordan were suffering. I wanted to do something to help."

"So you moved in right next door to me?" I whisper, my mind reeling from this . . . this . . . nightmare.

He followed the trial. He bought a house in my hometown. He lived next to me for two months before we started talking.

"You stalked me!" I gasp.

"I just wanted to help, Kelcie. I tried to fight my feelings for you, but—"

"Is that why you kept pulling away?" I ask, feeling so stupid for pursuing him.

Oh. My. God. I . . . I . . . I . . .

A dry sob tears from me.

Someone knocks, and when I don't answer, they begin banging on the door. "Kelcie. Let me in. You deserve to know the truth," Colby shouts.

When I step toward the door, Levi begs, "Don't listen to him. Let's talk about this."

Ignoring his plea, I unlock the door and yank it open. Giving Colby the darkest glare I can conjure to my face, I snap, "Get off my property. The next time you come near me, I'm calling Sheriff Williams, and I'll have you arrested for trespassing."

"Kelc—"

I slam the door shut again, engage the locks, and walk to the kitchen to put some distance between Levi and me.

When he takes a step in my direction, I shake my head. "You stay right there. Don't come any closer."

My mind races to process everything.

I remember every memory Levi shared with me and realize he never said his family's names. It was always stepfather, mother, or half brother.

"Baby," Levi groans.

My eyes snap to him, and I begin to feel torn. Part of me wants to do everything in my power not to hurt him, but the other half feels betrayed and so, so very heartbroken.

"You lied to me." A tsunami of pain tears through my chest. "You inserted yourself in my life and made me fall for you. You . . . you . . . you . . ."

My breathing becomes choppy as my emotions spiral into chaos, and I blindly move toward the cupboard. I can't get any air into my lungs, and it feels as if I'm suffocating.

Levi darts past me and quickly grabs my medicine from the cupboard. He pops one of the pills out and pushes it past my dry lips.

My vision grows spotty, and I'm not aware of what happens for the next few minutes.

When the severe panic attack begins to ease, I smell cedarwood and citrus.

"I'm so sorry," Levi groans, sounding as if he's in physical pain. "I love you with everything I am. I never meant to hurt you."

My face is pressed to his chest, and his arms are steel bands of safety around me.

But the moment only lasts a few seconds.

I yank away from him, and when he lets go of me, I stagger backward until I hit the wall.

"You tricked me. You played me for a fool," I sob, unable to handle all the heartache eating me up alive.

What else is he capable of?

Fear slithers through my veins, and I don't know what my expression looks like, but it has Levi holding his hands up in front of him.

"I will never hurt you. Please don't look at me like that."

"Leave," I whimper.

"Kelcie." His arms fall limply to his sides, the most heartbreaking expression I've ever seen settling on his face. "I didn't play you. Everything between us was . . . is real. The memories I shared with you were the truth. I left that family when I turned sixteen." He lifts his arms again and scrubs his palms over his face. "I shouldn't have kept from you who my half brother was, and I'm so sorry I did."

His expression turns pleading again. "I didn't want to lose you."

While Levi talks, I can't keep myself from remembering every moment we shared.

My head begins to pound from all the tension, and I wrap my arms around myself.

"I need time alone. I have to process it all. I can't do this with you right now."

Levi takes a cautious step toward me, and when I begin to shake my head, he sucks in a shuddering breath before saying, "I'll give you all the time you need." His eyes burn into mine. "I never meant to hurt you, Kelcie. Your beautiful nature and warmth drew me in, and I couldn't fight it. Getting to know you has been the greatest gift I've received in my life, and whatever you decide, I'll always treasure every second I got to spend with you."

When he slowly begins to move closer again, I don't have it in me to tell him to stop.

"Can I hold you, please?" he begs. "If this might be the last time I see you, can I be selfish and ask for one last hug?"

Tears overwhelm me, and as I begin to cry, his arms gently wrap around me and pull me against his chest. His scent envelops me, and I weep because the happiness I managed to find with Levi has just been cruelly ripped away from me.

I don't think this is something I'll ever recover from.

LEVI

Unbearable pain keeps dragging me back down into the darkness that's followed me throughout my thirty-three years of life on this godforsaken planet.

Kelcie is the only warmth and love I've ever felt, and I can't bear to think I might lose her.

I hold her as tight as I can without hurting her, and as her tears wet my shirt, my eyes burn like they're on fire.

It feels as if someone is ripping my heart clean from my chest.

"I love you," I groan, buckling under the severe heartache. "I'm so sorry."

There's nothing I regret more than hurting Kelcie.

The instant I laid eyes on Rene, the woman who gave birth to me, the ground might as well have opened up beneath my feet. I was bombarded with every destructive emotion she and my stepfather have ever made me feel. The abuse I suffered at their hands tightened like a noose around my throat, threatening to once again squeeze the life from me.

During my entire childhood, they destroyed me, and now she has come back to destroy the happiness I've finally managed to find.

"I'm sorry," I say again, hoping Kelcie believes me.

She begins to calm down, lost sobs drifting over her lips, and then she wraps her arms around me and holds me tightly.

"I love you, Kelcie. More than you'll ever know. It might not matter, but please don't judge me for what Wesley did. Please try to understand, I was terrified of losing you, and that's why I kept quiet about being related to him. I haven't seen my family since I was sixteen."

"You deceived me." She sounds broken, and it crushes my heart to dust.

Kelcie lowers her arms and pulls away. Knowing I have no choice, I move a couple of steps backward and desperately take in every inch of her face.

When I see all the strength drain from her and a grief-stricken expression dull her eyes, I know I've lost her.

Her light fades away, and it feels as if I'm dropped in the middle of the Arctic desert.

My entire body trembles as I quickly dart forward, and framing her face with my hands, I lean down and press a kiss to her forehead. Against her skin, I vow, "I will always love only you, Kelcie. You own all of my heart."

I duck down lower and kiss her soft lips before I force myself to let go of her.

I rush out of the back door, and as blinding pain engulfs every part of my being, I somehow make it back to my house.

I feel Lick nudging her head against my hand, and when I drop down on the couch, she jumps up and lays her head on my chest, her big eyes locked on my face.

Fuck.

I gasp as the pain keeps intensifying.

Lifting my arms, I grab hold of Lick and bury my face against her fur. She whines as if she can sense my distress.

I just lost Kelcie.

I let go of Lick, and unable to sit still, I dart to my feet and begin to pace up and down the living room for God knows how long.

When I hear an engine start, I stop by the window, and seeing Kelcie's car backing out of her driveway, I rush to my front door and rip it open. As I run across the yard, she drives by and keeps going.

Jesus, she's in no state to drive anywhere!

I stop in the road and lift my hands to the back of my head, my breaths exploding over my lips as worry for her safety floods me.

"Levi!"

I glance over my shoulder, and seeing Rene, I turn away and walk back to my house.

"Please," she cries.

The next second, she grabs hold of my arm, and I just react, yanking away from her while growling, "Don't fucking touch me."

I'm instantly filled with disgust so thick, it threatens to suffocate me.

Lick barks threateningly, and it has Rene quickly retreating a couple of feet. "I just want to talk to you."

"I have nothing to say to you."

I go inside my house, and as I wait for Lick to come in, Rene says, "We lost everything to pay for your brother's lawyer. I wouldn't ask for money if I had any other choice, but we're family. We read you made millions from your books and the movie."

You have got to be fucking kidding me.

My eyes lock with her desperate ones.

For a split second, I thought she was here to ask for forgiveness. To tell me she missed me.

But instead, she's here to ask for money?

It feels like I'm losing my mind, and a dark chuckle escapes me. My voice sounds foreign to my ears as I say, "You come to my house with a reporter and ruin the most important thing in my life, only to ask for money?" I shake my head hard. "Even if you were dying of hunger, I wouldn't give you the trash I throw out every week."

I keep eye contact with her and let her see every ounce of hatred I feel for her. Only when I see the realization that she's not getting a dime from me register in her eyes do I shut the door.

With every step I take through the living room, my body trembles more and more, and by the time I move in beneath the scorching hot spray of the shower, there's nothing left of the man I was this morning.

I sink down until my ass hits the tiles, and lowering my head, I stare at nothing.

I've lost Kelcie.

My chest shudders, and for the first time since I ran away from home, I break down.

Chapter 20

KELCIE

For the first time in my life, I'm driven by a desperate need to get away from Verona.

With the radio on and an old Kenny Rogers song blasting in my ears, I struggle to focus on the slippery road. My thoughts keep jumping from one thing to another, and my emotions feel like they're stuck on a crazy roller coaster ride.

I have no idea how long I've been driving when a news broadcast comes on. I turn the volume down, and when the car slips on the ice, I quickly grab hold of the steering wheel with both hands.

For what feels like the hundredth time since I found out Levi is related to Wesley Porter, my heart breaks into a zillion unrecognizable pieces.

How could Levi do that to me?

How could the man who was so patient and understanding with me lie to me every day?

I hear Levi's name on the radio and turn the sound up again.

"... the bestselling author of *The Elimination Project* is related to Wesley Porter, a convicted murderer. More about this at five. Stay tuned for ..."

I switch the radio off, and just then the tires slip on the icy road, and my car begins to slide.

"Oh God!" I grab the steering wheel tightly, but there's nothing I can do as I slam into the embankment on the side of the road. Snow splatters all over my windshield, and the car jerks before the engine stalls.

Breaths burst over my parted lips, and I blink through the shock. The next second, I burst out into tears and begin to ugly cry. I lean forward and press my forehead against the steering wheel.

Agonizing sobs rip through me, and it feels as if I've lost all reason for living.

A knock on my window startles the crap out of me. I quickly wipe my cheeks and try to rein in the tears before I let the window down a couple of inches.

"Are you okay?" a man with gray hair and a Santa Claus beard asks. "I saw you go off the road."

I nod, and my voice sounds like it's been put through a grater as I reply, "I'm fine."

"Is there anyone I can call for you?"

I reach over to the passenger seat and pick up my bag. Digging my phone out, I check that I have a signal, then say, "You're so kind, but I'll call my brother."

"Okay then. Take care."

"Thank you for checking on me."

When he walks away, I let the window up to keep the cold out.

I slump back in my seat and stare at the pile of snow on the hood of my car. Only then does a trembling creep deep into my bones.

White puffs of air come from my mouth, and somehow I think to start the engine again so the heat will work.

It takes a minute or two before I'm able to calm down enough to dial Jordan's number.

After a few rings, he answers, "Hey, what's up?"

"I need you . . ." I suck in a desperate breath before trying to continue.

"Kelcie!"

"I need you." I burst out in tears again and have to squeeze the words out. "I crashed into an embankment. I don't think I can drive further. Please come get me."

"Send me your location," he says, his breaths rushing over the line. "I'm on my way."

Even though he can't see me, I nod. I end the call and send him my live location. Seconds later, my phone rings.

"Did you get it?" I ask.

"Yes, but you didn't have to hang up. Stay on the line with me." I hear his car start, then Jordan says, "Jesus, Kelcie. What are you doing near Rockford?"

"I'm on my way to you."

"What happened?"

I shake my head, and squeezing my eyes shut, I begin to cry again.

Jordan's tone is gentle, even though it's filled with worry. "I'm on my way. Shh . . . I'm coming."

"Okay," I whimper.

"Talk to me, Kelcie."

I try to form the words, but I can't.

"Did something happen between you and Levi?" he asks.

"Uh-huh."

"Is it bad?"

"Yeah," I sigh as exhaustion hits.

We're quiet for a long while, and I manage to calm down eventually. I dig tissues out of my bag and blow my nose.

"I'm ten minutes away," Jordan informs me.

God, I have no sense of time anymore.

I clear my throat before replying, "Okay."

"I'm going to go so I can call a tow truck to collect your car."

"Thank you."

"Just sit tight."

We hang up, and I plug in my phone charger so the battery doesn't die.

A police car slows down as it passes me, and the officer pulls over in front of me.

I let my window down and dig my driver's license and papers out so I have them ready.

"Are you okay?" the officer asks when he reaches my door.

"Yes. My car lost traction."

"Have you called a tow truck service?"

"Yes, and my brother is on his way. He'll be here any minute."

His sharp gaze flits over my face. "Do you have any injuries?"

"No, I'm just having a really bad day."

"I'm sorry to hear that." He pats the roof of my car. "I'll stay with you until your brother gets here."

"Thank you. I really appreciate it."

Just as the officer walks back to his patrol car, I see Jordan's SUV coming from the opposite direction.

I let the window up, and grabbing my phone and charger, I put them in my handbag before shoving the driver's door open. Climbing out, I glance up and down the stretch of road before I jog across to where Jordan comes to a stop.

He gets out and stalks toward me, his arms opening. I slam into my brother's chest, and then I completely lose it.

"I'm here. I've got you."

"Are you her brother?" I hear the officer ask.

"Yes. Jordan Woodruff. A tow truck is on the way."

"I just want to make sure she's safe," the officer says. "You should get her inside your SUV so she can stay warm."

Jordan steers me to the passenger side and opens the door. He bundles me into the seat, then leans in and presses a kiss to my temple. "Let me just deal with everything, then we'll get out of here, okay?"

I nod and keep my head lowered as he shuts the door.

While Jordan takes care of my mess, the day's events flash through my mind.

How easy it was for Colby to rip the ground from under me and destroy my life.

Seeing Wesley Porter's mother again.

Finding out Wesley is Levi's half brother.

Levi deceived me for months.

The back door opens, and Jordan places the single piece of luggage I haphazardly packed on the seat. He shuts the door and opens the driver's side. When he climbs in behind the steering wheel, I glance at the other side of the road and see the tow truck drive away with my car.

"I told them to take it to Verona and leave it at Woods' Auto Repair. I called Malakai, and he said he'll keep it there for you."

"Thanks." I'm too exhausted to manage anything more than a whisper.

Jordan starts the engine and makes a U-turn, then he asks, "Did you and Levi break up?"

"Yes." I begin to shake my head, then whimper, "No." Looking down at my hands clamped together on my lap, I admit, "I don't know."

"We have time. Wanna tell me about it?"

I lean the side of my head against the window and stare at the white landscape passing us by.

"Levi lied to me."

"About?"

I look at Jordan as I say, "He's related to Wesley Porter. They're half brothers."

"What the fuck?" Shock ripples over Jordan's face. "How did you find out?"

"Colby came to my house with a cameraman and that murderer's mother. She's also Levi's mother, and Colby decided it would make great news by telling me who Levi is while recording it." I gasp as pain slices through my heart again.

"Fuck." Jordan's eyes flick to me, anger burning in his eyes. "Colby is such an asshole. If he puts that on the news, I'm suing him for invasion of privacy."

"Can we do that?"

"Definitely. I looked into it when all those reporters were hounding us after the attack. What Colby did was intrusive, and it caused you harm." Jordan overtakes a semitruck before he asks, "Is Levi really related to that bastard?"

"Yes." My tongue darts out to wet my lips, and remembering I have lip balm in my handbag, I dig the tube out and quickly put some on.

Suddenly, my phone rings, and when I see Levi's name, I don't know what to do.

"Are you going to answer?" Jordan asks.

"It's Levi."

"Put it on speaker. I'll talk to him."

I take the call, and my brother says, "It's Jordan."

"Is Kelcie with you?" Levi's voice is gravelly, and just hearing him sends a wave of goose bumps over my skin.

"Yes."

"Is she safe?"

"Yeah," Jordan replies.

There's a pause before Levi asks, "Is she okay?"

Jordan glances at me. "Not by a long shot. Why are you calling, Levi?"

"She left hours ago, and I got worried. I just wanted to make sure nothing happened. Thanks for taking the call, Jordan. I appreciate it."

Levi hangs up, and a sob sputters from me. Covering my face with my hands, I cry, "It hurts so much."

"I'm sorry, Kelcie," my brother murmurs.

Once I manage to rein in my tears again, a weird calmness settles over me. It was the same after I learned Mom, Dad, and Sage died.

"Did Levi know who you were when he started a relationship with you?"

I nod and let out a heavy sigh before I reply, "He came to Verona because he felt bad about what happened. Apparently, he wanted to help us." I look at Jordan again. "But seriously, who moves in next door to the woman your half brother and his druggie friends tried to kill?" I shake my head wildly. "Levi followed the trail. He inserted himself into my life. He made me love him."

My voice cracks, and I suck in deep breaths, the shock of what Levi did hitting me for the umpteenth time.

I close my eyes and whisper, "I trusted him, and he broke my heart."

Silence falls between us, and by the time Jordan pulls up to his house, it feels like I've lost a fight against a grizzly bear, and my head is pounding something fierce.

The garage door rolls up, and after he parks the SUV, I shove the passenger door open and climb out.

"Oh, sweetie," I hear Natalie say, then she comes around the back of the SUV and pulls me into a hug. "Are you okay? Did you get hurt?"

I shake my head and struggle to keep my tears back. When she lets go of me, I ask, "Is it okay if I visit for a little while?"

"You know you don't have to ask."

I follow her into the house while Jordan brings my luggage.

When we walk into the kitchen, the aroma of pot roast fills the air.

"Dinner is almost ready," Natalie says, her worried gaze drifting over my face. "Can I get you anything to drink?"

Not wanting her to wait on me, I reply, "I'll make some tea."

"Auntie Kwelsie!" Brady hurries toward me as fast as his little legs can carry him.

"Hi, buddy," I coo as I crouch down.

He wraps his tiny arms around my neck, and as I pick him up, he says, "I missed you."

"Aww. I missed you too."

Jordan comes into the kitchen and asks, "Should I bathe him quickly?"

"Please," Natalie replies.

I hand Brady over to his dad, then walk to the counter and start making tea. "Do you want some?"

Natalie shakes her head. "I'm good." Her eyes sweep over me again. "I'm here if you want to talk."

"Thanks." I soak the tea bag and watch the water change color. "Did Jordan tell you I started seeing someone?"

"Of course. He couldn't stop talking about Levi."

"I think we broke up," I tell her the awful news.

"What?" she gasps. "But Jordan said you looked madly in love on Saturday."

"We were." I pick up the cup and walk to the island in the middle of the kitchen. Taking a seat on one of the stools, I say, "Turns out Levi is related to Wesley Porter. They're half brothers."

"Are you serious?"

"Yep."

I look at my sister-in-law, taking in her stylish bob and clear blue eyes. It was love at first sight for her and Jordan.

I take a sip of the warm liquid before I continue, "Levi hasn't had contact with his family in seventeen years, but he knew who I was and what his half brother did to us when he initiated contact between us."

"Oh dear."

"He came to Verona and bought the house next door to me. He says it's because he felt guilty and wanted to help."

"Well, that changes things, doesn't it?"

I meet Natalie's eyes and shake my head. "How does that change anything?"

"He didn't have to do anything. It's not his fault his half brother became a cold-blooded murderer." She takes a seat across from me. "Just like it isn't my fault my father is locked up for fraud."

"Levi hid it from me," I whisper.

"Yeah, he shouldn't have done that," she agrees.

I let out a sigh and brush my hand over my hair, which must look a mess. "I just need time to process it all."

Natalie gets up to check on the food while saying, "You take all the time you need."

My phone beeps, and stretching to reach my handbag, I drag it closer and dig the device out. Seeing a message from Levi, my heart squeezes painfully, and when I bring my finger to the screen, I notice my hand is trembling.

Sucking in a deep breath of air, I hesitate for a few seconds before I tap on the screen to open the text.

Levi: I'm so sorry about everything. I did so many things wrong, but if there's one thing I don't regret, it's getting to know you. After I moved in next door to you, I had no intention of talking to you. But the longer I watched you, the more I saw how strong and amazing you were. I also saw how much you were suffering, and I could not just stand by and do nothing. Then we talked, and it felt like we clicked. You opened up to me, and it was as easy as breathing to open up to you. I didn't mean to fall in love with you, but you can't fault me for that. I will never regret loving you. Every time I got to touch you, kiss you, and hold you, it felt heavenly. Thank you, Kelcie. Thank you for showing me what love is and for giving me a chance, no matter how short or long, to experience it. You will always be my happiest memories. I hope you can find it in your heart to forgive me. I hope we can have another chance. But I'll understand if you can't be with me. I won't reach out to you again, so you can have your space. Once you decide whether you want to end things or try again, please let me know. I will love you until the day I die. There will never be another.

Getting up from the stool, I go to the guest room and shut the door behind me.

I sit down on the side of the bed and read the message over and over until tears blur my sight, making it impossible for me to see.

I don't know what to do. How do I even begin to process everything?

Chapter 21

LEVI

The past twenty-four hours of my life have been a living hell.

The second the piece Colby recorded aired on his YouTube channel, it went viral.

My agent called and he tried to get me to agree to do an interview with one of the big networks, but I refuse to talk about my personal life on national television. My agent and publicist said they would get the footage of what happened outside Kelcie's house taken down.

It's too late, though. Last time I checked, the video had over two million views. Everyone now knows I have a murderer for a half brother.

I don't give a flying fuck whether my sales go down the drain and the publishers cancel their contract with me.

I want Kelcie back. I don't care about anything else.

Pain rips through my chest like a category five hurricane, obliterating everything inside me.

I load my last bag into my car, ignoring the stares from the neighbors who are suddenly interested in taking evening walks in the middle of winter.

Going into the house, I make sure all the windows are shut and the back door is locked. I check every room for anything I might've left behind, then pat my thigh for Lick to follow me.

When I open the car door so she can jump onto the back seat, my eyes go to Kelcie's house.

For a long while, I stand and stare at her place, remembering every special moment I got to spend with her.

"Jesus," I gasp, the pain too much to handle.

I shut the back door before getting in behind the steering wheel. When I start the engine, I look at both houses where I found a taste of happiness.

That's what makes this so unbearable. I now know what it feels like to be loved, and it will be so much harder to return to my old life.

I reverse out onto the street, aware there's a very good chance this might be the last time I drive through this town.

I might never see Kelcie again. Which will mean I'll never feel her touch again.

Even as relentless heartbreak drowns all the light from my life, I know with dead certainty I'd do it all again just for the chance to experience being loved by Kelcie.

She's worth all the hell I'll have to endure for the rest of my meaningless existence.

I stop at the gas station to fill my tank, and while I glance in the direction of the auto repair shop, I see Kelcie's sedan in one of the bays. There's damage to the bumper, and it has chills racing down my spine.

No!

My heart stutters in my chest, and my mouth goes bone dry. I jog toward the repair shop as Malakai begins shutting the doors.

"What happened to Kelcie's car?" I ask.

His head whips in my direction. "Oh, hey, Levi. It slid off the road into an embankment. They had the car towed here for repairs."

Icy air fills my lungs as I gasp, dread coiling around my heart. "Did Kelcie get hurt?"

Malakai shakes his head. "Jordan said she's fine."

Thank fuck!

I probably called after the accident happened, and that's why Jordan answered.

As I turn around and walk back to my car, I rub my hand over my chest, my heart beating a mile a minute from the fright I just had.

I put in gas, and after paying, I get back into my car and drive out of town. It's a five-and-a-half-hour drive to Grand Rapids, and I don't plan on making any stops unless Lick needs a toilet break.

As I put one mile after another between me and Verona, my thoughts revolve around Kelcie. I alternate between thinking about how I could've done things differently so I ended up with the woman I love, and reliving the happy moments we shared.

But let's face it. If I had introduced myself to her as Wesley Porter's brother, she wouldn't have given me a snowball's chance in hell.

Instead, I did the selfish thing and took what I could get from her. But at what cost?

I can't lay the blame at Colby's feet. I'm the one who hurt Kelcie. This time her pain is all on me.

As more miles fall behind me, my chest begins to tighten until it feels like I might suffocate. I jerk the steering wheel to the side and make a U-turn before bringing the car to a stop.

I can't leave Verona. I can't drive five and a half hours away and never see Kelcie again.

I don't have that kind of strength in me.

Pushing down on the gas, I begin to drive back, hoping and praying to all that's holy, I'll get another chance with the woman I love.

If not, living near her would be better than having Lake Michigan between us.

Instead of going back to the house, I find a motel in the next town over and get a room for the next few days.

I only grab one of my bags and my laptop, and once I've placed them in the room, which is so outdated, the wallpaper is peeling in the corners, I take Lick to the open piece of ground behind the motel that's covered in snow.

I lean back against the wall and cross my arms over my chest while staring at my dog as she searches for the perfect spot to pee.

My phone buzzes in my pocket, and I dig the device out as quickly as possible. When I see a message from Kelcie, my heart begins to hammer in my chest.

Earlier, I sent her a text, trying to convey everything I wanted to say to her, and I'm incredibly nervous to read her reply.

Sucking in a cold breath of air, I let it out slowly before I open the message.

Kelcie: What happened with your mother?

I frown because I wasn't expecting her to ask that question at all.

Levi: She wanted money. I told her to go to hell.

Kelcie: I'm sorry you had to deal with her after being no-contact for so many years. It must've been a shock to you.

Shock is the understatement of the year. I was rattled to my core.

Kelcie: I saw everything on the news.

Levi: My publicist and agent will take care of it all.

Kelcie: Are you okay?

Levi: Not at all. You?

Kelcie: Same.

Kelcie: You knew it would hurt me when your secret came out. Why did you do it?

Levi: At first, I approached you with good intentions. I wanted to make things better for you, and when I saw it helped you to spend time with me, I decided to stick around until you were able to heal enough to go on with your life. But then I started healing as well. The more time we spent together, the more I wanted to get to know you. Before I knew what was happening, I was head over heels in love with you, and I couldn't pull away anymore.

Kelcie: Why didn't you tell me before we kissed?

Levi: I was scared I'd lose you.

Kelcie: Were you ever going to tell me?

I read her question four times before I bite the bullet and type my honest reply.

Levi: No.

Kelcie: Thank you for responding to all my questions.

Levi: I'm here if you need more answers.

It shows that she reads my message, but she doesn't send another one and instead goes offline.

I let out a heavy sigh and tuck my phone back into my pocket before watching Lick jumping excitedly around in the snow.

When she's soaked through, I indicate for her to come, and we head to the motel room. I place my phone on charge, then grab one of the towels. Sitting down on the floor, I lean back against the bed and begin to rub Lick's fur dry.

She lets out a little whining sound as she keeps looking at me.

"I know, girl. I miss her too." Lick lies down on her side, exposing her belly to me. "I don't know where we go from here," I whisper as I pet her.

After a while, I drag my sorry ass up and change into a pair of sweatpants and a hoodie. I switch off all the lights and slump down on the bed. Lick jumps up and takes the spot beside me, resting her head on a pillow as if she's a little human.

Lying on the lumpy mattress, I stare up at the dark ceiling, trying to figure out what I'm going to do next.

My thoughts keep returning to the shit show that happened and some of the special moments I experienced with Kelcie.

The first time I kissed her. God, my entire world shifted on its axis when I tasted her and got lost in the feel of her soft lips.

The memories we shared. Besides my fucked-up family, she's the only one who knows some of what happened to me.

With Kelcie, everything was different. For the first time in my life, it felt good to be touched. That alone changed my world. Never mind the desire she made me experience. She made me feel like I belonged. Like I finally had a purpose in life.

To love her.

KELCIE

For the past week and a half, while everyone is at work and Brady is at day care, I lie in bed with the covers pulled over my head. I only get up before they all come home, so I don't cause them unnecessary worry.

Every half an hour or so, the urge to reach out to Levi becomes a torturous battle.

I want to beg him to tell me it was all a hallucination. That none of it really happened.

But it did.

"Kelcie," Jordan murmurs from the doorway.

I startle out of my deep thoughts, and surprised he's home so early, I quickly throw the covers back.

He walks closer and sits down on the side of the bed. "I've given you time. You can't keep bottling things up. Talk to me."

"Don't wanna," I groan, like a petulant teenager.

When I begin to pull the covers back up, he stops me and shakes his head. "I'm not going to stand by and watch you fall back into depression. I might not be Levi, but I'd like to think I can help in some way."

I sit up and lean against the pillows before locking eyes with my brother. "I don't know what to do. I'm torn in two."

Jordan gives me an encouraging smile. "Tell me what you're torn up about and maybe we can figure something out together."

"My rational side knows what Levi did was way over the line. He stalked me. He inserted himself into my life and deceived me. Even though he says his intentions were good, I don't even know if I can believe that."

When I'm quiet for a few seconds, Jordan tilts his head. "And how does your heart feel about it all?"

"My heart . . ." My chin begins to tremble, and I shake my head. "My heart wants to run to him because I know it must've hurt him so much to see his mother after seventeen years. I want to comfort him and—" My voice cracks, and a sob sputters over my lips. "And I want him to hold me and tell me we can get through this, because I still love him."

Jordan scoots closer and gathers me into a hug. He pats my back like he does whenever he tries to soothe Brady.

"Deep down, I know Levi never intended to hurt me," I admit. "But he deceived me."

"Did he say why?"

"He was scared he would lose me if I learned the truth." I pull back and let out a forlorn sigh. "He admitted that he never planned to tell me."

"I can understand where he's coming from," Jordan says. "He was scared we would judge him for what Porter did, and maybe we would've."

I shake my head but stop when I'm forced to admit Jordan is right. I never would've given Levi a chance had I known he was related to Mom's killer.

Jordan lifts his hand to my shoulder and gives me a comforting squeeze. "I think what you should focus on is whether you can forgive Levi. Do you love him enough to give him another chance, or do you end things and move on with your life?"

Knowing he's right, I nod. "Yeah."

My brother leans forward and presses a kiss to my forehead, the way Dad used to do with Sage and me.

"Take your time to think about it."

I nod again, then meet his eyes. "Thank you for being the best brother ever."

Emotion washes over his face, and his voice grows a little hoarse as he murmurs, "I love you, buttercup."

Hearing the term of endearment our parents used to call me makes tears jump to my eyes. "I love you too."

"Now get your butt dressed. I'm taking you out for lunch." Jordan climbs to his feet. "Getting out of the house will do you a world of good."

Not arguing, I drag myself out of bed, and while I change into warm clothes, I think about the conversation we just had.

Jordan is right. I need to figure out if I can forgive Levi or not.

Chapter 22

LEVI

Since the disaster of Kelcie learning the truth about me, I've been a hopeless case. Poor Lick has had her job cut out for her, but she does her best to comfort me.

I moved to a better motel that's not as run down as the previous one. It's all I've been able to do because I can't stop thinking about Kelcie long enough to figure out what to do with my life.

I'm lost without her.

This morning, while I took Lick around to the side of the motel to do her business, an idea popped into my head. I'm going to buy the farm Kelcie wanted.

It's something that should keep me busy for a while, and once I have everything ready, I'll give it to her as an apology gift.

At least this way, it will feel like I'm doing something worthwhile.

I've spent the entire morning searching for a realtor who can help me sell my two properties and look for a farm in the Sugar River Valley area. In the meantime, this motel room will be home for the unforeseeable future.

At least it's quiet here and there aren't a lot of guests. I'm half tempted to book out every room to guarantee I don't have to run into any people.

Sitting at a small-as-fuck desk, I scroll through available farms on my laptop, when my phone rings. Not recognizing the number, I almost let it go to voicemail but, at the last second, figure it could be the realtor.

"Hello?"

"Mr. Graye? It's Tish Sanders. You sent me an email regarding two properties you'd like to sell?" The woman sounds old and sweet, and for some reason, her tone sets me a little at ease.

"Hi, Tish. Yes. More importantly, I want to buy a farm in the Sugar River Valley area." I glance at the photos of a two-hundred-and-fifty-acre farm that looks like something Kelcie might like. It even has its own lake. "Can I send you a link to a property I've found?"

"Sure. Let me look at it and see if I can arrange a viewing for us."

"Thanks."

"When we meet up, we can get the paperwork going for the sale of your two properties."

"That works for me," I agree.

We end the call, and I share the link to the farm with Tish before reading more about the property. When I read that it's situated across a huge area of protected green space, I'm sold. It means there won't be many neighbors to worry about.

I'm surprised when my phone rings so quickly after hanging up, and I accept the call.

"Hi, Mr. Graye. Tish again. We can view the farm today. How does your schedule look?"

"It's wide open."

"Oh, good. It's a thirty-minute drive from where I am in Verona. Would you like to ride together or meet up at the property?"

"I'll meet you there."

"Great. We can meet at the entrance to the farm."

We hang up again, and I quickly rise to my feet, patting my thigh for Lick to follow as I leave the motel room.

During the drive to Old Stone Road, I notice the houses are gradually situated farther apart. Eventually, I don't even see any kind of dwellings, and by the time I pull up to the farm, I'm sure this is the one I'm going to buy.

Not long after I get to the property, a blue sedan arrives, and an elderly lady with a friendly smile gestures for me to follow her.

As we head up a long stretch of dirt road, I glance at the white blanket of snow that stretches out all around me.

Kelcie will love it here. I'm going to get her every damn animal her heart desires and create a little slice of heaven where she can be happy.

I bring my vehicle to a stop behind Tish's car when she parks near a house that seems to be in desperate need of maintenance.

The place will look so much better with a wraparound porch.

When I get out and open the door for Lick, I look at the realtor and say, "Don't worry. She's friendly."

"Oh my gosh, aren't you the prettiest fur baby I've ever seen." Tish coos while bending at the waist to pat Lick's head. "What's her name?"

"Lick."

"Well, Lick, let's see if we can convince your daddy to buy this land so there's plenty of space for you to have zoomies." Turning her attention to me, she begins to reach her hand out to me.

My tone is much gentler than it would usually be as I say, "I'm sorry. I don't touch other people."

Tish quickly stops and pets Lick again. "No worries. I have a sister who's the same. She'll slap you two ways to Sunday if you try to hug her."

I have a feeling I'm going to get along with Tish.

"I think we should walk through the house before taking a look at the rest of the property. We can also get the paperwork out of the way for your two houses."

As I follow her up the steps, I say, "You can just show me the house and the lake. We're not going to use the land for farming," I explain. "My . . ." Not knowing what to call Kelcie, I go with what feels natural. "My wife loves animals. She wants mini–Highland cows, goats, and horses."

"Remind me to give you a number. I have a cousin who breeds mini–farm animals. He's up in Montana, though."

"I'd appreciate that."

We enter the house, which has clearly been standing empty for a long while.

"As you can see, no one has lived in the house for a few years. I was told the owners retired to Florida."

I slowly walk through the house, making mental notes of what I want to change, and when I stop in the living room area, I decide to do the work myself.

I don't want another person working on my love project for Kelcie. Locking eyes with Tish, I say, "I'll take it."

Her gaze widens. "You haven't seen the lake yet."

I shake my head. "I've seen photos." With determination lacing my words, I repeat, "I'll take the farm, Tish. Tell the owners I'll pay cash. I'd like to get to work on renovating the place as soon as possible."

A wide smile spreads over Tish's face. "I'll get in touch with their lawyer and let you know when the paperwork is ready. I'm sure they'll be open to you paying rent and starting with renovations while we wait for the sale to go through."

"I'd appreciate that."

"I just need you to sign a couple of documents so we can get started on selling your two properties." Tish sets an envelope down on the worn surface of the counter and pulls all the contracts out.

We fill out all the information about the two houses, and I sign everywhere there's an X before I say, "If possible, I'd like to include the furniture currently decorating the houses in the sale."

"I can add it, but what do you want to do if a buyer doesn't want the furniture?"

"I'll arrange for some charity to collect it."

Tish jabs a thumb over her shoulder. "Let's go take a look at the lake anyway. It's walking distance."

We leave the house, and as we trudge through the few inches of snow, Lick runs around, letting out a happy bark every couple of minutes.

"Well, the place has Lick's stamp of approval," Tish says. "Just let me know when you would like to bring your wife for a viewing."

"It's a surprise for her."

Tish's eyebrows dart up. "A three-point-five-million-dollar surprise? Wow. She's one lucky lady."

I shake my head as we approach a lining of trees, and I see the smooth surface of the lake through the branches. "I'm the lucky one."

Or, at least, I was.

We stop to look at the body of half-frozen water, and Tish says, "It's a beautiful piece of land. I hope you and your wife will find happiness here."

Me too. But if Kelcie ends things between us, then I hope this farm will bring her all the joy I can't.

Glancing at Tish, I ask, "Would you mind if I stayed here for an hour or so?"

"Not at all. Take your time and have a good look around." She turns to head back to where our cars are parked. "I'll be in touch."

"Thanks, Tish."

When she walks away, I shove my hands in my coat pockets and stare at the winter wonderland around me.

I've never been the praying kind, but as I stand out in the cold air, I send up a prayer.

Please let Kelcie forgive me.

KELCIE

My sleep routine is so messed up. It's already midnight, and my mind won't come to a rest.

I can't stop thinking about Levi. Tonight is especially bad because I keep remembering the memories he shared with me.

That family was horrible to him long before his brother destroyed my life.

Half brother.

I grip my phone tightly, my heart beating faster and faster as I think of calling him for the hundredth time.

As much as I'm upset about him keeping the truth from me, I'm also worried about how seeing his mother has affected him.

Unable to stop myself, I unlock the screen and press dial on Levi's number. The instant the call connects, my heartbeat speeds up drastically.

Listening to the ringtone, I begin to second-guess my decision, but as my thumb moves to cut the call, Levi's voice suddenly bursts over the line. "Hi."

My lips part, and when the words don't come, he asks, "Kelcie? Are you there?"

"Uh-huh." I squeeze my eyes shut when the urge to cry hits hard.

I wish I could run into his arms right now. I need comfort so bad, and he's the only one who can make things better.

"Hey, baby," he murmurs, his tone gentle. "How are you holding up?"

"Not good," I force the words over my lips. A second later, a sob sputters from me.

"I'm here."

I curl into a small ball and keep the phone pressed to my ear as I soak in the sound of his voice.

"Want to talk to me about what happened?" he asks.

"No." I suck in a trembling breath. "I want to know how you're doing after seeing your mother."

"She's not my mother," he says, tension creeping into his tone. "I'm doing okay. I'm more worried about you."

I keep quiet for a few seconds before I ask, "Memory for a memory?"

He lets out a sigh. "I don't think tonight is a good time for that."

"Please."

"Okay. Do you want to go first?"

"No." I clear my throat. "You go first."

Levi's quiet for close to a minute before he talks again. "I would always walk home from school, whereas Wesley would take the bus. One day, he didn't get off the bus at the stop, and when I got home thirty minutes later, Rene was hysterical. We searched everywhere for him, and eventually, the bus driver brought him home. He fell asleep in the back, and the driver only realized when he walked through the bus." Levi takes a deep breath and lets it out slowly. "Dennis, my stepfather, was so pissed off with Wesley, but instead of taking his anger out on his own son, he came after me. He made Wesley watch while he whipped my back with a belt. While the buckle tore up my skin, he told Wesley I'd be hurt like that every time he messed up. I was lying in a puddle of blood by the time he stopped, and when Dennis walked away, Wesley just stood there smiling at me as if he was reveling in the sight of me beaten half to death."

"Jesus," I whimper.

"Anyway, as soon as I healed enough to walk, I left."

Levi suffered so much at the hands of those people.

"I'm sorry," I say, my voice hoarse.

I wish I could hug him right now.

"Your turn," Levi reminds me.

"I was at the end of my rope when I met an incredible man." My throat strains, and the tears start to drip onto my pillow. "He understood me in ways no one else could. It felt like he healed me, and I fell head over heels in love with him." A sob escapes me before I'm able to continue, "But then I found out he deceived me, and I don't know how to get past it."

When Levi speaks again, his tone sounds forlorn. "I'm so sorry I kept the truth from you. Do you think you'll ever be able to forgive me?"

"Forgiving you for keeping it from me that Wesley's your half brother isn't the hard part."

"Then what is?"

I shake my head and fight hard to keep the tears from overwhelming me. "I need more time to figure out if I can be with someone who stalked me before inserting himself into my life, while knowing one of his family members killed my mother right in front of me. That's the part I'm struggling with."

"I understand," he murmurs. "Take all the time you need, Kelcie, but while you're deciding what to do, please remember every good moment we shared the past few months."

I nod, pressing my lips together to keep a sob back. It takes a few minutes before I'm able to say, "I have to go."

"I love you more than anything, Kelcie," he says, sadness creeping into his voice.

I love you too.

"Bye, Levi," I whimper before I quickly end the call.

As I begin to cry my heart out, I sob, "I miss you so much."

Chapter 23

KELCIE

I've resorted to making a pros and cons list, and as I stare at what I've written under each column, I scrunch my nose because this isn't working.

With every passing day since I last saw Levi, it feels as if a fist is closing tighter and tighter around my heart. When everything is said and done, I still love him, and I don't know what that makes me. A lovestruck fool?

It's been almost two weeks since I called him, and things haven't gotten any better. I miss him so much, and even though I know what he did was wrong, I just can't stop thinking about the time we spent together and the huge difference he's made in my life.

I'm a mess, and realizing I'm not going to come to any kind of decision by hiding at Jordan's house, I let out a sigh. I have to return to Verona. Maybe when I see Levi again, I'll be able to find some clarity.

Leaving the bedroom, I find Jordan and Brady in the living room where they're playing with building blocks. Natalie is taking a long, relaxing bath before dinner.

"Hi," I say while I sit down on one of the couches.

"Hey." Jordan glances at me before turning his attention back to his son.

"I think it's time for me to go home."

My brother's head snaps up, surprise flashing over his face. "Are you sure?"

I nod, then explain, "I need to talk face-to-face with Levi. Hiding here isn't going to solve the problem."

"I can take you back tomorrow."

I shake my head. "I'll take the bus."

Instantly, Jordan frowns. "The bus is easily a five-to-six-hour drive with all the stops, instead of just two and a half! Let me take you."

I stand up, and moving closer to him, I give his shoulder a squeeze. "I want to take the bus."

"When are you leaving?" Jordan asks.

"Tomorrow morning." I walk toward the kitchen. "So tonight I'm making dinner as a way to say thank you for letting me invade your space the past three weeks."

"Can you still make those crispy roasted potatoes the way Mom showed you?" Jordan gets up and comes to sit at the island where he can talk to me and still keep an eye on Brady.

My heart clenches as I answer, "I can try to make them, but I don't promise they'll be as good."

I grab two knives and the bag of potatoes, and while we peel them, Jordan glances at me. "Which way are you leaning? Break up or try again?"

I keep my gaze trained on the potato skins. "Would I be an idiot to give him another chance?"

"No." Jordan leans to the side to get me to look at him, and when I do, he says, "You do what's right for you, Kelcie. You've suffered so much the past year and a half. If being with Levi makes you happy, then try to see if you can forgive him. Maybe start from scratch." He sucks in a deep breath before he adds, "Levi never meant you any harm, and he's not responsible for what his half brother did. As for him not telling you his true reasons for being in Verona? I can understand why he hid it from you. Neither of us would've given him the time of day if he had walked up to us and introduced himself as Porter's brother."

"I had that same thought," I admit, letting out a sigh. "We'll see what happens when I talk to Levi again."

Jordan sets down his knife and gets up from the stool.

"Hey, where are you going? We're still peeling potatoes," I say.

"Nope. You're peeling potatoes." He shoots me a playful grin. "I'm going to lie down on the couch and watch an episode of *Storage Hunters*."

The corner of my mouth lifts, but as I continue to get everything ready for dinner, the worry that's been my constant companion the past three weeks slithers through my mind.

What if this is something Levi and I can't come back from, and things are really over between us?

When the cab I took from the bus station pulls up to my place, I immediately look toward Levi's house. Seeing a realtor's sign with the word SOLD in big, bold red letters across it, shock shudders through me.

No. Levi sold his house?

I've only been gone three weeks! How did he sell so fast?

After settling my cab fare, I hurry to climb out of the car and haul my luggage out of the back seat. Leaving the bag in my driveway, I quickly jog to Levi's front door.

I had hoped to take a shower so I could wash off the grimy feel of sitting on a bus for five and a half hours before going over to talk to Levi.

The SOLD sign has me feeling completely rattled as I ring the doorbell. I listen closely for Lick's bark, but when I don't hear anything and Levi doesn't open, I try knocking.

"Kelcie." Hearing Jill call me, I glance in her direction. "You're back." She rushes toward me and hugs me hard. "My God, I heard about what happened. Are you okay?"

"Yeah. I just took some time away from Verona to process everything."

Jill looks at Levi's front door, then says, "Levi left the same day as you, and no one has seen him since. A few days later, the FOR SALE sign went up, and it sold for next to nothing last week. Even I was tempted to buy it, but I'm not ready for that kind of commitment. Yesterday, a moving truck came, and they emptied out the house." She pauses to take a breath before adding, "I think a newly married couple bought the place."

"No one's seen Levi in town?" I ask to make sure I heard right.

"No. He probably moved to a new place where no one knows who he is." She glares at the Adamses' house, and we see the drapes move.

"Mrs. Adams is probably being nosy and watching us," Jill mutters. "Let's go inside."

As we walk to where my luggage is standing, I'm still a little in shock. I shouldn't be surprised Levi decided to move, but the fact that he didn't even mention it to me during our call two weeks ago makes me worry even more.

"Ahh . . ." I take hold of my bag's handle and give Jill a rueful smile. "I've just spent the past five and a half hours on the road. Can we catch up another day?"

"Oh yeah. Of course."

I dig my house keys out of my bag, and while I walk to the front door and unlock it, I wonder if Levi went back to Grand Rapids.

God, Levi probably couldn't get away from Verona quickly enough. I don't blame him. This town hasn't been kind to him.

After I shut the door behind me, I glance over the living room and kitchen. The place feels empty.

Letting out a sigh, I search for my phone in my handbag, and when I find it, I drop the bag on the kitchen counter before preparing a cup of tea for myself. While the tea bag soaks a little, I send Jordan a quick text to let him know I'm back home so that he won't worry.

After taking a much-needed sip of my tea, I open the chat I share with Levi.

Kelcie: Hi. I know it's been a while, but I just got back to Verona and see you've sold your house. It was a bit of a shock. Anyway, I hope you're doing okay. If you've got a minute, shoot me a text. I'd love to talk.

I read the message a few times before I press send. I watch as one tick appears, and when a minute passes and there's no second tick to show it's been delivered, I scowl at the device in my hand.

Be patient, Kelcie.

I walk to the living room and put my phone on charge before grabbing my luggage and dragging it up the stairs.

The empty bedrooms on the second floor make me feel lonely, and for the first time since the attack, I think about moving back to my parents' house. At some point, I'll have to gather the courage.

But that day is not today.

I grab a fresh set of clothes from the closet in the main bedroom and head into the en suite bathroom. Switching on the faucets so the water can warm up, I get undressed. When I step beneath the spray, my thoughts revolve around Levi and the fact that he's sold his house. There's a sad pang in my chest because we've had so many happy memories within those walls.

What if Levi gave up because he didn't hear from me again after our call?

God, what if he's done with us and decided to build a new life for himself?

Panic floods my veins, and my heartbeat speeds up.

Don't overreact yet. Talk to Levi before you jump to conclusions.

I hurry through my shower routine, and after getting dressed, I brush my teeth and hair before rushing out of the bathroom and heading downstairs.

When I grab my phone and enter the chat, I see the text still hasn't gone through. I press dial on Levi's number and nervously wait for the call to connect.

Only it doesn't, and I get his voicemail instead.

'You've reached Levi. You know what to do.'

"Hi. It's Kelcie. Um . . . can you give me a call when you get this message? Ahh . . . thanks."

As I lower the phone from my ear, fear coils around my heart.

Levi sold his house, and his phone is off.

What if he's cut all contact?

Since the day I found out he's related to Wesley, I've tried to imagine a life without Levi. Not once did it hurt as much as it does right now, because I never really believed it was over between us.

Deep down, I knew I'd come back to him.

I realize I was never going to break up with Levi. I just needed time to process everything.

But what if the choice isn't mine? I never considered that Levi would want to end the relationship.

I slump down on the couch and go back into the chat, willing that second tick to appear.

When I lost my parents and Sage, I thought I'd never recover. Then Levi came along, and he made life worth living again.

If I've lost him . . .

No.

I begin to shake my head as my face crumples.

I won't survive losing him. I can't even begin to imagine a life where I'm not with him.

Out of sheer desperation, I call his number again, and when it goes straight to voicemail once more, I wait for the beep.

"Levi, it's me again. I don't know if you'll get this message, but if you do, please . . ." My voice cracks and I have to swallow hard on the tears threatening to fall. ". . . please call me back." My breaths start coming too fast. "Don't . . . just . . ." A sob bursts from me as more fear pours into my chest, and a panic attack hits hard, making it next to impossible for me to get air into my lungs.

I end the call, and it feels like an elephant is sitting on my chest as I get up and hurry to the kitchen. My vision blurs, and horrible, strangled sounds come from me every time I try to inhale.

Yanking open the cupboard, my fingers fumble with the box, and I drop it. Sinking down to my knees, my panic increases until I begin to see spots dancing in front of my eyes. Somehow, I manage to get a pill out, and with a trembling hand, I shove it into my mouth, swallowing it dry.

I move onto my butt and lean against the cupboards, shutting my eyes tightly while I desperately try to breathe.

Feeling woozy, I struggle to remain conscious until the medication finally starts taking effect. When I manage to take deeper breaths, I'm so worked up that I burst out in tears and sob my heart out.

I just want to talk to Levi.

LEVI

After I've washed my hands, I stand back and glance over the bathroom. I tiled the walls, put in a shower, and installed a new toilet today.

I used timber panels on the wall by the tub and for the floor, and the other two walls are covered in light granite.

Loving the finished look, I smile as I walk to the front of the house.

Since I've started working on the place, I've gotten a lot done. I spend every day on the farm and only go back to the motel to sleep.

The sellers were very happy with my offer, and Tish is doing her best to push everything through as quickly as possible. She's hopeful the land will be transferred over to me in the next month or so. It would've been sooner, but with the holidays, everything is delayed.

She's sold my house in Verona, and she's dealing with another agent to sell the property in Grand Rapids.

A court case has been opened against Colby, but God only knows what will happen there. Honestly, I have zero interest in the matter.

The only thing missing from my life is Kelcie, and I haven't heard anything from her since she called two weeks ago. Every passing day, it gets harder not to reach out to her, but she asked for space, and I have no choice but to give it to her.

I pat my thigh for Lick to follow as I leave the house and lock up behind me.

We head to the truck I bought two weeks ago, because the sedan couldn't handle the dirt road anymore. The snow is coming down hard, and I hurry to get Lick into the cab before I climb behind the steering wheel.

Lick shakes her body to get rid of the snowflakes and curls up on the seat while I start the engine and carefully steer the truck toward the road.

Midway to Paoli, where the motel is, my phone starts beeping like crazy. I dig the device out of my pocket, thinking the messages are from Tish.

Seeing Kelcie's name, I'm so surprised, I almost steer the truck off the road. I quickly pull over and put on my hazards before opening the message and devouring the words, then my fingers move as fast as possible as I type out a reply.

Levi: It's so good to hear from you. Let me know when works for you. I can come over, or we can meet somewhere.

Guiding the truck back onto the road, a smile spreads over my face while I check my voice messages.

'Hi. It's Kelcie. Um . . . can you give me a call when you get this message? Ahh . . . thanks.'

Jesus, hearing her voice is everything, and it has my smile widening as the next message begins to play.

'Levi, it's me again. I don't know if you'll get this message, but if you do, please . . . please call me back.' The panic in Kelcie's voice has me frowning, then her breathing speeds up, a clear indication that she's having a panic attack. *'Don't . . . just . . .'*

"Fuck!"

When she begins to sob, I floor the gas and head for Verona. I exit my voice messages and quickly press dial on her number, then impatiently listen as the call connects.

"Levi!" Kelcie's gasp comes over the line.

"Are you okay?" I ask, worry for her making my voice deeper than usual.

"Thank God you got my messages."

"Are you okay?" I repeat my question.

"Yes. Sorry for rambling on your voicemail."

While relief pours through me, I say, "It sounded like you were having a panic attack."

It's so good to talk to her.

"I did, but I took my medication, so I'm okay." She pauses for a few seconds, then her tone sounds apprehensive as she asks, "How are you?"

"I'll be fine when I see you. I'm on my way to your place. Is that okay?"

"Yes."

The smile returns to my face, and I suck in deep breaths of air.

"So I'll see you soon?" she asks.

I check where I am, then reply, "I'm five minutes away."

"Okay. I'm going to hang up."

She ends the call, and I drop the phone on my lap while grinning at Lick. "We're going to see your mom soon."

Her ears flick, and her head perks up as if she understands what I'm saying.

When I pull up Kelcie's driveway, I can't switch off the engine fast enough, and I hurry to climb out of the truck. Lick jumps out, and I slam the door shut.

The front door opens, and the sound has my eyes darting to where Kelcie is standing in the light spilling from the living room behind her.

It feels like my soul manages to finally take a deep breath after drowning for the past three weeks.

As I close the distance between us, Lick runs ahead and jumps up against Kelcie. She gives my dog pets before looking at me again, a nervous smile tugging at her mouth.

My eyes roam over every beautiful inch of her, and unable to stop myself, I grab her into a tight hug against my chest.

"Jesus," I groan, and my body shudders from the indescribable feeling of finally getting to hold her again.

Totally overwhelmed by the emotions filling me, I press kisses to her hair and take deep breaths of her flowery scent.

Kelcie's arms wrap around me, and I feel her grip hold of my sweater. Her breathing hitches, and then she hides her face in my chest.

"I missed you so much," I murmur, my tone raspy. "Fuck, I missed you."

"I missed you too," she admits before pulling away. "Come inside."

After I step into the house, she shuts the door behind me. Our eyes meet, and I search for any signs that she's not doing okay.

I can't get a read on her emotions, and ask, "You wanted to talk?"

"Yeah." She gestures at the couch. "Let's sit."

Worry creeps back into my chest as I take a seat beside Kelcie, turning my body to face hers while Lick lies down by her feet.

All I want to do is reach out and touch her.

"I've thought a lot about everything," she says, her gaze flicking to Lick. She rubs my dog's head before she continues, "I can understand why you didn't tell me you're related to Wesley, because I probably would've judged you unfairly. When we met, I wasn't in a good place, and I wouldn't have given you the opportunity to explain about your past and that you haven't had any contact with your family for years." She sucks in a breath before looking at me. "I had to think about whether we could make it work."

Her voice begins to quiver, and it gives me the impression she's going to end things between us. I clench my jaw and try to brace for the worst.

"My trust in you has been shaken," she whispers.

When a tear rolls down her cheek, I can't hold back, and I gently brush it away with the back of my fingers. It hurts like a bitch to listen to what she has to say, but I keep my eyes locked with hers.

"I don't know where we go from here. I just know I can't imagine a life without you."

It takes a moment for her words to get through to me. My lips part as I inhale a sharp breath, surprise rippling through me.

"So what are you saying exactly?" I ask as I waver somewhere between hope and fear.

"I'd like to give us another chance." Her eyebrows draw together. "That's if you want to."

I nod like crazy as I lift my hand and cup her cheek. "I want to, Kelcie. More than anything."

Her features ease with relief, then she says, "You can never lie or keep anything from me again."

"I promise."

She covers my hand with hers and leans her cheek into my palm. When another tear rolls down her cheek, I shift closer and gently pull her into my arms.

I have her back. She's mine again.

"I'm so sorry for what I've done." I begin to kiss her hair and forehead, soaking in the feel of having her in my arms. "I will spend the rest of my life making it up to you."

"Jordan said I have to make you grovel."

I let out a chuckle. "He's right."

Closing my eyes, I hold her tighter and thank all that's holy that she hasn't given me the boot.

Chapter 24

KELCIE

There are still some things we have to talk about, but for the moment, I just revel in how amazing and right it feels to be in Levi's arms again.

His embrace gives me the comfort I've desperately needed the past three weeks. What he did was wrong, but he's the only one who can repair the damage done to my heart.

Minutes pass before Levi pulls back enough to see my face. His gaze drifts lovingly over me, then he says, "You've lost weight."

"Just a couple of pounds. I'll gain them back soon enough."

I can't tear my eyes away from his. "You sold your house."

He nods.

My heart clenches. "Are you moving back to Grand Rapids?"

"No. I'm selling that property as well."

"Oh." The word pops over my lips. "So where are you moving to?"

Levi glances at Lick when she yawns, then he clears his throat. "Currently, I'm staying at a motel in Paoli."

The corner of my mouth lifts. "So are you going to look for a place in Paoli?"

At least that's just ten minutes away from Verona.

When Levi shakes his head, I start to feel confused.

He looks at me again, then says, "I bought a farm."

My eyes go wide as saucers. "You did what?"

"Well, technically, I bought the farm for you." He gives me a lopsided grin that looks so cute, my heart melts. "I've been fixing up the house for the past couple of weeks, but the place still needs a lot of work."

When I recover from the initial surprise, I gape at him. "You bought a farm? For me?"

He lowers his head, and his teeth tug at his bottom lip before he lifts his eyes to me again. "If you ended things between us, I would've given it to you, but seeing as you're giving me another chance, I'm kinda hoping it's a project we can work on together." He gives me a hopeful look as he adds, "Maybe we can make the farm our home. When you're ready, of course."

While I was trying to decide what to do, Levi bought us a farm, which tells me he never gave up. He made a big financial commitment to our future, not knowing whether we would even have one together.

He begins to look unsure, then says, "I needed to do something. I couldn't sit still while I gave you the space you asked for."

"So if I said things were over between us, you would've given me a farm? Why?"

"Because I want you to be happy, Kelcie. Even if it's not with me."

That right there is why I love him and couldn't give up on us. Levi might have gone the wrong way about it, but at the end of the day, everything he's done has been for me.

I dart forward and wrap my arms around his neck, and he doesn't miss a beat as he returns the hug.

I inhale his cedarwood and citrus cologne, which is mixed with his natural scent, and press as close to him as I can get. Levi shifts on the couch, pulling me onto his lap, and I position my legs on either side of him.

His fingers grip my jaw, and he nudges my face up. When I see the love shining from his eyes, emotion wells in my heart until it feels like it might burst.

"I love you, Kelcie." His gaze lowers to my mouth, and it makes anticipation spark to life in my abdomen. "I never want to be separated from you again. I won't survive it a second time. Without you, there's only darkness."

We move at the same time, and our mouths collide with so much longing and heat, I gasp. Levi kisses me as if I'm his beginning and end, as if he'll cease to exist without me.

I feel the same way. He's rescued me from the claws of despair. He's the glue that keeps the shattered pieces of me together. I'm only whole because of him.

Like I've said before, I learned a hard lesson to appreciate every single moment I have with a loved one because they can be ripped away from me in a heartbeat. I don't want to waste a single second with Levi.

As we kiss, things feel right again.

When he nips at my mouth and pulls back to press his forehead to mine, I say, "Thank you for buying us a farm."

A symbol that even when I walked away, he didn't. He kept his promise to me that he would only leave if I asked him to.

"I think you're going to love it so much. We even have a lake."

I let out a chuckle. "Yeah?"

He nods and gives me another gentle kiss. "And there are no neighbors close to us."

Laughter bursts from me. "Perfect."

I lean back so I can see his face, and my smile fades as I ask, "How have you been? Have you heard from your mother again?"

He shakes his head. "Don't call her that. She's not my mother."

I see the pain in his eyes, and my heart squeezes for him. "Did seeing her trigger you?"

Levi glances away and brushes his palms up and down my thighs. "She touched me." His features draw tight. "I sat in a hot shower until the water ran cold, and it still didn't remove the feel of her hand on me."

"Where did she touch you?"

He holds up his right arm. "My wrist."

I wrap my hands around his wrist and forearm, pressing a kiss to his palm.

The tension eases on his face, and he tilts his head while a smile tugs at the corner of his mouth. "All better. My miracle."

Figuring we can both use something to drink, I move off his lap and climb to my feet. "I'm going to make us some hot chocolate."

"Actually, I'm in desperate need of a shower." He gets up, and my heart sinks at having to say goodbye so quickly. He can no longer just go next door.

"You can shower here," I suggest.

Levi shakes his head. "I need clean clothes."

"Oh. Right."

Feeling dejected, I begin to walk toward the front door. "Thanks for—"

"I was hoping you would consider coming back to the motel with me," he interrupts me, and I stop dead in my tracks.

When I turn around to look at him, he adds, "No pressure. I want to spend more time with you, but I'll understand if you're not ready."

I glance around the living room and the lone couch, then nod. "Let me just grab my bag."

I walk to the stairs, and when Levi follows, I say, "Upstairs is pretty . . . empty. I never bought furniture."

As we reach the landing and walk down the hallway, Levi glances around. He stops in the doorway of the main bedroom, and a frown forms on his forehead.

"You don't have a bed," he comments.

"I slept on the couch." I grab my luggage, thankful I haven't unpacked yet.

Moving closer, his eyebrows draw together as he lifts his hands to frame my face. "You never made this place home."

I shrug. "Because it wasn't. It was just meant to be a place where I could stay until I was ready to go home."

"Your parents' house?" Levi asks.

I nod.

He leans down and presses a tender kiss to my lips, then he takes the bag from me. "Let's go, my muse."

As we leave the room, he holds his other hand out to me, and I quickly link our fingers. His grip is firm as he leads me down the stairs and out of the house.

Noticing the truck again, I ask, "When did you get the new ride?"

"A couple of weeks ago. The road to the farm is too uneven for a sedan. I also needed something to transport all the materials when I started fixing up the house."

"So you've been doing renovations?"

He nods and lets go of my hand to open the passenger door for me. "I'll take you tomorrow so you can look around and tell me what you want done."

Suddenly, Lick jumps up, and I smile as she makes space for me to sit beside her. I grab hold of the door and put my foot on the step, but then Levi's hands settle on my hips, and I'm lifted into the cab.

He shuts the door, and I hear him place my luggage in the truck bed before he comes to get in behind the steering wheel.

I put on my seat belt, then give Lick a hug. "I missed you."

"She missed you too," Levi murmurs.

After starting the engine, he reverses into the road, and my eyes land on the Adamses' house. I see Mrs. Adams peeking through the drapes, and it gives me the creeps.

"I'm going to cancel the lease for the rental," I tell Levi. "I can't live across from Colby's family anymore."

"You can stay with me at the motel." He glances at me. "What do you think?"

"Or . . ." My tongue darts out to wet my lips. "We can go to my family home and stay there until the farmhouse is ready."

Levi's eyes widen. "Are you ready to take that step?"

Lick lies partially on my lap, and I begin to brush my hand over her soft fur. It gives me a moment to think about temporarily moving into my parents' house.

"I won't know until I try," I answer honestly.

Levi reaches across Lick and gives my hand a squeeze before he pays attention to the road again.

"I hope to have the living room on the farm ready by the end of December." A frown line appears between his eyes. "Unless we're still going to Jordan's for the holidays?"

"I forgot about that." Then my eyes widen. "Oh my God. Christmas is in five days."

"We can still drive through and spend a day or two there," Levi suggests.

"I'll give Jordan a call tomorrow and hear what he thinks," I reply.

LEVI

After I park the truck in my spot right in front of my room, I switch off the engine.

"Wait in the cab. I'll unlock the door, then you and Lick can come. I don't want you standing in the snow."

Kelcie releases her seat belt while I get out of the truck. I'm hit with a blast of cold and quickly unlock the door to the motel room.

"Come, Lick," I hear her say.

I glance at Kelcie, and when she jumps over a puddle of slush, she loses her footing. I dart forward, and as she begins to fall backward, I grab hold of her arm and yank her against my body. My other arm locks around her waist, and as her hands grip my shoulders, I lift her off her feet and carry her into the room before setting her down again.

"That was a close call," she chuckles.

I quickly go back out to get her luggage, and when I shut the door behind me and look at her, the smile on her face is blindingly beautiful.

Kelcie is here with me.

We're still together.

I get to feel her love and touch for the rest of my life.

The realization keeps hitting me upside the head every few minutes.

I want to kiss her until I forget my own name, but I'm in desperate need of a shower.

"I'll be quick," I say as I walk to the bathroom. I gesture at the bed and TV. "Make yourself comfortable."

Before I shut the door behind me, I see Kelcie taking off her coat and sitting down on the foot of the bed.

I switch on the faucets in the shower, and while the water warms, I brush my teeth. Stripping out of my clothes, I fold every item neatly and place it in the laundry bag.

As I step beneath the spray, I think of Kelcie sitting on the bed, and a smile spreads over my face.

She came back to me. Fuck, I'll never do anything to risk what we have.

My thoughts don't leave her for a single second while I shower. Once I'm done, I switch off the faucets and reach for a towel so I can dry myself. I glance at the counter, where I usually set down my sweatpants and hoodie and grimace when I realize I forgot to bring the clothes.

I wrap the towel around my waist, and opening the bathroom door, I look at Kelcie. "Can you pass me a pair of sweatpants from the closet?"

"Sure." She jumps up off the bed and disappears from my sight. "Damn, Levi. Your closet is neat." I hear her clear her throat, then she asks, "Do you need underwear as well?"

"Just the sweatpants."

She appears with the pants draped over her arm, but as she comes closer, her eyes lower to my chest and her lips part. Desire instantly tightens her features, and she murmurs, "Suddenly, I wish I was a drop of water."

A chuckle rumbles from me as I take the sweatpants from her. Kelcie's attention remains locked on my chest, her pupils dilating, and it has me growing hard in a split second.

Dropping the sweatpants, I barely remember to keep hold of the towel as I lift my free hand, wrapping my fingers around the back of Kelcie's neck. I tug her closer, and her heated gaze darts to my face right before my mouth crashes against hers.

Her palms settle on my chest, and when she starts roaming them over my skin, she lets out a moan that has a direct link to my cock.

Fuck the towel. I let go of the fabric and place an arm around Kelcie.

Her palms move to my sides and brush down to my hips. "Oh God," she moans against my mouth. "I could get drunk on touching you."

I grab hold of her sweater and pull the fabric off her. Ducking my head, I drop hungry kisses to her jaw and neck while my fingers work to unbutton her jeans.

Our movements grow more desperate by the second as we hurry to get her undressed.

Once I have Kelcie naked, I take a step backward so I can see all of her. My eyes roam over every breathtaking inch of her body.

She's even more beautiful than when I last got to go down on her, and it fills me with a ravenous hunger.

My eyes lift to Kelcie's face, and I see she's looking at me with something that can only be described as awe.

"I'm on birth control," she thinks to tell me. "Just in case you wanted to know."

The corner of my mouth lifts, and with one step, I eliminate the distance between us. As my body pushes against hers, I lower my head and kiss her with all the hunger she makes me feel.

We move blindly toward the bed, and I lift my arms, brushing my hands over her cheeks and the sides of her neck. I revel in the feel of her silky skin as I keep moving down until I grip hold of her hips. Kelcie wraps her arms around my neck and squashes her breasts to my chest as she lifts herself on her tiptoes so she can press kisses to the scruff on my jaw.

Nothing has ever felt as good as having Kelcie's naked body rubbing against mine.

"I love the feel of your skin on mine," I groan while I grip a fistful of her hair, tugging her head back so she'll tip her face up to me. My mouth nips at hers, my teeth tugging her plump bottom lip, and it draws another groan from me. "I'm starving."

She pulls back, and it looks like she does a double take before she stammers, "You want to eat? Now?"

A chuckle rumbles from my chest, and I push her backward until she's forced to sit down on the bed. "Lie down, baby. I'm starving for you."

"Oh." A grin spreads over her face as she does what she's told.

Placing my knee on the mattress, I grip hold of Kelcie's thighs and push them wide open. My eyes feast on her clit, and seeing how wet she is for me has me losing my mind.

I duck forward and swipe my tongue over her, desperate to taste her.

"God," Kelcie gasps, her hips lifting and her thigh muscles tightening.

My shoulders force her legs wider apart, and as I get comfortable, I grip hold of her hips to keep her in place. I lick and suck to my heart's delight, savoring every drop of arousal she gives me.

Kelcie's body begins to tremble, her breaths nothing but short gasps. I glance up, and the sight of her hands fisting the covers as her back arches off the bed has my cock jerking and becoming painfully hard.

"Levi," she whimpers, her body tensing as I keep pushing her toward an orgasm.

My eyes lock on Kelcie's breasts, and as I continue to feast on her clit, I can't tear my gaze away from her nipples.

They're begging for my teeth.

I groan against Kelcie's sensitive flesh, and it sends her over the edge. A cry tears from her, and she begins to convulse, her hips gyrating as she desperately rubs herself against my mouth and chin.

I've never experienced anything hotter in my life than watching my woman orgasm. Going down on Kelcie has officially become my favorite thing to do.

Chapter 25

KELCIE

When Levi crawls up my body, I greedily take in every perfectly sculptured inch of him before my eyes stop on his manhood. I've only seen that part of a man once before, and I don't remember it looking so big . . . and beautiful. Like velvet stretched over steel.

"Levi," I gasp while trying to catch my breath. My gaze drifts over his abs and chest, and my fingertips ghost over his warm skin and the beautiful tattoo. "You are so attractive. I could stare at you for hours and not get tired."

He lies down on top of me, and it looks like he's savoring the feel of our bodies touching. Minutes pass before he slowly lowers his head and kisses me as though he might die if he doesn't, and I get swept up into a world where there's only the two of us.

I feel his hardness pressing against the sensitive spot between my thighs, and it makes me desperate to feel him inside me. He rests his forearms on either side of my head while his mouth devours mine until I'm breathless again.

When he ends the kiss and lifts his head, he stares down at me with so much love, it brings tears to my eyes.

With his tone raspy, he murmurs, "You're so beautiful, sometimes it hurts to look at you. I love you, Kelcie." His words create a bubble where it's just us, and the outside world doesn't exist. "You're not just my muse. You're my miracle, my reward for surviving thirty-three years of darkness."

My heart.

I lift my head and seal our mouths together again. Slowly, the kiss turns passionate, and I push my hand down between us until I'm able to wrap my fingers around his hard manhood. His skin is silky soft, and when I stroke him, his body shudders and he groans against my lips.

Needing to become one with him, I position him at my entrance. Levi breaks the kiss and lifts his head so he can look into my eyes as he pushes against my opening.

I move my hand to his hip and brush my thumb along the sharp V that has a way of making me stupidly turned on for him.

Levi's expression turns tender, and he brings one of his hands to my face, cupping my cheek.

As our love for each other fills the air all around us and we stare into each other's eyes, he slowly pushes inside me. The moment is insanely intense, and I can't stop a tear from rolling into my hairline.

I begin to feel impossibly full, and unable to keep still, I lift my hips. The movement makes Levi sink much deeper, and while he groans, I gasp from the sting in my abdomen.

His voice is gravelly and deep as he asks, "Are you okay?"

I nod quickly. "Yes."

Then he thrusts even deeper, and my head tilts backward, air bursting over my lips from the unexpected pain. It didn't hurt as much when I lost my virginity, but then again, that guy wasn't half Levi's size.

Levi drops kisses all over my face and neck. "I'm sorry, baby."

I suck in a few breaths while the sting fades, then I say, "I'm okay."

Levi's eyes are glued to my face as he slowly pulls out before easing back into me. When the sting returns, I do my best not to react to it because I don't want him to stop.

On the third thrust, he asks, "Does it feel better?"

"Yes," I answer truthfully, and lifting my head, I begin to pepper kisses on his stubble. "You don't have to hold back."

Levi's mouth finds mine as he draws out of me again, and this time when he fills me, it's harder. I ignore the sting and focus on how amazing it feels to have the man I love deep inside me.

The kiss quickly turns wild, and my hands start to roam over the muscled expanse of his back.

God, he feels amazingly good.

Levi reaches down, and pushing his hand beneath me, he grips hold of my butt cheek. His thigh moves in beneath my leg, and I quickly hook my calf over his hip. The position opens me wider, and as Levi begins to fill me with hard thrusts, the pain morphs into pleasure.

When I whimper because of how incredible it feels, Levi answers me with a rumbling groan.

I'm consumed by how he kisses me, and the way his strong body keeps moving against mine is like tidal waves crashing to shore.

"Kelcie," he growls, and it's the only warning I get before he uncontrollably begins to hammer into me.

My hands brush down until I reach his firm butt, and I dig my nails into his skin, loving the feel of his muscles tensing beneath my touch.

Levi hits a spot deep inside me, which has pleasure shooting through my body like fireworks, and a cry spills over my lips.

He breaks the kiss and presses his forehead to mine as I begin to orgasm, and I watch his features grow tenser with every deliciously hard thrust he gives me. He keeps hitting my G-spot, and it prolongs my orgasm until he reaches his climax.

Feeling Levi's body jerk and how he grows even bigger inside me is something I'll never forget.

While he empties himself deep in me, I know he is the only man I'll ever love. Levi was made for me.

"I love you," I whisper as he continues to lazily plunge inside me, giving me the impression he can't get enough of me. "I love you more than anything."

"I'll never do anything to risk what we have," he vows. "You've given my life purpose, and it's to spend every waking day making you happy."

When Levi finally stills, he presses a tender kiss to my lips. We stare at each other, our eyes making silent promises to each other.

After a while, he gathers me in a hug and buries his face against the side of my neck. "Thank you for giving me another chance."

I begin to trail my fingers up and down his back, and feeling scars all over his skin, I close my eyes from the stab of pain to my heart. I hate that he suffered and wish I could erase every mark from his body.

I kiss his shoulder while bathing him in loving touches.

"I'm going to fall asleep if you keep doing that," he mumbles drowsily.

I let out a chuckle. "You're still inside me."

"I don't want to move," he admits. "I want to stay like this forever." Lick jumps onto the bed, and Levi lets out a groan. "Who needs kids if you have a dog?"

When he pulls out of me, residual sparks of pleasure shoot through my abdomen. I watch as he climbs off the bed, and my gaze devours his body as I get to see him from behind for the first time. There's a tattoo of bare branches, and I notice the ink covers the skin where I felt the scars. I also notice the red marks I left on his way-too-hot butt.

"Damn, you look good from behind," I compliment him. "Do the tattoos mean anything?"

Levi shakes his head as he swipes his sweatpants from the floor and puts them on. "The one on my back was just something I chose to cover the haphazard marks left over from the whippings my stepfather gave me. The phoenix is to remind me to keep rising from the ashes, and it conceals the burn mark."

My heart clenches painfully in my chest as I sit up and spit out, "Those people are vile."

Levi grabs a hoodie from the closet and pulls it over his head.

When he puts on his boots, I say, "You look nothing like your mother."

"Just call her Rene. She's not my mother." His eyes flick to me, his expression growing grim. "I think I look like my father, but I've never seen him, so I can't tell for sure."

"You said you never knew your father. Do you know what happened to him?" I ask.

Levi shakes his head as he stands up again. "Rene never told me anything about him."

He shrugs on a coat, then says, "I'll be back in ten minutes." He gestures for Lick to follow, and when they leave the room, I climb out of bed and go to the bathroom.

While I'm washing my hands, my eyes lock on my reflection in the mirror, and I take in the post-sex glow on my face.

Unlike the first time I had sex, this time was damn near perfect.

I walk back into the room and dig a pair of leggings and an old shirt out of my bag. I put on the clothes, then straighten the covers on the bed and fluff out the pillows.

When I sit down on the mattress again, I think about Levi's horrible family. It's difficult to believe such an extraordinary man came from all that abuse and darkness.

We both survived their evil ways, and it makes me feel even closer to Levi.

A while later, the door opens, and Lick darts into the room to escape the cold. Levi comes in with two paper cups, steam billowing from them.

"I grabbed us coffee and tea from the reception area."

"You're the best," I gasp as I shoot up to take my cup from him. I sip on the tea and let out a moan. "So good. Thank you."

"You moan like that again, and I'm going to fuck you straight through the night."

His words have my eyes widening and the cup stopping midway to my mouth.

Holy crap, that's hot.

"It also doesn't help if you look at me like that," he warns me, a smirk tugging at his lips.

I drink more of my tea while Levi's eyes remain locked on mine. He takes a sip of his coffee, then places his cup on the small table where his laptop is.

My tea is forgotten as he slowly begins to prowl toward me, his gaze never leaving mine. He takes the cup from my hand and sets it down on the bedside table before his head dips and his teeth tug at the sensitive skin beneath my ear.

My eyes drift closed from how hot and amazing the moment feels, and when Levi begins to remove my clothes, my abdomen greedily clenches, desperate to have him inside me again.

Once we're both naked, we fall onto the bed, and with wild kisses and loving touches, we get lost in each other once more.

Chapter 26

LEVI

As we drive out to the farm, I'm nervous as fuck. I really hope Kelcie falls in love with the place like I did.

Her phone begins to ring, and she quickly digs it out of her handbag. "Oh, it's Jordan!" I listen as she answers, "Hi. Thanks for calling back."

I realize she's put Jordan on speaker when I hear him say, "How are things between you and Levi? Did you get to talk to him?"

"Yes. Everything is good between us," she answers. "Levi reminded me about Christmas. We're still coming through to you, right?"

"Hell yes," Jordan replies.

"But we'll only drive through on Christmas Eve. I already took over your house for three weeks, so we won't visit for a week like we initially spoke about."

"I understand."

It's only then that I realize Kelcie never told Jordan he's on speaker, and he probably has no idea I'm listening in on the call. It tells me Kelcie isn't worried that Jordan will say anything bad about me, and it goes to show what good people they are.

"Hi, Jordan," I greet him.

"Oh, hey. How are you?"

"Much better now that your sister has forgiven me."

Jordan lets out a chuckle. "You struck gold with her, but please be gentle with her heart."

I glance at Kelcie, who's grinning from ear to ear. "I'll treasure her."

"Are we good?" I ask him.

"Yeah. It was a shitty thing you did, but I don't hold it against you for being related to that bastard."

More tension eases from my body. "Thanks, Jordan."

"So I'll see you on Wednesday?"

"Yes. Is there anything we can bring?" I ask.

"Just yourselves and empty stomachs because Natalie is planning to cook up a storm."

"Yummy." Kelcie glances around the area, then says, "We have to go. See you soon."

They end the call as I turn off the main street. While I steer the truck up the dirt road leading to the farmhouse, I keep stealing glances at Kelcie so I don't miss her reaction to seeing the farm.

I love the emotions flitting over her face, everything from amazement to excitement. "Oh my God, Levi. It's beautiful out here."

The two-story farmhouse comes into sight, and Kelcie's chin begins to quiver. "Our home."

The two simple words wrap tightly around my heart, and I'm filled with a sense of belonging because this place will be the first *home* I've ever had, and I'll share it with the woman I love. It won't just be a soulless house like the other places I've lived.

I bring the truck to a stop and chuckle when Kelcie can't get out fast enough. I climb out and watch as Lick sets off over the snow-covered yard.

Just as I turn my attention back to Kelcie, she lets out a happy shriek and launches herself at me. "It's perfect!"

I catch her while laughter escapes me, and holding her tight, I twirl her in a circle before I set her down on her feet. "Yeah? You like our farm?"

"I want to see all of it. God, there's so much space." Kelcie pulls away from me and looks over the yard in the direction of the lake.

"Come," I say as I take hold of her hand. I lead her toward the line of trees and watch her reaction as the lake comes into view.

"Holy crap. We have our own lake," she breathes, then her eyes light up with more excitement. "We can ice-skate!"

"I might fall on my ass and break something, but I'm willing to give it a try for you," I joke as we look at the frozen surface. We're quiet for a little while, then I say, "The day I put in an offer to purchase, I stood here for hours wondering if I'd ever see you again."

"Levi," she whispers as she turns to face me. "Of course you would've seen me again. I wouldn't have ghosted you."

The pain I felt while I was separated from Kelcie flickers through my chest. "I didn't know that at the time, though."

Her eyebrows draw together, and she moves closer until our bodies touch. Lifting her gloved hands, she frames my jaw and locks eyes with me. "No matter what happens, I won't leave you unless you explicitly tell me to." She makes the same promise to me that I made to her over Thanksgiving.

"I really needed to hear those words," I murmur, my entire soul letting out a sigh of relief. "And I will never tell you to leave. You're kinda stuck with me forever."

Her mouth curves up, and she gives me a quick kiss before she pulls back. "Show me our house."

"Remember it's a work in progress," I remind her as we walk hand in hand to the farmhouse.

Lick lets out happy barks as she zooms all over the place, loving the open space.

"She's so cute," Kelcie chuckles. "We're going to have to bathe her when she's done playing in the snow."

"I gave her a bath two days ago, so we can just dry her off when she comes inside," I reply as we take the stairs up to the front door. "I want to build a wraparound porch."

"That's a lot of work, Levi," Kelcie says. "Are you going to hire help?"

I shake my head. "I don't want a stranger touching our house." I glance at her as I pull the keys out of my pocket. "Sorry, I know it sounds weird."

Kelcie rubs a hand up and down my back while I unlock the door. "I understand, and it's not weird."

When we step into the house, my eyes are glued to her face. Her lips part, and I watch as she falls in love with our home.

Thank God.

She slowly moves forward, her gaze sweeping over the living room. I had the movers bring my furniture from the house in Verona, but everything is covered with plastic sheets to protect it from dust.

She keeps quiet as she walks through the room toward the kitchen.

"I want to knock out that wall so it's all open plan," I mention. I stay a few steps behind Kelcie. "And I'm thinking of replacing everything with mahogany cupboards. We can put a dark marble slab on the island and counters."

"It will look beautiful," she whispers, emotion tightening her voice. She trails her fingertips over the worn wood, then she asks, "Can I make the cupboard doors?"

Remembering she used to whittle and she hasn't done it since the attack, I realize what a big moment this is for Kelcie.

I move closer to her and place my hand on her lower back. "Of course you can. Just tell me what you need, and I'll order everything."

She shakes her head. "I have a contact who always supplied me with the best quality wood. I'll use them."

We head up the stairs, and as we walk from room to room, Kelcie takes her time to look at every nook and cranny. When we reach the main bedroom, she gasps.

Looking at the walk-in closet where I've put up shelves, drawers, and hanging space for clothes, she says, "God, Levi. Did you do all this?"

"Do you like it?" I ask. "I can change it if you want to add or remove something."

Her head snaps to me. "Don't you dare change a thing. I love it." She gives me a teasing look. "So this row of shelves is yours, and the rest of the closet is mine, right?"

I let out a chuckle and follow her to the en suite bathroom. She scrunches her nose at the strong smell of glue, mortar, and paint.

"I finished this yesterday. The smell will fade soon."

Kelcie trails her fingers over the counter and tiles. "You're so talented. It looks like it was done by a professional." She shoots me a look of warning. "Take the compliment."

"Yes, ma'am," I reply playfully. "Thank you."

She grips hold of my hand and pulls me into the shower. We both fit comfortably, and there's plenty of space to move around.

Kelcie wags her eyebrows at me. "The things I plan to do to you in this shower should scare you."

The corner of my mouth lifts. "Yeah? Like what?"

She reaches for my jeans and pops the button before she pulls down the zipper, then she purrs, "I think it's better if I show you."

Fuck. That's one hell of a turn-on.

As she pushes the fabric down my thighs, I harden at the speed of light. Her fingers wrap around my cock as she presses a kiss to my neck, and then my woman moves down to her knees.

I never allowed my ex to give me a blow job, so this is a new experience for me.

Actually, everything with Kelcie is new.

I stare down at the love of my life and watch her lips wrap around me. The pleasure is instant, and my lips part on a harsh breath.

I slap one hand against the tiled wall, and with my other, I cradle the back of Kelcie's head.

Her tongue swirls around my shaft as if she's licking a fucking lollipop, and then she sucks me hard, and her cheeks hollow out.

"Fuck," I groan, the erotic sight of Kelcie going to town on my dick and the pleasure she's making me experience pushing me closer to the edge. "I'm going to come," I warn her, heavy breaths rushing from me.

Her fist tightens around my base, and she sucks harder, her head bobbing and tears forming in her eyes.

The orgasm hits so hard, I sway on my feet and stop breathing altogether. My fist tightens in her hair as I ride the wave of pure ecstasy while I get to watch her swallow every drop of my release.

When Kelcie frees my cock from her mouth and climbs to her feet, I slump back against the tiles and try to catch my breath. My eyes don't leave her as I fix my jeans and pull up the zipper.

"How did I do for my first time?" she asks.

Knowing I'm the only man she's sucked off fills me with overwhelming satisfaction. "You blew my mind, baby."

A happy grin spreads over her face.

I move closer and press a soft kiss to her mouth before saying, "Like I said, you're a damn miracle, and those lips of yours are the gates to heaven."

Kelcie beams at my praise as we leave the bathroom, and when we're back in the living room, I quickly get the fireplace going to warm up the place.

As if she has a sixth sense, Lick comes in from outside, and I shut the door behind her to keep the cold out. I walk to the coffee table, and picking up her towel, which I dropped there yesterday, I hand it to Kelcie. "Wanna dry her while I fix us something for lunch?"

"We have food here?" my woman asks as she sits down beside Lick, who's made herself comfortable in front of the fire.

"Yes. I spend most of my days here and only go back to the motel to shower and sleep."

"As soon as the smell of the fresh paint fades, I think we can move in," Kelcie mentions while she rubs the towel over Lick's fur.

"There will be a lot of dust and noise while we renovate," I remind her. "But I love how eager you are to live here."

"I can't wait. It's the best Christmas present ever."

I put together a couple of ham and cheese sandwiches and grab two bottles of water before joining Kelcie on the floor.

While we eat, I tell her, "Tish, the realtor who sold me this place, has a cousin who breeds mini–Highland cows. He's up in Montana. I've reached out to him, and he said he'll have calves early spring."

Kelcie just took a bite of bread, and with her mouth full, she begins to bounce right where she's sitting while her face lights up like the Fourth of July. Once she's swallowed, she exclaims, "Mini cows! How many can we get? Oh my God!"

Laughing, I enjoy every second of her happiness. "As many as we can fit onto two hundred and fifty acres. He also breeds goats and miniature horses, so keep some space for those."

Kelcie squeals, and abandoning her sandwich, she practically throws herself at me, kissing me with so much love, it warms every part of my body and soul.

Chapter 27

KELCIE

I've contemplated waiting until after Christmas to see if I can go into my parents' house without losing it, but after only two nights in the motel, I'm already tired of staying there and don't want to live in my rental either.

Levi brings his truck to a stop in front of my family home, and after turning off the engine, he takes hold of my hand and just sits in silence beside me.

My gaze slowly moves over the house where I had the happiest childhood. Until that horrific night, this house was my little slice of heaven.

My heartbeat speeds up, and I pull my hand free from Levi's when my palm begins to grow sweaty. I suck in deep breaths of air before I shove the passenger door open and climb out of the truck.

I hear Levi move, and when he comes to wrap his arm around my shoulder, he asks, "Are you ready?"

"As ready as I'll ever be," I whisper.

"I have your medicine and water, and I'm not leaving your side. Take your time, my muse."

"Some muse I am," I say, a nervous chuckle escaping me. "You haven't written in weeks."

"We can talk about my writing later." When I glance at him, he says, "Right now, let's focus on you. This is a big moment."

He's right.

I look at the house again and take another deep breath before slowly walking toward the porch.

The image of Mom opening the door flashes through my mind. When I take the steps up and I glance at the hanging chair, I picture Mom and Dad enjoying a glass of wine at sunset.

I turn my head and look at the wooden floor, but I don't see any sign of blood.

Jordan said he had everything cleaned.

When I bring my gaze back to the front door, Levi unlocks it before stepping to the side. "You're doing great, Kelcie."

I reach for the handle and push down on it, and when the door creaks open, my breaths come a little faster. Feeling very emotional and apprehensive, I take cautious steps forward.

"I'm right behind you," Levi murmurs.

Keeping my eyes lowered, I walk past the formal sitting room and dining area. I fist my hands at my sides, and when Lick comes to nudge her head against my thigh, I lift my head and look up the staircase to where I last saw Mom.

Instead of getting a flashback of Mom dying, I hear her laughter as she wrapped Christmas decorations around the banisters.

I glance at the living room and see the couches have been pushed back into their original positions, and the lamp stands upright.

There's no sign of the destruction that happened in the room when Sage and Dad were killed.

Instead, I picture Sage lying on the couch with a bowl of popcorn resting on her chest while she judges every participant on some reality show.

Buttercup, I'm getting some ice cream for me and Sage. You want some? I hear Dad ask, and my head snaps to the left where the kitchen is.

The flashback is so clear, for a moment it feels like he's really standing at the counter, scooping spoonfuls of chocolate ice cream into a bowl.

Tears gather in my eyes as I remember him eating directly from the tub and Mom chastising him.

No, Harry! Dish some up instead of eating like a barbarian.

A weird mixture of a sob and laughter splutters from me, then I feel Levi's arm wrap around my shoulders, and I'm pulled out of the past. I turn into his chest as the tears come.

Levi holds me, and I feel him dropping kisses on my hair. "I'm here, baby. I've got you."

I take the comfort only he can give me, and when the tears stop flowing, I keep resting my cheek against his chest while letting more memories of my family flutter through my mind.

"We were so happy here," I whisper.

"I can still feel that happiness in the house," Levi mentions.

I pull back and look at the staircase again. Gathering courage, I take the first step, and then the second. I glance at our family photos on the wall, and seeing my parents' and Sage's faces for the first time in over a year, tears silently roll over my cheeks.

Levi stops to stare at one of the whole family. We're all wearing matching Christmas sweaters. "There's so much love in this photo that I can feel it."

When I reach the landing, I notice the entire carpet has been replaced.

Before I know what I'm doing, I sit down on the top step and lean my head against the wall. Closing my eyes, I imagine Mom as she sat here and bled out.

"What if the last thing my mom saw was me running away?"

Levi crouches in front of me and tilts his head. "If I were in your mom's position and I saw you run, I'd be filled with relief, Kelcie. It would've been much worse if she had to watch you die. It would break me, and knowing how much your mother loved you, it would've destroyed her."

My eyes focus on Levi's face as I hear what he's saying. "She didn't know Sage was dead. Maybe she had hope that we both survived. Maybe she heard Dad telling me to run, and she thought he would survive too."

Levi places his hand on the side of my neck and nods. "I like those maybes."

"It's so much better than Mom dying thinking we were all killed," I whisper.

His thumb brushes over my skin in a soothing way, and I lock eyes with him. "You didn't have to come here to try and fix what Wesley destroyed."

"I had no choice in the matter. I took one look at your smiling face, and I just had to make sure you got the chance to smile like that again."

"My smiling face?"

"There was a photo of you in one of the articles," he explains. "There's also a part of me that wondered if things would've turned out differently if I hadn't left Wesley behind."

"Did they abuse him too?" I ask.

Levi shakes his head. "No, but they're responsible for turning him into a cold-blooded monster. His father taught him to laugh whenever he hurt me." His expression fills with hatred. "But that doesn't excuse what Wesley did, and he deserves the life sentence he received."

"It's hard to believe you grew up in the same house as him. You're complete opposites, and I'm so thankful for that." I lean forward and press a kiss to Levi's mouth. "I have one more maybe."

"Yeah? What's that?"

"Maybe my parents and Sage found a way to send you to me because they knew we would be able to heal each other."

Levi's mouth curves into a heartbreakingly beautiful smile. "I like that maybe a lot."

I climb to my feet, and when Levi straightens out, I take his hand and pull him toward my bedroom. When we step inside, I glance around at everything that's so familiar yet so foreign after being away for a year and a half.

Levi pulls his hand free from mine and walks to the wall that's decorated with floating shelves. My most prized and sentimental wooden pieces are on display, and he takes his time looking at every single one. "You made these?"

"Yes. I made half of them with my dad's help."

I move closer to the five oval-shaped pieces that have an intricate pattern carved into them. "These took me a year to make." I twist off the top piece, and as I lift it, it reveals a miniature statue. "This is Sage."

"Jesus, Kelcie." Levi leans closer, admiring the detail. "Your work is amazing."

I show him the statues of Dad, Mom, and Jordan, and I love how he inspects every inch of wood.

Levi locks eyes with me, then asks, "Will you ever whittle again?"

"I'm going to make our kitchen cupboards and take it from there."

"Will you show me your workshop?"

Nodding, I walk out of the room. I glance at my parents' bedroom, the door standing open. I pause for a moment before I go inside.

"It doesn't smell like them anymore," I whisper to myself.

I move closer to the dressing table, and picking up a half-full bottle of perfume, I squirt some into the air and inhale deeply.

Mom.

I keep the bottle and go look for Dad's cologne in the bathroom. Again, I spray in the air and take a deep breath.

"That's what home smelled like," I tell Levi as I meet his eyes. "Now home smells like cedarwood and citrus." Seeing he doesn't understand, I add, "Your scent."

His features soften, and he closes the distance between us, engulfing me in his arms. "You're my home too. Flowers, bright light, and beautiful smiles."

I shut the front door of the rental behind me and glance around the space where I licked my wounds.

Levi dropped me off, and he's heading to the motel to pack his belongings, then he'll come back to pick me up.

We've decided to temporarily move into my family home because I want to slowly work my way through every room and decide what I'm keeping and giving away.

I'll tell Jordan when I see him and hear if he wants to come through to look at everything as well. I think he'll be very happy to hear about the progress I've made.

Time to pack and say goodbye to this place.

Heading toward the stairs, I remember to lock the door and quickly turn around. I reach for the deadbolt, but the next instant, the front door opens.

For a second, I think it's Levi, but when I see Colby, I'm instantly angry and scowl at him. "You can't just barge into my house."

He doesn't listen and comes in before slamming the door shut behind him.

"Leave right now. I have nothing to say to you," I snap, my body starting to tremble from all the anger I feel.

"I just want to talk to you, Kelcie," he says, but when he engages the deadbolt, fear slithers through me.

"We can talk outside." I take a step toward the door and reach for the lock, but Colby grabs hold of me.

God!

I let out a startled shriek when he lifts me off my feet, forcing me deeper into the living room, before he throws me down on the couch.

I hiccup from shock, and twisting, I scramble to get away from him as my mind struggles to catch up to what's happening.

"Just fucking stop!" Colby shouts as he grabs hold of my hips, hauling me back onto the couch and beneath him.

I begin to hit every surface of his body I can reach while screaming bloody murder.

He manages to grab hold of my forearms and lock them to my chest. "Why, Kelcie?" he roars in my face. "What does he have that I don't? I fucking did so much for you. Do you know what it took to find that bitch mother of his and convince her to come here? I showed you what kind of monster he is, and still you fucking picked him."

When he stops yelling, our rushed breaths are all that can be heard for a few seconds before I buck my hips up in an attempt to get Colby off me. My heart thunders against my ribs, and it feels like I'm having an out-of-body experience.

I twist my arms, fighting to free them, and when I get my right hand loose, I don't hesitate and punch Colby as hard as I can on the jaw.

His head whips to the side, and I fight like crazy to wiggle from beneath him. When I drop onto the floor, I dart to my feet and run for the back door, while I dig my phone out of my coat pocket. My attention is split between running and finding Levi's number.

Just as I press dial, I also manage to slide the deadbolt back, but before I can open the door, Colby grabs hold of my shoulders and yanks me backward.

I lose my footing and fall to the floor between the kitchen and the living room, my phone flying from my hand and sliding beneath the couch.

No!

My head snaps back to where Colby is securing the deadbolt, and I catch a glimpse of a gun tucked into the back of his pants.

Oh, Jesus!

I scramble to my feet, and instead of running away, I lunge at Colby in an attempt to get ahold of the gun. Something connects hard with my chin, and I bite my tongue, a coppery taste quickly filling my mouth.

"Fucking. Stop," Colby roars before he slaps me so hard, I swear I see stars for a few seconds.

Those precious seconds are all it takes for him to tackle me off my feet. As my side slams into the hard floor, the air whooshes from my lungs, and my vision goes spotty.

Colby forces me onto my back and straddles me, then grips hold of my jaw. He leans down until his breath hits my face. "Why do you love him? Why do you give him what's always been mine?"

My tone is biting as I sneer, "Because Levi is everything you will never be."

A look of heartache tightens Colby's features, and I'm so freaking confused when tears roll over his cheeks. "I love you, Kelcie. I'll do anything for you." He leans closer, and I begin to slap him again when he tries to kiss me. "Pick me," he breathes against my mouth, and I squeeze my lips tightly together while letting out a strangled shriek.

Nothing I do helps to get him off me, and I cry, "Stop, Colby!"

"No. I'll make you see we're meant to be. You just need to give me a chance."

When I feel his hands working to undo the button of my jeans, a fear I had hoped to never feel again floods my body.

I scream my head off, and I fight harder than ever to get away from him.

I hear barking, and the relief hits me so hard, I begin to cry hysterically. There's a crashing sound somewhere behind me, and as Colby finally moves backward, Lick flies right over me and sinks her teeth into Colby's arm, her body slamming him onto his ass.

I scramble away until I reach the couch while Levi charges Colby, who's pulling the gun from behind his back.

"Noooooo!" I scream, my hand flying to my mouth.

It feels as if time slows down. I hear Lick viciously snarling as she lets go of Colby's arm, darting around him to get to his other side. I see the dark metal of the gun and hear the crushing blows of Levi's fist connecting with Colby's face.

The gunshot is so loud I jerk. Lick whines, and the men freeze.

God. No. Please, no!

I crawl to them as Levi lets go of Colby and sinks back onto his haunches while Lick crawls to him, her ears pulled back.

"Levi?" I whimper, and as I get closer, I see blood flowing from a hole beneath Colby's ear.

Levi pets Lick as he turns his head toward me, his breaths rushing over his parted lips. There are droplets of blood on the side of his face, and I use my hand to wipe them away before I curl up against his chest. When Levi's arms wrap like steel bands around me, a wail tears loose from the deepest part of my soul.

I thought Lick was shot. Then I thought Levi was shot.

Those two thoughts are the reason I break down. Not because Colby attacked me, but because there was a chance I could've lost them.

Chapter 28

LEVI

Keeping ahold of Kelcie, I climb to my feet before I lift her bridal-style into my arms. When I back away from Colby's body, I hear sirens.

I contacted the sheriff's department after I got the call from Kelcie and heard muffled sounds of her and Colby fighting. Hanging up on her so I could let the police know what was happening is officially the hardest thing I've ever had to do. It felt like I was abandoning her.

Turning around, I walk out of the house and take Kelcie to the truck, where I bundle her into the passenger seat. I indicate for Lick to jump in before instructing her to stay with Kelcie.

Lick lies down partially on top of Kelcie's lap, her ears pulled back, which tells me she's still in attack mode.

"Good girl," I say as I pat my dog's head so she'll relax.

I press a kiss to Kelcie's temple, and as the sheriff's cruiser comes to a screeching stop, I say, "I'm going to deal with the mess. Stay here."

Tears keep spilling over her cheeks, and seeing the angry red handprint on her face makes it unbelievably difficult to walk away from her.

"Colby is in the house," I tell Sheriff Williams just as Mrs. Adams comes jogging across the road.

Sheriff Williams points at her and shouts at his deputy, "Keep her back, Jonas."

Deputy Stone darts toward Mrs. Adams and grabs hold of her, which has her screaming, "Where's Colby?"

Deputy Stone pulls her back to the house across the road while Sheriff Williams hurries into Kelcie's house.

Fuck. I can't believe what happened.

I let out a sigh as I walk to the front door, watching as he checks Colby's pulse.

"Jesus," he mutters while he uses his pen to pick up the weapon.

"You'll only find Colby's fingerprints on the gun," I tell him. "He shot himself."

Crouched near Colby, Sheriff Williams shakes his head. "Do you know if Kelcie's security cameras still work?"

"They should. I'll check with her quickly." I walk back to the truck, and when I see how she's trembling, I shrug out of my coat and drape it over her. "Do your security cameras still work?"

She nods her head, her teeth clattering from shock. "M-my phone is under th-th-the couch. S-Sheriff Williams knows h-how the app works."

I brush my hand over her hair and wish I could stay with her, but once again, I have to force myself to walk away. "Her phone is under the couch. Can I move it?"

"Yes," Sheriff Williams answers.

I lift the couch and set it aside, then crouch and pick up Kelcie's phone. I hand the device to the sheriff.

"Thank God I installed the cameras for Kelcie," he tells me as he goes into the app. "I only did it because I thought it would help her feel safe."

He goes silent, and I walk closer to watch the security footage with him, praying to God that it shows my hand wasn't near the gun.

When I see Kelcie fighting Colby, who's almost twice her size, I begin to feel sick with disgust and anger.

Lick jumps over Kelcie and begins to maul Colby's arm, and then it shows me punching the bastard. He moves his right arm, trying to point the gun at me, and Lick darts around, biting and yanking at his wrist. The barrel points at Colby's face just as he pulls the trigger.

"Jesus. That's one hell of a dog you have there," Sheriff Williams mutters.

"Can I go wait with Kelcie?" I ask.

"Yes. Stick around, though. We need your statements, and the ambulance should be here already. Have them check Kelcie."

I nod before jogging out of the house. I hear Lick growl as a paramedic examines Kelcie's face.

"Is she okay?" I ask the first responder.

She glances at me. "Are you her partner?"

"Yes," I answer while I indicate for Lick to relax.

"Kelcie will have some bruising, but she should be fine. I'll give her an ice pack to help with the swelling. Keep an eye on her for the next twenty-four hours, though."

"I will." I place my hand on Kelcie's knee, where she's sitting sideways on the passenger seat of my truck. When the paramedic walks back to the ambulance, I duck my head to catch Kelcie's eyes. "Sheriff Williams just wants our statements before we can leave."

She blinks a few times before her face crumples, and she reaches up to wrap her arms around my neck. I hold my woman, thankful none of us were seriously injured.

"Are you okay?" Kelcie asks as she pulls back to take hold of my hand so she can look at my knuckles. They're busted, but I don't give a shit. "Let Brooklyn look at your hand before she leaves."

Assuming Brooklyn is the paramedic, I shake my head. "I'm not letting her touch me. I'll take care of it myself."

I hear Mrs. Adams screaming across the street, but I can't make out any of the words. The front door opens, and I see Deputy Stone struggle to hold her back as Mrs. Adams cries, "You killed my son! You murderer! You killed my baby!"

Lick begins to bark, and I quickly silence her with a command while pulling Kelcie back against my chest. I press kisses to her hair and say, "We'll leave soon."

Deputy Stone finally gets Mrs. Adams back into the house and shuts the door. I watch as the paramedic jogs across the road, and I hope she'll give the woman something to calm her.

Snow begins to fall around us, and I let go of Kelcie. "Move back into the truck. I don't want you to get cold."

She does as she's told, and I pull my coat over her.

"God, this weather is miserable," Sheriff Williams says as he comes out of the house to take our statements.

We spend the next ten minutes recounting everything we can remember, and when the sheriff seems satisfied for the time being, he says, "You can't stay here today. Do you have anywhere else you can go?"

"My parents' house," Kelcie answers.

Surprise flickers over the sheriff's face. "Okay. I'll find you there if I have any more questions."

I think to add, "We're going to visit Jordan for Christmas. We'll be gone three days at the most."

Sheriff Williams nods. "That's not a problem. You folks try to enjoy the holidays."

"Thank you, Sheriff," Kelcie murmurs. "You too."

When he walks away, I shut the passenger door and jog around the truck before I climb in behind the steering wheel.

KELCIE

I can't believe what happened.

My mind is reeling as Levi ushers me into the motel room. When we drove away from the crime scene, Levi mentioned neither of us had any clothes at my family home. He let Sheriff Williams know where we'll be staying tonight.

I'm only half aware that he shuts the door behind us and locks it.

Lick pads over to her spot in front of the bed and lies down, and following her, I crouch so I can brush my hand over her head.

I hear Levi switch on the faucets in the shower and watch as he moves around the room, gathering clean clothes for us. He takes it all to the bathroom before coming back and holding out his hand to me. "Come, my muse. Let me get you cleaned up."

I place my palm in Levi's and let him help me to my feet, then follow him into the bathroom, where he removes my coat before pulling my sweater over my head.

He continues to undress me, then gets rid of his own clothes, and as he tugs me into the shower, my eyes remain locked on his face.

Levi begins to wash my body, and as I feel his hands move over my skin, it erases some of the shock I suffered today. His gentle touch is soothing, but then I notice a muscle jumping in his jaw.

"Are you okay?" I whisper.

"I just need to erase his touch from your body," he says.

"It feels good," I tell him in a soft tone. Levi's eyes flick to mine, and I quickly add, "Having your hands on me."

When he's done washing me, he moves in behind me and shampoos my hair. After he's worked conditioner into the strands, his fingers massage my scalp, and my eyes drift closed from how comforting it feels.

Levi rinses my hair until the water runs clean, then I finally get my turn to wash his body. I give him the same love he showed me, and I'm careful when I clean his bruised knuckles.

We get out of the shower, and Levi dries us. Once I'm done getting dressed, I walk to the doorway, just wanting to crawl into bed.

"Hold up. I'm not done yet." He grips my hand and pulls me toward the counter.

Picking up the brush, he gently works all the knots out of my strands, then he pulls a hair dryer out of a drawer and plugs it in.

God. This man is everything.

Watching Levi in the mirror as he takes care of me erases some of the trauma I was forced to endure today, and the corner of my mouth lifts.

His eyes lock with mine every few seconds, and I swear I fall in love with him all over again.

"Feeling any better?" he asks as he switches off the hair dryer and sets it down on the counter.

"Much. You have a miracle touch that has a way of soothing me."

"Yeah?" He places his arms around me, and keeping eye contact with me in the mirror, he kisses the red handprint on my cheek.

"Thank you for saving me, Levi," I whisper.

"Lick did most of the saving."

I shake my head to silence him. "Thank you for coming to Verona and moving in next door to me. Thank you for talking to me and becoming my friend." My eyes tear up, and my voice grows hoarse as I continue, "Thank you for giving in and loving me." I turn around so we can be face-to-face as I say, "You saved me in so many ways. Mentally. Emotionally. Physically. You brought me back to life."

Emotion fills his hazel eyes, and he rubs his palms up and down my arms while he takes in every inch of me, as if he needs to keep checking I'm really okay after the attack.

"You've done the same for me, Kelcie." As his gaze meets mine, I see my entire future in him. "You make life worth living. You've given me purpose, hopes, and dreams." He shakes his head reverently. "You'll always be my miracle."

"We can be each other's miracles," I whisper as I wrap my arms around his neck.

Levi pins me to his body, and with his eyes hardly leaving mine, he moves us out of the bathroom and lays me down on the bed.

We take our time undressing each other, and when we're naked and Levi's body covers mine, he says, "You're the only person I love, Kelcie. You're my entire world."

I frame his jaw, taking in the feel of his bristles against my skin. "I'm the luckiest woman, Levi. I'm going to spend the rest of my life giving you happy memories."

He lowers his head and presses another soft kiss to the bruising on my cheek. Then his mouth finds mine, nipping at me in a hot way that has my abdomen clenching. His tongue brushes over the seam of my lips, and as I part for him and he strokes over mine, we both groan.

This man's kisses are everything to me.

His hands begin to roam over my body, and when his palm covers my breast, I arch into his touch. He moves, placing heated kisses down the column of my neck before he sucks my right nipple into his mouth.

"Fuck," he groans against my skin, the deep rumble from his chest making my entire body greedy to feel all his touches and kisses everywhere. "You taste like heaven, baby."

He takes his sweet time giving my nipples so much attention that I'm desperate to feel him inside me.

"I need you," I whimper, ravenous for my man.

Levi braces one of his arms beside my head, and reaching down, he positions his hardness right where I need him most. Our eyes lock, and as he surges into me in a single thrust, my lips part and the air bursts from my lungs.

He grips my hip in a biting hold and begins to take me with punishingly deep strokes. I'm inundated with pleasure, not knowing if I'm coming or going. My hips lift, trying to meet his brutal pace, but in the end, all I can do is wrap my arms tightly around him and hang on for dear life.

"Oh God," I gasp against the side of his neck. "Levi."

He dips his head, the bristles on his jaw scratchy on my sensitive skin, then his mouth claims mine, the kiss wild and filled with so much heat, it creates an inferno between us.

Levi's chest rubs against mine, his fingers digging into my hip, and as he keeps driving harder and deeper inside me, cries spill from my mouth to his.

"Yes . . . oh . . . Levi . . . please," I resort to begging, not knowing exactly what I'm asking for. "Please. Please. Please. More."

Levi rips his mouth away from mine, and moving to his knees between my thighs, he hauls my butt into the air before filling me so roughly, the entire bed shakes.

He hits that spot deep inside me, and as I claw at the covers, my head tilts back, my body arches, and I come so hard, I lose all my senses except for feeling the unadulterated ecstasy seizing me.

I feel Levi jerk inside me as he finds his own release with a harsh growl, making my orgasm so much more intense. The pleasure just keeps hitting me, and when he falls over me, squashing me to the bed, I grab hold of him and sob.

Even though we're both coming, he doesn't let up and prolongs the intensely intimate moment between us.

Only when my bones turn to Jell-O and I feel like a limp noodle does Levi slow down. He continues to fill me with leisurely strokes, sending spasms of residual pleasure through me.

Lifting his head, he meets my gaze, and all I can do is let out a satisfied chuckle.

His mouth curves into a sexy smirk. "You're so fucking beautiful when you come." He dips his head, and his mouth nips at mine. "You take me so well, baby. My cock fits perfectly inside you."

"Holy crap," I gasp before I start to laugh. "You can't get me all hot and bothered again. I need at least an hour to recover."

He playfully bites my jaw, then presses a kiss beneath my ear before groaning, "I want to stay buried inside you."

Like the greedy hussy my abdomen is, it clenches, and Levi groans again. "So fucking good when you squeeze me like that."

I wrap my arms and legs around him, and brushing my palm up and down his back, I say, "You don't have to pull out. Stay inside me."

For the next thirty minutes, he keeps pressing lazy kisses over my neck and jaw, and I draw patterns over his skin with my fingertips.

Ever so slowly, Levi's hips begin to move again, and while we touch and kiss each other, he makes love to me once more.

Chapter 29

LEVI

Sheriff Williams just called, telling us it was okay to go back to the rental.

"I'll be quick," I say to Kelcie. She's sitting cross-legged on the bed with Lick cuddled up beside her. "The two of you stay here. I don't want you anywhere near that house."

"Can I pack your clothes while I wait?" she asks.

"I'd appreciate that." I tie the laces of my boots and climb to my feet. Striding over to Kelcie, I give her a quick kiss. "Love you, my muse."

She grins up at me. "I love you too."

I ruffle Lick's fur, then leave the room, shutting the door behind me.

Hit in the face with an icy blast, I grumble, "Jesus." I quickly jog to my truck and climb in. Starting the engine, I set the heat high before I pull out of my parking spot.

The ten-minute drive goes by quickly, and I glance at the Adamses' house across the street as I pull into the rental's driveway, parking beside the sheriff's cruiser.

I didn't like Colby, but I feel for his parents. What happened yesterday was such an unnecessary waste of life.

After climbing out of my truck, I hurry to the front door and quickly open it. Sheriff Wilson is standing in the kitchen, drinking a cup of something hot.

"I just made coffee. Want some?" he asks.

"I'm good, thanks." I look at the bloodstain on the wooden floor, and the memory of seeing Colby on top of Kelcie flashes through my mind. I shudder to think what would've happened if she hadn't managed to call me.

My jaw clenches, and not in the mood to chat, I mumble, "I'm going upstairs to pack."

"How is Kelcie handling everything?" he asks as I turn toward the staircase.

I pause and look at him again. "She's doing okay."

Sheriff Williams stares at me for a few seconds. "You take good care of that girl. She's suffered enough."

"I will." I go up the stairs two at a time, not giving the sheriff time to say anything else.

In the main bedroom, I find several moving boxes and see that some already have clothes packed in them. I open the closet doors and get to work, folding every piece of clothing neatly. When I'm done, there are still two empty boxes, and I take them down to the kitchen before heading back to the main bedroom so I can load everything into my truck.

Just as I'm loading the last of Kelcie's clothes into my truck, I hear Mrs. Adams scream, "You're a monster!" My head whips to the left, and I see her coming toward me, not even checking the road for traffic as she crosses it. Her tone sounds downright manic as she cries, "You killed my baby. You should rot in jail with that brother of yours."

As I turn to face her, Sheriff Williams comes jogging past me. "Hey, now. Let's get you back home, Darlene."

Mrs. Adams keeps glaring at me with an insane expression, making her look unstable. She repeatedly hisses, "You killed my baby."

"Come, Darlene." Sheriff Williams takes hold of her and pulls her back toward her house, but she cranes her neck to keep glaring at me.

I let out a sigh while I head back inside to clear out the kitchen.

Hearing footsteps, I glance at the sheriff as he comes into the house. "She's just grieving. Don't take anything she says personally."

I make a noncommittal sound and continue to place the tableware in a box.

Sheriff Williams looks at the lone couch and probably notices there is no other furniture because he asks, "Kelcie never really moved in here, did she?"

"It wasn't home to her," I murmur, emptying the drawer containing all the silverware.

"Are the two of you moving into her folks' place?"

I shake my head. "We'll only be staying there for the time being while Kelcie packs everything."

"Oh." His eyebrows lift in surprise. "Is she going to sell the place?"

Fuck, he talks a lot.

"Probably. Kelcie mentioned it's what Jordan wants."

When I lift a full box, Sheriff Williams comes closer, saying, "I'll grab the other one."

"You don't have to hang around. I've got this," I mention, hoping he'll take the hint.

"Nah, if I go back to the office, my wife will have me filling out loads of paperwork." When I give him a confused look, he explains, "Libby is the receptionist at the sheriff's department. That's where we met."

While we load the last of the boxes into my truck, Sheriff Williams glances at the Adamses' house. "Just as well you're clearing out today. Colby's death hit Darlene hard."

"I can only imagine," I grumble before walking back into the house to make sure I have everything.

Sheriff Williams follows me through the house, saying, "If Kelcie and Jordan sell their folks' place, where will she live?"

"With me." I shut the door to each room as I'm done checking it. "I bought a farm in Stoughton."

"Oh wow. So it's the farm life for you? Can't really see Kelcie fitting in on a farm."

"It was her idea." My feet make quick work of the stairs as I head down them.

"Will you be back for the couch and TV?" Sheriff Williams asks.

"No. I'm taking them now." I unplug the TV, and carrying it outside, I load it onto the passenger seat, making sure it's secure and won't topple over during the short drive to Kelcie's family home.

When I go back for the couch, the sheriff says, "I'll grab this end. You take the other."

Appreciating the help, I smile at him. "Thanks."

It takes some pivoting and nudging, but we get the couch into the truck bed.

"I'll follow you to the Woodruffs' place and help you offload."

Letting out a chuckle, I say, "You must really hate paperwork."

"You have no idea." While he watches me lock up the place, he adds, "A word of advice? Never work with your wife."

I give him a chin lift as I climb into my truck, and while I reverse out of the driveway, I see Mrs. Adams glaring at me through the window.

Kelcie

I've decided to live out of boxes because I'm too lazy, but Levi is insisting we unpack everything.

"It will be quick," Levi says.

My teeth worry nervously at my bottom lip. I have a growing sense of urgency to get out of Verona. There's been too much death, and I can't risk running into Colby's parents. I know what happened yesterday wasn't my fault, but I feel bad for the Adams family.

"Or we can leave it like this and move to the farmhouse when we get back from visiting Jordan," I say, giving Levi a hopeful look.

"It will be dusty while we do renovations," he reminds me.

"The main bedroom is ready. We can keep the door shut." I move closer. "I want to get out of this town, Levi. Please, can we move to the farm?"

The corner of his mouth lifts, and his features soften. "If that's what you really want, my muse."

"It's the only thing I want," I tell him, giving him a thank-you kiss. "Oh, and I want to go to the cemetery. Would you mind taking me? Malakai said my car will only be ready the second week of January."

"Why are the repairs taking so long?" Levi asks.

"They're closed for two weeks over the holidays."

"Right." I watch as he neatly stacks the boxes on top of each other so they're not scattered all over the place, then he asks, "When do you want to go?"

"Seeing as we're leaving early tomorrow to head to Naperville, I was hoping I could visit today." When Levi's gaze meets mine, I add, "I'd like to introduce you to them."

The corner of his mouth lifts. "Yeah? What are you going to introduce me as?"

"Oh, I don't know," I tease him. "My friend. My neighbor." I toss around a couple of ideas. "My stalker." I snort. "They'll get a kick out of that one."

Levi comes to wrap his arms around me, and staring into my eyes, he asks, "How about you introduce me as your husband?"

My lips part, but an instant later, I scowl at him. "You want to skip the whole wedding and go straight to being my husband? That's cheating, mister."

He chuckles, then says, "Okay. Then how about you tell them I'm your fiancé?" Before I can give him my thoughts on that, he continues, "Tell them I bought a farm to show how invested I am in us. Tell them I can't live a single day without you." My eyes begin to fill with tears when I realize what he's doing. "Tell them I would be the luckiest man on the face of this planet if you agreed to marry me. I want you as my wife, Kelcie."

"Levi," I whisper.

Standing in the house where my happiest memories are, I add another one to them as I ask, "Is that a proposal?"

The corner of his mouth lifts, and with emotions swimming in his eyes, he brings his hands up to frame my face. "Will you marry me, Kelcie?" A tear escapes, and as it rolls over my cheek, Levi leans in to catch it with a kiss. "Please. I'm only half a soul without you."

A sob sputters over my lips as I nod. "Yes, I'll marry you."

He seals our special moment with a kiss, and when he finally lifts his head, he says, "We can buy your ring while we're in Naperville and celebrate with your brother."

"I'd like that."

"But first." He pulls away from me and grabs our coats from where they're hanging near the front door. "Let's go so I can ask my soon-to-be in-laws for their blessing."

While I shrug on my coat, I ask, "How soon?"

"As soon as you'll let me." Levi indicates for Lick to come. "I'll marry you today if you give me half a chance." When Lick just stares at us from her warm spot on the couch, he asks, "Are you staying?"

Her reply is to curl up and go back to sleeping.

Laughter tumbles past my lips as I open the door. "Let her stay. We'll only be an hour at most."

I step out onto the porch and put on my gloves while I wait for Levi to lock up behind us. We walk to his truck, and when his phone buzzes, he digs it out and checks the message that came through.

"I think that's the first time I've seen you get a message," I mention.

"It's my agent. He's just wishing me a happy holiday and not so subtly asking when I'm sending the manuscript."

I give him a worried look. "Have you gotten any writing done the past month?"

Levi shakes his head while we climb into the truck, and as he starts the engine, he replies, "I couldn't write while we were apart. Don't worry. I still have eight months before the deadline."

"Oh, that's good." I place my hand on his thigh, then say, "I'm sorry all the nasty business messed up your writing schedule. We can set up a writing corner for you in the main bedroom until we have the study ready."

"I was just going to sit on the couch, but I like your idea better."

The drive to the cemetery is quick, and when we get out, I glance over all the headstones that are covered in snow. "It's actually so peaceful here."

Levi meets me at the front of the truck and takes hold of my hand. "Where are they?"

I point at the big tree that's a hundred yards or so away. We trudge through the snow, and when we stop in front of the three graves, I pull my hand from Levi's and brush the headstones clean with my gloved hand.

"Hi, guys. Sorry, I haven't visited for a while. Things got a little crazy, but it's nothing for you to worry about." I move back to Levi's side and hug his arm. "This is Levi."

He pulls his arm free from my hands and places it around my shoulders. "I wish I could've met you all," he murmurs. He's quiet for a while, then he clears his throat and says, "I'm sorry for what my family did to yours, but I want you to rest in peace knowing I'll take care of Kelcie and love her with all my heart."

I place my hand on Levi's chest and lean into his side as I smile at the graves. "Isn't he the best? I knew you'd love him."

I hear a car's engine, but I don't pay it any attention.

"Levi bought us a farm, and we'll be moving in soon. I'll take everything that was special to you with me, but Jordan and I are going to sell the house. I hope you're okay with that."

"I'm sure they understand," Levi says.

"You killed my baby!" Mrs. Adams suddenly shouts behind us, and shocked by the sudden attack, our heads turn to look at her. "Monsters! It should've been you instead."

"What the hell?" I gasp, my heart sinking. I don't have it in me to handle an argument with Mrs. Adams.

"Jesus," Levi snaps. "I'm so over this fucking shit." He pulls his keys out of his pocket and shoves them into my hand. "Get in the truck. I'll deal with her."

"I'm not leaving you alone," I argue. "Besides, you hate dealing with people."

Sucking in a deep breath, I look at Mrs. Adams. "This has to stop."

Her cheeks are flushed, and there's a mean look in her eyes as she glares at me. "You should've died with them." She points at my family's graves. "I told Colby he was too good for the likes of you, but that boy just wouldn't listen to me. He could've made it big in life, but no, he stayed in Verona, chasing after you."

"That's enough!" Levi's voice thunders, and he moves partially in front of me.

A deranged expression makes her look scary as hell, and I grab hold of Levi's arm as she spits the words out as if they're poison. "You played him like a fiddle, and you loved it, didn't you? You . . . YOU . . ." She gasps for air before she screams, "My boy just kept giving and giving, and you walked all over him. You broke his heart, but that wasn't enough. Why did you have to kill him? What did he ever do to you to deserve that?"

Levi takes hold of my hand in a firm grip and pulls me in the direction of the truck while telling Mrs. Adams, "We are done here. You need to get help, lady."

Suddenly, there's a crack in the air, and as something slams into the snow near us, I let out a shriek.

As I realize Mrs. Adams just fired a gun at us, shock shudders through me.

"Have you lost your—" My sentence is cut short when Levi hauls me off my feet and runs for his truck.

My bear of a man makes quick work of putting some distance between us while I cling to him, my eyes locked on Mrs. Adams.

She points the gun at us, and when another gunshot fills the air, I scream, "Levi!"

Chapter 30

LEVI

There's a burning sensation on the side of my neck, and cradling Kelcie tightly to my front, I duck behind the truck. A bullet slams into the metal on the other side of the vehicle, and a second later, there's another blast in the air.

"Jesus Christ," I gasp, my mind racing to come up with a plan.

"Come out, you cowards!" the bat shit crazy woman shouts.

"We need to get in the truck," I tell Kelcie while quickly peeking through the side windows to see where Mrs. Adams is standing. "As soon as we're inside, you have to duck down. Okay?"

My heart is thundering against my ribs, my mind racing to stay ahead of the situation.

"Y-you're b-b-bleeding," Kelcie stammers, her teeth clattering violently as she lifts a trembling hand to my neck. Her gloved fingertips brush over my skin, the wool coming away bloody, and her eyes grow wide with terror.

"I'm fine," I say to set her at ease. "The bullet just grazed me."

My arms tighten around Kelcie as I check where Mrs. Adams is, and seeing she's getting close to us, I snap, "Fuck. We have to run."

Kelcie's breaths come too fast as she starts having a panic attack, and not wasting another second, I grip her to me as I lunge forward, running for the wooded area behind a mausoleum.

"Stop!" Mrs. Adams yells. "Stop and face what you've done! Come back here!" Her voice grows shriller with every sentence.

I hear sirens as I dart between the trees, and when she fires another shot, I duck to my right and press my back against a large trunk.

Thank God! Someone must've heard the gunshots and called the sheriff's department.

"I will kill you if it's the last thing I do."

Breaths saw over my dry lips as I look down at Kelcie, and seeing she's unconscious and her lips are blue, the air is ripped right out of my lungs.

"No!" I crouch down and let go of her lower half so I can check her for bullet wounds. "Kelcie! Baby?"

There's another shot, and it slams into the bark behind me. I instinctively duck while my hand keeps roving over Kelcie, but I don't see any blood.

"Darlene!" I hear Sheriff Williams shout. "Drop the weapon and let's talk about this. No one needs to get hurt. There's been enough killing."

"No!" she spits the word out. "You let them kill my baby and even helped that monster move out while Colby's blood was still wet on the floor."

"Don't, Darlene!" The sheriff's voice is tense. "I don't want to shoot you. Please. Drop the gun. Let me help you."

"The way you helped Colby? No! That good-for-nothing girl should've died with her family. Instead, she got to live and destroy my boy."

I pat Kelcie's cheek, willing her to come to. "Open your eyes, baby. Please."

"Noooo!" Sheriff Williams hollers, followed by two gunshots, and I lean over Kelcie to keep her shielded from any stray bullets.

Seconds later, I hear Mrs. Adams cry, "Get off me. Let go. I have to kill them." I hear her sob hysterically. "I have to. Get off. Noooo. They need to pay."

"I've got her restrained," Deputy Stone calls out.

Boots crunch, and as I glance around the tree, I see Sheriff Williams jogging toward us.

I adjust my arms and pick Kelcie up bridal style. When her head falls against my shoulder, her lashes begin to stir, and I freeze. "Baby? Open your eyes. Come on." Finally, she comes to, and when I get to see her beautiful brown irises, a relieved smile spreads over my face. "There you are."

"Is Kelcie okay?" Sheriff Williams asks.

"What?" Kelcie mumbles, then her eyes lock on the blood coating my neck, and they go wide as saucers.

"I'm fine," I say quickly. "It's just a scratch." I sink down to my knees and cradle her. "It's over. We're safe."

"Did either of you get hurt?" Sheriff Williams asks as he places his hands on his knees and leans over to look at us.

I lock eyes with Kelcie. "Are you hurt anywhere?"

She shakes her head while she sits up a bit straighter, then she rips off her glove, and her fingers probe the area on my neck where the bullet grazed me.

"I'm really okay."

Her chin begins to quiver as her hands move all over my chest before she grips hold of the lapels of my coat.

"Come on," Sheriff Williams says. "The ambulance is here. Let the paramedics take a look at you."

When I climb to my feet with Kelcie still cradled in my arms, she says, "I can walk."

I ease her onto her feet but quickly place my arm around her to keep her close to me.

"This way," the sheriff says, gesturing where we should go.

Up ahead, I see Deputy Stone half forcing, half dragging a hysterical Mrs. Adams toward one of the cruisers.

When we break through the lining of trees and walk past the mausoleum, the same paramedic from yesterday jogs toward us, carrying an emergency bag.

"What are we dealing with?" she asks the sheriff.

"It looks like a bullet grazed Levi, and they're rattled, but other than that, they both seem to be fine," he answers her.

When the paramedic comes toward me, I stop walking and say, "You're not touching me."

"She needs to look at your wound," Kelcie says.

"No. I'm fine." The paramedic comes too close, and when she reaches for my neck, I duck and back up. "Keep your fucking hands off me!"

"It's okay, Brooklyn," Kelcie says as she steps between the paramedic and me. "Tell me what to do."

"We need to clean the wound so we can see if he needs stitches," Brooklyn says while shooting me a scowl.

"Fine. I'll do it," Kelcie says.

"Don't be stubborn, Levi," Sheriff Williams mutters. "Let them fix you up."

Knowing Kelcie will understand, I look at her and say, "I can't handle being touched right now. Not after what just happened."

Kelcie nods, then she holds her hand out to Brooklyn. "No one is laying a finger on my fiancé. Give me an antiseptic wipe so I can clean his wound."

Only feeling the effects of the shock now, I sit down on the side of the paved lane that runs through the heart of the cemetery and close my eyes. Sucking in a deep breath, I try to come down from the adrenaline still rushing through my veins.

"It's okay, Levi. It's me touching you," Kelcie whispers to warn me before she gently wipes the side of my neck. When it begins to burn, I clench my jaw.

Brooklyn sounds dangerously close when she says, "It's not too bad. We'll put on some ointment and a bandage. It should heal quickly."

My eyes snap open, and I see that Kelcie's on her knees beside me. She places her hand on my shoulder and presses a kiss to my forehead while we wait for Brooklyn to hand her the ointment.

It takes another few minutes until Kelcie sticks the bandage to my skin, then she climbs to her feet and smiles at Brooklyn. "Thank you for helping."

"No problem," she replies before heading to the ambulance.

Sheriff Williams lets out a heavy sigh. "It's too cold to stand out here. Let's get this over with quickly. Walk me through what happened."

Wanting to spare Kelcie the trauma of reliving the ordeal, I quickly climb to my feet. "I'll do it. Kelcie was unconscious. Can she wait in the truck, where it's warm?"

"I dropped the keys somewhere," she mutters while glancing around.

"You can sit in my cruiser while we search for them," Sheriff Williams suggests.

Once I have Kelcie safely in the sheriff's vehicle, I walk to the truck and find the keys lying by the left rear wheel. I gesture to where the Woodruffs are buried. "We were standing over there when Mrs. Adams arrived."

We head to the graves, and I point at where the first bullet hit the snow. "That was the first shot she fired." As I glance over the cemetery, I add, "I didn't keep count of how many times she fired the gun, but one hit my truck as well."

"We'll collect all the rounds for evidence," Sheriff Williams informs me, then he asks, "Where's that dog of yours?"

"She's at home."

"Just as well," he sighs. "At least she was out of harm's way."

I nod in agreement, then spend the next thirty minutes going through everything with the sheriff.

When we come to stop near his cruiser, Kelcie gets out.

"I don't want you to worry," the sheriff tells us. "This should be an open and shut case."

"What will happen to Mrs. Adams?" Kelcie asks.

"By the looks of things, she'll probably go to a mental hospital where she can get the help she needs." He sighs again, then mutters, "Hopefully that's the end of this unpleasant business."

Kelcie pulls her hand free, and stepping closer to the sheriff, she hugs him. "I hope so too. Thank you for everything."

When she pulls back, he looks at Kelcie with fondness. "You take care of yourself, sweetheart."

Kelcie nods as she presses close to me, and I say, "Let's get out of here."

"Drive safely." Sheriff Williams tips his head, then walks off to check the area again with the crime scene investigators who arrived a few minutes ago.

As Kelcie and I head to the truck, exhaustion sets in. We're quiet as we climb into the cab and during the drive home, but when we step into the house, Kelcie lets out a shaky breath, and the tears come.

Lick pads closer, excited to see us.

I make sure to lock the door behind us before I pull Kelcie to my chest. Holding my love while she cries again because people just couldn't leave her the fuck alone, I say, "I think we should move to the farm tomorrow. I'm sure Jordan will understand if we cancel. I want to get you out of Verona."

Kelcie clings to my coat as she nods. "Okay."

Bending, I pick her up and carry her into the living room. I sit down on the nearest couch and cradle her to me. Lick jumps up beside us and nudges her head against Kelcie's legs.

We both pet our dog while we sit in silence, processing the shit we just went through.

"It's insane," Kelcie whispers. "It feels like I've been living in some evil kind of twilight zone."

I inhale a deep breath, then slowly let it out. "I hope to God it's all over now, or I'm buying us an island."

A mixture of a sob and laughter sputters from her. "I just want to move to the farm and forget the outside world exists for the next year or so."

"I agree," I murmur before pressing a kiss to her forehead.

Her eyes lower to the bandage. "When I saw the blood on your neck, I had a flashback of my mom. I'm sorry I passed out on you." Her gaze lifts back to mine. "What happened after I passed out?"

"Nothing worth repeating." Lifting my hand, I place my palm over the faint red mark from where Colby slapped her yesterday. "We're both okay, and it's all that matters." I take in every inch of her face, my tone soft as I say, "What I feel for you transcends love. I've written so many words, and I can't think of one to describe the emotion you evoke in me."

Lowering my head, I seal my mouth to hers, and instead of trying to explain, I show her how I feel.

Chapter 31

KELCIE

Three months later . . .

The aroma of sizzling bacon draws Lick and Rocket out of their beds and to the kitchen.

We got Rocket a month after we moved to the farm. The puppy had zoomies twenty-four seven, and Levi almost named him Zoom. But I saved our new addition to the family and gave him a more badass name. There was no way I was naming our baby after an online app.

While Lick stares at me with a cute look I find hard to resist, begging for a piece of bacon, Rocket drops his ball right by my feet. He lives for playing catch. I swear it's all he'd do if we gave him half a chance.

Opening their treat cupboard, I give them each a chew stick that's good for their teeth. While Rocket devours his right on the spot, Lick takes hers to her bed, enjoying the treat at a much slower pace.

"Something smells good in here," Levi says as he comes into the kitchen.

He was up until two this morning, writing the ending to his book. He still has editing to do before he can send the manuscript in, but at least he finally typed "The End." It was such a big moment for him, he looked a little emotional.

"Why are you out of bed?" I give him a playful scowl. "I told you to rest today. You worked your butt off and deserve a lazy day before you start with edits."

Gripping hold of my chin, he presses a kiss to my mouth, then meeting my eyes, he replies, "I got up because you're not in bed." He leans past me and steals a slice of bacon. "And I smelled food."

"I'm making a big breakfast to celebrate you finishing the book," I tell him.

The corner of his mouth lifts, and a happy emotion flashes over his face. "You are?"

God, I hate that Levi had such an awful childhood. Every time I do something that's as natural as breathing to me, he has this stunned reaction. Then I just want to hold him, and that leads to sex and no work getting done.

"I am." I grin at my man while keeping an eye on the bacon, eggs, and hashbrowns. "My parents taught me to celebrate every achievement and special day."

"I like that." Levi grabs some coffee, then leans back against the counter and sips on it while watching me. "You're spoiling me rotten. Thank you, my muse."

"Ooooh, this is just the start. We're celebrating you all day long. I even got you a gift."

I almost whittled my fingers to the bone to get the surprise ready on time, and I can't wait to see his reaction.

Levi straightens up, curiosity lighting up his eyes. "What did you get me?" When I shake my head, he moves closer. "Food can wait." I shake my head again, and it has him setting down his mug and folding his arms around the front of me while resting his chin on my shoulder. "You can't tell me you have a gift for me and expect me to wait."

"I can," I chuckle as I place the bacon on paper towels so the oil can drain. "The growing suspense is the best part about getting a present."

"I don't like suspense," he grumbles, pressing a kiss to my cheek. "Please."

"Nope."

Another kiss is dropped beneath my ear. "Pretty please."

Laughter bursts from me as I check the hashbrowns before dishing them onto our plates. "You're getting it tonight," I tease him.

One of his hands moves up to massage my breast, and his voice drops low as he seductively murmurs, "Please."

I stop cooking, because whenever he uses that tone with me, I'm instantly turned on. "Fine. Maybe you can have it late this afternoon."

His other hand moves down and slips beneath the stretchy fabric of my leggings. "Please."

I quickly switch off the stove and place the eggs on our plates, then teasingly murmur, "Maybe you can get it at two."

Levi lightly bites the side of my neck while his fingers part me to get to my clit, then the word rumbles from him, and I'm done for. "Please."

I lean against his chest, my arms moving back so I can rub my palms up and down his thighs. "I'm open for negotiation."

His pointer finger drags through the arousal at my entrance. "Hmm . . . I can feel you are." Then he pulls away from me with a dark chuckle.

I swing around, ready to jump his bones if I have to, but I freeze when Levi sucks his finger into his mouth.

Holy hotness.

Not wasting a second, I shove my leggings and underwear off. Levi slowly unbuckles his belt while he watches me with what can only be described as fuck-me eyes.

"I'm so liking this side of you," I say.

"Take off your shirt and get on the island," he orders with a dominant tone, making tingles scatter through my body.

As quickly as possible, I perch my butt on the side of the island.

Levi flicks the button of his jeans open while stepping closer. He takes hold of my ankles and sets my feet on two stools, the position spreading me wide for him.

"Lean back and brace yourself with your arms." He gives me another seductive order.

I do as I'm told, then watch as my man pulls his zipper down and frees his deliciously hard manhood. My mouth salivates just looking at his velvety skin stretched over the steel that's going to pleasure the hell out of me.

His fingers wrap around his hardness, and the sight of him stroking himself has my abdomen clenching unbelievably hard.

"Please," Levi groans.

"One p.m."

He steps right up to me and drags the swollen head over my needy clit. "Please."

"Twelve," I moan.

Levi teases my opening, only giving me half an inch. "Please."

"Eleven."

Shoot. What's the time?

My eyes dart to the clock on the wall, and I see it's seven a.m.

His other hand shoots up, and he grips me by the front of my throat, his touch firm enough to get my attention without hurting me.

"Eyes on me," he commands.

My gaze instantly locks with his, and it feels like he's rewarding me when he pushes an inch deeper inside me. My lips part, and my lashes lower slightly from how good it feels.

"Please," he rasps.

With his other hand, he grips my hip to keep me in place.

My core flushes with heat as I say, "Ten thirty."

Levi surges inside me with so much force, my body jerks, and his hold on me is the only thing stopping me from shifting back on the island.

His hand around my throat eases and brushes down the front of my body, the hungry look he's giving me downright sinful.

"Please," he growls.

My reply is nothing but a mere gasp. "Ten."

Slowly, he pulls out before forcefully thrusting forward.

"This little impromptu game might just be the end of me if you don't start moving faster," I say.

Levi chuckles, a hot smirk tugging at his mouth as he once again unhurriedly eases out of me. "Please."

My inner thighs begin to tremble from the relentless need he's creating in me. With my gaze still locked with his, I purr, "Nine thirty."

While he yanks my butt toward him, he fills me hard, hitting so deep my arms give way and I slump back onto the island. This time, I'm the one begging, "Please."

Levi's fingers dig into my backside, keeping me hoisted right where he wants me as he starts taking me rough and fast.

"Nine," he growls.

My back arches, my hands blindly searching for something to hold onto as I whimper, "Please."

"As soon as I'm done coming inside you, you'll give me the gift."

He finally angles himself to hit my G-spot, and I cry, "Yes!"

The orgasm reduces me to a whimpering mess as my body convulses.

Suddenly, Levi pushes an arm beneath my shoulders and hauls me up against his chest while his other hand keeps a tight hold of my butt. He buries his face in the crook of my neck and lets out a groan that has more pleasure spiraling through me.

His body shudders against mine as he empties his release deep inside me.

I cling to him, trying to catch my breath, and once my orgasm fades, I draw patterns on his back while he comes down from his high.

My lips curve up into a satisfied smile. "I vote we have morning sex in the kitchen every day."

Levi chuckles, and he sets me down on the island again before pulling out of me. "I second that."

He fixes his jeans, then picks up my clothes, placing them beside me.

I jump off the marble top and go to the guest bathroom to clean up. When I return, Levi finishes wiping off the island and picks up my panties before coming to crouch in front of me.

My man begins to dress me, and once he's done, he gives me a tender kiss. "Breakfast first, then my gift."

"Okay." I quickly finish plating the food and carry it to the island. When we're both sitting, I ask, "How does it feel now that you've finished writing?" I scoop some hashbrowns into my mouth, my eyes on Levi.

"Once I'm done with editing and send in the manuscript, I always feel lost for a couple of weeks." Grinning at me, he adds, "But I get the feeling that won't be the case this time."

"Yeah? Why?"

"I have you and the farm to keep me busy until the next plot starts to form in my head."

"Oh, I'll keep you busy," I tease him.

The instant I take my last bite, Levi gathers our plates and loads them into the dishwasher. "Gift time."

Loving his excitement, I slip off the stool and say, "Close your eyes. I'm going to lead you to it, and you're not allowed to peek."

His eyes snap shut, and the smile forming on his face is so happy, I take a few seconds to commit it to my memory.

Taking his hand, I carefully pull him through the kitchen and out the back door, warning him, "Careful of the steps."

I lead Levi across the yard to my workshop, which he built for me last month. The second floor is still a work in progress, but I'm able to use the first floor.

I haven't opened for business yet. I've been too focused on making the kitchen cupboards and Levi's present. It will probably be another two months before I start taking orders again.

I push the door open and guide Levi to where I want him before I say, "You can open your eyes."

The instant Levi sees the bookshelf, his lips part. I whittled his book covers onto the side panels, and the titles are in cursive on every shelf.

He walks closer and brushes his fingers over the cedarwood. "Kelcie," he whispers, sounding like he's awestruck. "How did you hide this from me?"

"You were lost in your writing, so it was easy."

Suddenly, Levi spins around and stalks to me. Framing my cheeks with his hands, he kisses me with so much passion, I'm breathless and in a daze by the time he lifts his head.

His eyes look deep into mine, and I can see he means every word as he says, "Thank you for giving me the best gift ever."

"You're welcome."

"I love the shelf." He shakes his head. "But I'm talking about this extraordinary life you're giving me. Every day, I get to wake up next to you. I get to hear your laughter in the house. I smell your floral scent lingering in the air."

His words hit me so deep I feel them in my soul, and my sight blurs as tears threaten to fall.

Levi takes a breath before he continues, "Thank you for being mine."

I wrap my fingers around his wrists and bathe in the love he's giving me.

"An extraordinary life for an extraordinary man. You have no idea how amazing it is to love and be loved by you." I push up on my tiptoes and kiss him tenderly. "You are my source of comfort, strength, and every beat of my heart. I live only for you, Levi. Now and until my very last breath."

Epilogue

LEVI

Six years later . . .

Sitting on the porch with my laptop resting on my thighs, I'm supposed to be writing, but my eyes are locked on my wife as she comes walking back from the lake after feeding the ducks.

Starburst and Skittles, our two mini–Highland cows, follow behind Kelcie, stopping every few feet to graze on some grass.

Lick lifts her head and barks, which has Rocket leaving Kelcie's side and running ahead. His tongue is lolling out of the side of his mouth, and as he lies down beside Lick, he pants from all the exercise.

"How's the writing coming along?" Kelcie asks as she climbs the steps to the porch.

I set the laptop aside and get up from the chair. Brushing my palm over her heavily pregnant belly, I lean in to give her a kiss. "It's not."

Suddenly, there's a dripping sound, and both our heads snap down to the floor.

"Oh crap," Kelcie gasps. "My water just broke."

"We've got this," I say, instantly jumping into action.

I've done so many practice runs with Kelcie, we're well prepared for this moment.

Placing my arm around her to make sure she doesn't slip and fall, I guide her into the house and to the restroom. I grab a washcloth, and while Kelcie takes off her wet dress and underwear, I wipe off her legs and feet.

She hands me her clean panties, and I help her put them on before I grab the dress she's chosen to wear to the hospital.

Once we're done, I pause to press a kiss to her lips, then I take in her flushed cheeks and a panicked look in her eyes.

"I'm going to be with you every step of the way. You can do this, baby," I say to encourage her.

She nods, but a second later, her features tighten, and she lets out a gasp as her arm cradles her belly. "Oh God."

I move to her side and rub her lower back and hips as I wait for the contraction to pass, keeping my mouth shut while she deals with the pain. The last thing I want today is to annoy or upset her.

"Okay." She sucks in deep breaths of air as she begins to walk. "Let's move."

I shoot into the living room and grab my set of keys and Kelcie's hospital bag.

As we step out onto the porch, I look at Lick and Rocket. "Stay." I add a hand signal to make sure they understand, then I go to open the passenger door. I place the bag inside and turn to help my wife onto the seat.

"I'm just rinsing off the porch real fast," I tell her before jogging to where the hose is. It takes me a minute, then I'm climbing in behind the steering wheel.

Stay calm. Panicking won't help shit. Focus on the road and get your wife and unborn child safely to the hospital.

After giving myself a quick talking-to, I start the engine and steer the truck away from the house and in the direction of Madison.

During the thirty-minute drive, Kelcie's contractions start coming faster, and each time she digs her nails into my thigh while doing her best to breathe through the pain.

Jesus, and this is only the beginning?

When I pull up to the hospital, there's a fine layer of sweat on my forehead. I wipe it off on my sleeve while getting out, then run around the front to help Kelcie out of the truck.

Grabbing the bag, I keep an arm around her as we head inside. Seeing as we made all the arrangements ahead of time, we're quickly shown to our private room. I made it clear to our doctor that I'm willing to pay whatever it takes to make sure Kelcie gets the best care.

They already gave us a tour of the room, so I know where everything is. I set the bag down on the table by the window that overlooks the gardens situated on the side of the hospital. There's also a couch and a private restroom. Honestly, it's like a hotel room.

Kelcie sits down on the side of the bed so Amanda, our nurse, can take her vitals. While they're busy, I walk closer to the bedside stand and pour ice water into a glass so it's ready for Kelcie should she get thirsty.

"You can take off your clothes and change into the hospital gown," Amanda tells her. "I'm going to get you ice chips and make sure they've notified Dr. Carnick that you're here."

"Okay. Thank you," Kelcie replies, and as Amanda leaves, my wife says, "Call Jordan."

"Right!"

While she changes, I quickly dial Jordan's number, and when he answers, I say, "Hey, it's me. Kelcie's in labor."

"Man, you sound just as nervous as I was when we had Brady," my brother-in-law chuckles. "Deep breaths, buddy. You can't pass out on her. I did, and Natalie will never let me live it down."

A smile curves my lips. "Yeah, there's no way I'm passing out. Don't worry about that." I notice Kelcie is done and say, "I'm putting you on speaker. Talk to your sister."

Kelcie places her hand on her side as pain tightens her features. "Hold on. Contraction."

"You've got this, Kelcie," Jordan's voice comes over the line.

"Tell them to give you something for the pain," Natalie joins in. "Trust me. It helps a lot."

Standing beside my wife, I rub her lower back again until the contraction passes.

"I'm good," Kelcie gasps. "I think."

"We're leaving as soon as we hang up," Jordan says.

"Hang up already and get your butts over here," Kelcie grumbles. "But drive safely."

"Okay. See you soon," Jordan replies. "Levi, keep me updated."

"I will."

I end the call and set my phone on the bedside stand, then pick up the glass and hand it to Kelcie. "You need to stay hydrated, my muse."

She drinks some, then leans forward and presses her face against my shirt, whispering, "It's really happening."

I brush my palm over her hair, and the loose strands catch my attention. "Let me get your hair up." I pull away and dig a hair tie out of her bag, and gathering all the strands, I secure them in a messy bun.

With her face sweaty and flushed, she glances up at me. "Do I look as pretty as when you fell in love with me?"

I lean down and give her a kiss. "You've never looked more beautiful."

She lets out a chuckle. "Liar."

"Be right back," I say before I go to the restroom to get a washcloth. I wet it beneath cold water and squeeze the excess out, then head back to Kelcie and gently wipe her face and behind her neck.

When I'm done, I grab one of the chairs by the table and set it beside the bed. I sit down and rest my hands on either side of Kelcie's hips.

Locking eyes with my wife, I say, "I know I fought you on having a child, and this whole process started rocky, but thank you for wanting to have our baby."

When she first brought up the subject, I wasn't keen at all because crying babies give me anxiety. But seeing how much she wanted children had me agreeing. I still can't refuse her anything.

Over the past nine months, things have changed, and I've found myself getting excited to meet our baby. I now know with Kelcie by my side, I can face anything.

She places her palm on my jaw, but before she can reply, another contraction starts, and she grabs hold of my arm, her nails digging into me.

Amanda comes back with Dr. Carnick. Our nurse places the ice chips on the bedside stand, then seeing the washcloth, she says, "I'll get a bowl of cold water so you can keep rinsing it."

"How're my favorite parents-to-be doing today?" Dr. Carnick asks. "Ready to meet your baby?"

Kelcie nods while breathing through the pain, and I reply, "As ready as we'll ever be."

As soon as the contraction fades, Dr. Carnick says, "Lie down so we can see how far along you are, Kelcie."

I help my wife move onto her back and stay near her head when Dr. Carnick pushes her hospital gown out of the way.

Just like every other time he's been down there, I keep my eyes locked on Kelcie's face, trying not to lose my shit because another man is touching her.

That's been the hardest part about this whole process. I still can't stand it if anyone else touches my wife.

You can't do his job, so just suck it up.

"What time did the contractions begin?" he asks.

I check my wristwatch. "At eight forty-three, her water broke, and she had the first one about ten minutes later."

He glances at me from between her knees. "How far apart are the contractions now?"

"Five to seven minutes."

Just then, a contraction starts, and my attention is torn between Kelcie and Dr. Carnick, who is adjusting the gown around her before stepping away from the bed.

"Your baby is coming sooner than I expected and should be here in, give or take, four hours," he says. "I'm going to do my rounds, then I'll be back. Amanda will take care of you until then."

"Thanks, Doc," I say, then I focus on my wife, holding her hand and wishing I could take the pain on her behalf.

For the next few hours, we fall into a routine, and Kelcie dozes off as she grows tired from all the contractions. Jordan and his family arrived two hours ago and have made themselves comfortable in the waiting room.

When Dr. Carnick returns, things get really rough, and there are quite a few times I regret agreeing to having a baby. Seeing Kelcie in so much pain just doesn't seem worth it to me.

I remain by her side, and my hand loses all feeling at some point from how hard she's gripping it.

"Almost there," Dr. Carnick says. "Just one more push, Kelcie."

Already feeling overemotional, I keep quiet and wipe the cool washcloth over Kelcie's forehead and neck. Her face is torn with agony as she gives it her all while letting out a feral growl.

My eyes are locked on my wife when Dr. Carnick says, "You're the proud parents of a baby girl."

The next moment, I hear a cry, and my head snaps to where Amanda is tending to our baby. I have zero brain activity as I watch the nurse come toward us.

Then she places the tiny bundle in Kelcie's arms, and my entire world shifts on its axis. I'm hit with such a strong emotion as I look at my wife holding my daughter that tears begin to flow.

"Look, Levi," Kelcie says, still breathless from giving birth. "Look at our beautiful baby girl."

"I am," I whisper. Slowly, I move my hand toward the bundle, and when I touch her tiny fist, she takes hold of my fingertip.

A different kind of love I've never experienced before floods my entire being. It's instant and intense, knocking the air from my lungs.

As I take in every inch of our perfect daughter and she lets out a cry, there's no anxiety and only the need to hold and cherish her.

To protect her.

To give her everything I am.

I press a kiss to Kelcie's forehead, my eyes never leaving our daughter. "Thank you for giving me another miracle."

If you need someone to talk to, skilled, judgment-free counselors are available to provide compassionate support at **988 Lifeline**—https://988lifeline.org.

Thank you for reading *Every Single Broken Piece*.

If you want to hear all the news first, you're welcome to join my Facebook group, Michelle Heard's Readers Group (https://www.facebook.com/groups/118971435201074).

You can also sign up for my newsletter (https://landing.mailerlite.com/webforms/landing/p6m4o4).

Acknowledgments

Wow, this book took me on one heck of an emotional roller coaster ride, and I'm so thankful for my kids, who put up with me while I wrote, always making sure I ate and stayed hydrated.

Mom and Dad, thank you for the weekly calls to make sure I'm still alive.

Mark, your patience and guidance mean a lot. Thank you for always having my best interests at heart.

Maria, thank you for jumping on a call with me every time I needed to run through the plot with you. This book would not have happened without your guidance.

Sherrie, Leeann, and Sheena, thank you for always giving me your time, even if you're busy with your own lives.

Thank you to every reader and blogger. You're the cornerstone of this industry. Without you, stories would remain ink on paper. You're the ones who breathe life into the words we write.

Connect with me

Website
https://michelleheardauthor.com/

Newsletter
https://landing.mailerlite.com/webforms/landing/p6m4o4

Facebook Author Page
https://www.facebook.com/MHeardAuthor

Instagram Author Page
https://www.instagram.com/authormichelleheard/

TikTok
https://www.tiktok.com/@authormichelleheard

Amazon
https://amazon.com/author/michellehorst

BookBub
https://www.bookbub.com/authors/michelle-horst

Goodreads
https://www.goodreads.com/author/show/18108320.Michelle_Heard

About the Author

Michelle Heard is the *USA Today*, *Wall Street Journal*, and Amazon bestselling author of over sixty romance novels and counting. She specializes in love stories as heartwarming as they are heart-wrenching, about characters who would burn down the world for each other.

Before she began writing, Michelle had a career in banking. Now she lives happily in South Africa with her son—her right-hand man when it comes to all things publishing—and her daughter-in-law, who is also her best friend.